RISE OF
THE FIRST
WESSEX KING

RISE OF THE FIRST WESSEX KING

A J PROUDFOOT

The Book Guild Ltd

First published in Great Britain in 2024 by
The Book Guild Ltd
Unit E2 Airfield Business Park,
Harrison Road, Market Harborough,
Leicestershire. LE16 7UL
Tel: 0116 2792299
www.bookguild.co.uk
Email: info@bookguild.co.uk
X: @bookguild

Typeset in 11pt Minion Pro

Printed and bound by CPI Group (UK) Ltd, Croydon, CR0 4YY

ISBN 978 1835740 194

British Library Cataloguing in Publication Data.
A catalogue record for this book is available from the British Library.

*This book is dedicated to my family, and in
memory of my late parents, who inspired me to
pursue my family history.
Without them this book would not exist.*

*I need to thank my daughter, Zoë, for her help in
giving me feedback for my initial drafts, as well as
my publisher. I had a story to tell and they helped
me get this book out there for the world to read!*

PREFACE

Most people do not read the preface at the start of a book, because they just want to start reading the story.

However, tradition dictates that I tell you a little story about my motivation for writing this book. So, here goes...

This book is the culmination of over ten years of research into my own family history, which began by tracing my Scottish ancestors back to the first man to bear the Proudfoot surname, Gilbert Prúdfot, who served as Sheriff of London in 1115.

Gilbert was the son of an unknown Norman merchant, who migrated to England after the Norman Conquest, and established himself as a London merchant and city alderman. With no way to trace Gilbert's Norman ancestry in France, I set out to see how far back I could trace my family history through Gilbert's wife, to find my earliest ancestor in British historical records.

This task was initially made easier thanks to Gilbert marrying the daughter of a prominent Anglo-Saxon nobleman, whose family were part of the twelfth-century Norman London elite.

This family could trace their ancestry back to Burgræd, King of Mercia, who established an alliance with Wessex after marrying Æthelswith, daughter of Æthelwulf, King of Wessex, in the Wessex royal villa at Chippenham in AD 853.

King Burgræd's brother-in-law was Ælfred, King of Wessex, and it was Ælfred's obsession with his own Saxon pedigree, in commissioning the *Anglo-Saxon Chronicle*, that proved invaluable in tracing my family's ancestors as far back as the sixth century, before the authenticity of King Ælfred's ancestry is refuted by most historians.

According to the *Anglo-Saxon Chronicle*, and my own research, King Burgræd and Æthelswith can both trace their ancestry back to a chieftain, called 'Cerdic', who came to Britain in AD 495 and founded a new kingdom of the Gewisse that became the celebrated Anglo-Saxon kingdom of Wessex.

This made Cerdic, first King of Wessex, my earliest known ancestor.

Having spent several years on this project, I was intrigued by the fact that very little is known about the life of Cerdic, who was most likely a Romano-British nobleman and established this great Anglo-Saxon kingdom and the royal Anglo-Saxon dynasty that is still talked about over 1,000 years later!

However, when the *Anglo-Saxon Chronicle* writers were recording the history of King Alfred's house of Wessex, it would not look good to reveal that his royal Anglo-Saxon dynasty was established by a Briton.

Their solution was to change the narrative, creating an artificial Anglo-Saxon pedigree for Cerdic, all the way back to the Saxon god-king, Woden, 'Allfather of the Saxon

Kings'. The Anglo-Saxons then quietly let details about his early life fall into obscurity.

This became my final challenge… to tell Cerdic's story!

Whilst investigating the extensive research by historians, past and present, into various chronicles and documents written about the sub-Roman history of Britain, I became interested in the *Anglo-Saxon Chronicle*'s repeated claims that Cerdic was the 'son of Elesa', and the similarity with the Latin name of a regional chieftain, called 'Elasius', who welcomed bishop Germanus on his arrival on southern British shores in c. AD 447, according to the fifth-century biography of Saint Germanus by Constantius.

Other historians have identified a familial relationship between these men, so I developed my own theory about their lives, based on what is known about these two individuals, key events during that period and what motivated their actions, especially Cerdic's decision to expand his territory in only one direction, towards the southern shores of Britannia, before founding the kingdom of the Gewisse.

This novel is my interpretation of events during this period, how they impacted on two generations of a Romano-British family from the western province of Britannia and their role in the formation of the kingdom of Wessex in Anglo-Saxon Britain.

On a final note, for authenticity I have used the names of places that would have been in use at the time and provided a guide to their modern equivalent. However, I have not made any attempt to replicate the language used at the time of the book, unless relevant, because I want to make the story easier to follow for modern readers. Please forgive this concession to modernity.

A J Proudfoot

MAIN CHARACTERS

(in alphabetical order)

Ælle: fifth-century King of Suthseaxna (*Sussex*)

Æsc: Hengest's son, who succeeded him as King of Cantia (*Kent*), AD 488–516 (*also known as Oisc*)

Ambrosius Aurelianus: fifth-century Romano-British nobleman, who became King of the Britons after Wyrtgeorn's death

Arturius: commander of Ceredig's Gewisse warriors (*fictitious*)

Caradoc: Elisedd's eldest son, who died in his teens (*real person, but name unknown*)

Ceawlin: Cunorix's eldest son, who succeeded his father as King of the Gewisse, AD 560–591

Ceredig: Elisedd's youngest son, who became King of the Gewisse, AD 519–534 (*also known as Cerdic*)

Coel: Ceredig's commander of the citadel at Ventacaester (*fictitious*)

Constantius: monk from Lyon in Gaul (*France*), who wrote a biography on the life of Germanus, Bishop of Autissiodorum, called *Vita Germani*

Cunedda: Ceredig's youngest son, named after his grandfather's former commander of Portus Adurni (*fictitious*)

Cunedda: commander of Elisedd's Gewisse warriors (*fictitious*)

Cunorix: Ceredig's eldest son, who succeeded him as King of the Gewisse, AD 534–560 (*also known as Cynric*)

Cuthwulf: Cunorix's youngest son (*also known as Cutha*)

Eldad: Elisedd's youngest brother and fifth-century Bishop of Glevum (*also known as Eldadus*)

Eldol: Elisedd's younger brother and consul of Glevum

Elisedd: fifth-century ruler of the Gewisse and regional chieftain of southern region of Britannia, covering Oxfordshire, Berkshire, Hampshire and Sussex (*also known as Elasius*)

Erbin: fifth-century King of Dumnonia (*Cornwall and Devon*), AD 443–480

Euric: fifth-century King of the Vesi Goths (*Visigoths*), AD 466–484

Flavius: Ophelia's younger brother and chieftain of Darioritum in Armorica after Ceredig (*fictitious*)

Gereint: fifth-century King of Dumnonia (*Cornwall and Devon*), AD 480–508, son of King Erbin

Germanus: Bishop (*Saint*) of Autissiodorum (*Auxerre, France*)

Gruffudd: Hywel's son and commander of the Gewisse (*fictitious*)

Gwerthefyr: Wyrtgeorn's eldest son (*also known as Vortimer*)

Hengest: leader of Saxon mercenaries, who ruled Cantia (*Kent*), and elder brother of Horsa

Hildis: Cunorix's wife and daughter of a family of Jutes

Horsa: co-leader of Saxon mercenaries and younger brother of Hengest

Hywel: commander of Elisedd's Gewisse warriors (*fictitious*)

Lavena: Elisedd's wife (*real person, but name unknown*)

Madog: commander of the Gewisse warriors, under Elisedd and Ceredig (*fictitious*)

Nætanleoð: Saxon chieftain of a settlement called Onna (*near Nursling, Hampshire*)

Ophelia: Ceredig's wife (*real person, but name unknown*)

Pascent: Wyrtgeorn's younger son, who became King of Builth and Gwrtheyrnion (*also known as Pasgen*)

Rowena: Hengest's daughter and King Wyrtgeorn's second wife

Severus: Bishop of Trèves and colleague of Bishop Germanus

Trystan: chieftain of Portus Adurni, from AD 508 (*fictitious*)

Uthr: sixth-century King of the Durotriges, elder son of Ambrosius Aurelianus (*fictitious*)

Wihtgar: Hildis's cousin, a Jute who became chieftain of Onna

Wyrtgeorn Vitalinus: fifth-century King of the Britons, c. AD 425–456 (*also known as Vortigern or Gwrtheyrn*)

MODERN NAMES FOR PLACES FEATURED

(in alphabetical order)

Æglesthrep: Aylesford, Kent
Alaunacæster: Alchester, near Bicester, Oxfordshire
Alfoldean: old Roman settlement on Stane Street in
    West Sussex
Andredescæster: Pevensey, East Sussex
Andredeslea: The Weald, Sussex
Aquaesulis: Bath, Somerset
Armorica: Brittany, France
Autissiodorum: Auxerre, France
Badonbyrg: Badon hill, near Swindon
Belgae: Hampshire
Bituriges: fifth-century region around Bordeaux, France
Britannia Secunda: western province of Roman Britain,
    covering Wales, Shropshire, Herefordshire and
    Gloucestershire
Burdigala: Bordeaux, France
Caer Conan: Conisburgh, near Doncaster, Yorkshire
Calleva: Silchester, Hampshire
Cantia: Kent
Cerdicesleaga: Chearsley, near Aylesbury, Buckinghamshire

Chesle: Kingscote, West Sussex

Clausentum: Bitterne, near Southampton, Hampshire

Constantinopolis: Constantinople, Turkey

Corinium: Cirencester, Gloucestershire

Cunetio: Mildenhall, near Marlborough, Wiltshire

Darioritum: Vannes, France

Deva Victrix: Chester

Dumnonia: Cornwall and Devon

Durnovaria: Dorchester, Dorset

Durocastrum: Dorchester-on-Thames, Oxfordshire

Durocornovium: Wanborough, near Swindon

Durotriges: Wiltshire and Dorset

Durovernum: Canterbury, Kent

Elmet: kingdom in the north of England, comprising
    Yorkshire and Derbyshire

Est Engla: East Anglia

Estseaxna: Essex

Gallia Aquitania: Roman province, covering southwestern
    region of France

Gaul: western region of mainland Europe, mostly
    encompassing France

Glevum: Gloucester

Guenta: Gwent, Wales

Hafren (river): River Severn

Heardham: Hardham, West Sussex

Hispania: Roman province, covering most of Spain and
    northern Portugal

Lactodurum: Towcester, Northamptonshire

Letocetum: Lichfield, Staffordshire

Leucomagus: Andover, Hampshire

Lundein: London

Maesbeli: Salisbury Plains, Hampshire

Magnis: Kenchester, near Hereford

Namnates: Nantes, France

Natanleaga: Netley Marsh, Hampshire

Noviomagus: Chichester, West Sussex

Onna: Nursling, near Southampton, Hampshire

Ordinges: Worthing, West Sussex

Pagenses: Powys, Wales

Pontes: Staines-upon-Thames

Portus Adurni: Roman Saxon Shore fort at Portchester, Hampshire (*also known as Portuscæster*)

Portus Lemanis: Roman Saxon Shore fort at Hythe, Kent

Regni: Sussex

Rheged: Cumbria

Searobyrg: Old Sarum, near Salisbury

Suthseaxna: Sussex

Tamesis (river): River Thames

Tanat's Island: Isle of Thanet, Kent

Temple of Cor Gawr: Stonehenge, Wiltshire

Trèves: Trier, Germany

Vectis: Isle of Wight

Ventacæster: Winchester, Hampshire

Verulamium: St Albans, Hertfordshire

Vindomis: Alton, Hampshire

Wihtgarabyrg: Carisbrook, Isle of Wight

Wippidsfleet: Ebbsfleet, on the Isle of Thanet, Kent

INTRODUCTION

The *Anglo-Saxon Chronicle* records that, in AD 519, a chieftain called Cerdic founded a new kingdom and was initially known as 'King of the Gewisse'.

This kingdom, which was ruled over and expanded by Cerdic's descendants over the following five centuries, became the great Anglo-Saxon kingdom of Westseaxna, or, as we now know it, Wessex.

Historians have concluded that Cerdic's name is Brythonic, or Celtic, in origin, which had been anglicised over time. Therefore, his original Brythonic name was more likely to have been 'Ceredig'.

The Gewisse can be traced back to the fourth century as a Roman auxiliary unit, combining local warriors with foederati soldiers from conquered regions across the Roman Empire. They were based in the old Welsh kingdoms of Ergyng and Ewyas (*Ergyng ac Ewias*), which earned them the name 'men of Ewias', or 'Gewisse'.

The Gewisse came under the command of the region's client king, called Octavius Eudaf Hen, who was referred to by the Romans as 'Dux Gewissorum'. He was succeeded as ruler of the Gewisse by Magnus Maximus and Wyrtgeorn Vitalinus, before he became High King of the Britons.

King Wyrtgeorn's successor as ruler of the Gewisse would have been someone with a strong connection to the Gewisse and the western province of Britannia, most likely from a Romano-British family, as well as having a familial connection to the king.

The most likely candidate was a chieftain, known as 'Elasius', who was then sent by King Wyrtgeorn from Glevum to the southern coastline of Britannia, in command of the great Gewisse warriors, to deal with the continuing threat of attacks from Gaul, mostly by Saxons.

Some historians have concluded that Elasius was Ceredig's father, whom the *Anglo-Saxon Chronicle* repeatedly called 'Elesa', mostly based on the similarity between the Latin name 'Elasius' and the Old English name 'Elesa'. Given his likely background, Ceredig's father would also have borne a Brythonic name, like 'Elisedd'.

The following story about Ceredig's life starts several years before his birth, when his father, Elisedd, ruler of the Gewisse, was regional chieftain of southern Britannia responsible for protecting Britannia's southern coastline from invading Saxons.

1 ELISEDD THE REGIONAL RULER

In AD 447, a regional chieftain, called Elasius, welcomed
Germanus, Bishop of Autissiodorum, when he landed
on Britannia's southern shore.

"**D**o you want to live?"
The British chieftain who asked the question was
looking down at a group of five injured Saxon warriors, on
their knees with their hands tied behind their backs.

From their lowly position, this ruler looked like a
Roman commander, wearing a uniform similar to that of
a centurion, and appeared tall, imposing and threatening.
Surely the Romans have not returned to Britannia, thought
the Saxons' leader.

His men had been among a group of eighty Saxons
who had landed on the southern shores of Britannia,
about a week ago, and attacked five settlements, killed all
the men and children, then raped and killed the women at
their leisure. They had then ransacked these settlements
for supplies and any gold or silver.

Unfortunately for the Saxons, the local chieftain had
heard of their attacks and had come to put an end to their
plundering.

When a group of fifty British warriors found them, the Saxons thought the Britons were weak and were no threat to them, so decided to simply kill these Britons and resume their activities. However, they did not know whom they were facing and why they had made a big mistake.

These Britons were no ordinary soldiers. They were experienced, well-trained, elite warriors, who had learned the ways of the Roman centurion, combined with the battle skills of the best fighters from across the Roman Empire.

Their chieftain had led from the front of the attack by the Britons, who used swords instead of axes and fought as a single unit, moving in co-ordination, slicing, swinging and stabbing with their swords, and deflected the axe swings from the Saxons with their shields.

The Saxons were stunned by the Britons' skills and strength, like novices in their first battle. One by one, the Saxons were easily picked off, until there were only these five men left. They may have survived the initial attack, but not without suffering various injuries that left them unable to continue fighting.

"Do you want to live?" repeated the chieftain.

"Yes, we want to live," they all said, fearing death whilst unarmed.

"Good, because I need you to deliver a message to your people, from wherever you came. You will return there and tell them that Britannia is no longer yours to plunder. If there are any further attacks by your people on these shores, I will find them and next time there will be no survivors."

"Who are you?" pleaded the Saxon leader.

"I am Elisedd, ruler of the southern region of Britannia," said the chieftain.

"Take them to their ship, remove any plunder and weapons, then release them on the next tide," he told his men, then turned and walked away, knowing that his men would deal with the Saxons.

Once the Saxons had been put on their ship and were heading back out to sea, Elisedd led his warriors back to their base. He knew the Saxons would not turn back, so the region was safe for now.

*

As they neared the old Roman fort of Portus Adurni the following day, Elisedd and his men could see its white walls across the waters of the bay, shining in the sunlight. The fort had been built nearly 200 years ago on a peninsula of land, a day's march from the derelict Roman settlement of Noviomagus to the east.

Portus Adurni had been used to protect the southern coastline of Britannia until the Roman armies withdrew from Britannia nearly forty years ago. Without the protection of the Roman Empire, Britannia had come under continuing attacks from all quarters and, in the south, the threat was primarily from sea pirates and Germanic invaders, also known as the Saxons.

It was Elisedd's job to ensure that these threats did not go any further, so Portus Adurni was the ideal location for his activities.

The interior of the old Roman fort was more or less the same as it had been when the Romans were based there, including the stone-built Roman fort buildings that had survived intact. The only difference was that the Romans had closed off the north and south gates at some point.

The fort also boasted a port, so Elisedd commanded three ships to patrol the southern coastal waters, seeing off any sea pirates or potential invaders, most of whom were Saxons who crossed the calmer waters from Gaul.

Elisedd felt very fortunate to call Portus Adurni his home. He loved the approach to the imposing main gate of the fort and could often be found walking along the walls, taking in the views to the south over the estuary, especially as the waves lapped gently up against the shore and the smell of the sea was blown in by the southerly breezes.

*

Later that week, Elisedd walked towards the great hall of the old Roman Principia in Portus Adurni. He was looking for his only son, Caradoc.

Caradoc had been born just seven summers ago. Unfortunately, Caradoc carried a disability that affected his future prospects. His right leg was withered, the result of complications during his birth, which left him with a pronounced limp which was so bad that he was barely able to walk.

Caradoc's disability had been the primary reason why Elisedd and his wife, Lavena, had never had any further children and was the cause of many disagreements between them.

In normal circumstances, and despite his feelings for her, Elisedd would have banished Lavena for being unable to give him a natural heir and then taken a new wife. However, Elisedd was fully aware that his marriage to Lavena, a kinswoman of King Wyrtgeorn, had brought him great fortune as a result of this relationship with the king. Knowing the king as he did, ending his marriage to Lavena would have made his life impossible!

King Wyrtgeorn was the ambitious son of Vitalis, a high-ranking Roman consul in the civitas of Glevum during the last years of Roman rule. Before the Romans had withdrawn from Britannia in AD 410, Wyrtgeorn had been appointed to rule a small region to the west of Glevum, with command over an elite force of warriors, called the 'Gewisse'.

When Wyrtgeorn had achieved his dream of becoming High King of the Britons, he needed someone to replace him as commander of the Gewisse. He had higher ambitions for his sons, so who better than a kinsman like Elisedd.

Elisedd was no ordinary Briton. Like Wyrtgeorn, he was also from a highborn Romano-British family, based in and around Glevum. They had retained their Brythonic heritage, but assimilated into the Roman way of life, for the financial wealth and status that would bring.

When Elisedd had quickly established himself as a popular and successful commander amongst the Gewisse warriors, King Wyrtgeorn made the decision to relocate Elisedd and the Gewisse to protect the southern coastlines of the lands of the Belgae and Regni from the increasing attacks on Britannia by Saxons from their base in Gaul.

Elisedd and his Gewisse warriors immediately took control over the region and brought stability and peace there after defeating numerous attacks. Wyrtgeorn was delighted, so Elisedd was given overall rule of these kingdoms.

Portus Adurni was large enough to be a small town, so Lavena and the other families of the Gewisse joined their men there.

*

As he entered the great hall, Elisedd saw his young son sitting with Arturius, a young warrior who undertook administrative duties within the fort, as well as being Caradoc's friend and protector.

"Ah, there you are, Caradoc," said Elisedd. "I am pleased to see that your mother has dressed you well, for today we meet a great man, Bishop Germanus of Autissiodorum. He is here on an important mission, to investigate heretic religious practices in Britannia. He has a reputation for performing miracles, so I'm hoping to convince him to perform another one, this time on your leg."

A horn sounded from the port gate alerted Elisedd that a ship had been seen in the distance, heading into port. This was planned to allow time for Elisedd to bring Caradoc down to the harbour ahead of the ship's arrival.

"Time to go," announced Elisedd, and a small detachment of his Gewisse warriors, who had been called to the great hall by Arturius, formed up beside Caradoc.

Over the years, Elisedd had proven himself as a great warrior and leader, and had earned the respect and loyalty of the Gewisse, who would do anything to protect him and his family.

On this occasion, whilst it looked like these warriors were protecting Elisedd, they would be surreptitiously hiding a couple of spears being used to provide Caradoc with a bench to sit on whilst heading down to the port gate.

*

As the ship slowly manoeuvred up against the pier that reached out into the estuary, Germanus and his colleague Severus, Bishop of Trèves, stood at the bow watching closely as the port gate opened and a unit of armed warriors approached.

The emissary that Germanus had sent in advance of his visit had reported back that the region was under the control of a strong Romano-British ruler whose family had adopted Roman ways during the Empire's rule over Britannia. As a result, Elisedd was well educated and would understand Germanus if he spoke the language of the Church.

Germanus also learned that whilst Elisedd was not a Christian, his brother was Bishop of Glevum. The problem was that Elisedd did not have any issue with the Christian heretics, called Pelagians, who did not believe in original sin, and Elisedd was pragmatic enough to let them live in peace.

Pelagianism was a huge concern for the Church, as it gave people the right of free will, thereby reducing the influence of the Church on their lives, as they did not need to seek forgiveness for their sins, nor perform good deeds that benefited the Church.

Germanus knew he would have to tread lightly with Elisedd if he sought to get his help with his mission. However, Germanus had one more thing in his favour. He was aware of his reputation for performing miracles, and his emissary had reported that Elisedd had only one son with a crippled leg.

If Germanus knew anything about leaders, it was that they would do anything to have a healthy son and heir to succeed them. This was his opportunity, and he knew it would present itself if Elisedd brought his crippled son to their first meeting.

As if being granted a miracle of his own, Germanus watched as the warriors opened up their close quarter formation to reveal Elisedd, and his crippled son!

Germanus, Severus and their emissary disembarked and walked over to Lord Elisedd, identified by his position at the centre of the group, with the crippled boy by his side. Germanus took this opportunity to size up his host.

Elisedd was at least forty years old, with shoulder-length hair greying at the temples, like a Celt. He was taller than most men, with the stance of a man who felt at ease with his position and authority.

He looked too young to have known life under Roman rule, but it had clearly influenced his clothing, which signalled wealth and nobility. He wore the red cloak of a Roman commander, which was held in place by a large round gold brooch, with an unusual Celtic design and red glass insets in the centre.

Germanus thought that it must have been his father's cloak from when the Roman Empire ruled these lands, which Elisedd had inherited and clearly treasured.

Under the cloak, Elisedd wore a green tunic, with a leather overjacket, held in place with a belt. Attached to his belt was a high-quality sword, like a Roman spatha, about three feet long and relatively new, so it must have been made to a specific design for Elisedd.

The guard had been ornately carved, and the handle was covered in red leather. The pommel at the end of the hilt was round, with a bright green emerald stone built into the very tip, that glinted in the sunlight. The stone must have travelled from the other end of the Roman Empire to have ended up here in Britannia. The scabbard was covered in red leather, with a gold locket and chape at either end.

This was a very expensive sword, worthy of a ruler, and the red, white and green colours used in its manufacture were a very deliberate choice, so must have had meaning for Elisedd.

Germanus was confused. This chieftain looked more like a mixture between a Roman, a Saxon and a Celt. This man was a genuine enigma!

Meanwhile, Elisedd had sized up Germanus too. What he saw was a much older man, in his sixties or seventies, who had the look of a Roman nobleman, suggesting he was originally highborn.

Germanus was above average height, though not as tall as Elisedd, although he had the same build. Germanus was wearing the typical brown hooded cloak of a pious monk, but the gold cross on a chain around his neck showed his higher religious authority. However, underneath the monkish cloak, he appeared to be wearing the outfit of a Roman commander.

Elisedd's younger brother was Bishop of Glevum, so he knew what ordinary, simple monks looked like, but Germanus looked more like a soldier than a religious leader. This man was not entirely what he seemed, so Elisedd knew he would have to be careful with him.

Elisedd spoke first, in perfect Latin, saying, "I am Elisedd, overall chieftain of this region, and I welcome you to Britannia, Lord Bishop."

By using the language of the Church, Elisedd was letting Germanus know that he was an educated man with power and influence in that region.

Germanus was taken aback at Elisedd's very strong accent, believing that the people from this part of Britannia spoke with a softer accent. He reminded himself to find out more about Elisedd's background whenever the opportunity arose.

He realised that Elisedd would make a valuable ally whilst in country, but tried not to let the smile forming in the corner of his mouth show his good fortune in meeting a leader with a Roman background, instead of the uneducated warlords he was used to having to deal with.

"You will be my honoured guest in Portus Adurni for as long as you need," continued Elisedd. "You and your party will receive my protection whilst you are here. And this evening, I have arranged a banquet in your honour."

"I thank you for your welcome, Lord Elisedd," replied Germanus in the language of the Britons. "I would be delighted to accept your hospitality. God is most gracious in delivering such a powerful leader who is willing to help me in my mission on behalf of the Church."

Elisedd approached Germanus and offered his hand, which was reciprocated with a firm forearm handshake.

Elisedd then repeated the process with Bishop Severus, as well as the emissary, whom he already knew from his earlier visit.

"This is my son, Caradoc," said Elisedd, introducing the visitors to his son, who hobbled forward and exchanged forearm handshakes with the three men.

"Let us withdraw into the fort," said Elisedd. "I have quarters available for you, Bishop Severus and the emissary in my villa, the best I can offer, for your stay here."

The group started to walk towards the port gate, with Elisedd's guard reorganising themselves into a wider formation, although Germanus noticed that two of the guards had formed up at the back to provide Elisedd's son with his bench for the procession.

Inside the fort, Germanus took a quick look around the fort and saw a sizeable number of sentries on all walls. The fort was huge and looked like any other Roman fort he had visited, but with smaller individual houses that looked like family homes on the right side of the path as they walked, with women and children undertaking household duties.

Germanus turned to his left and saw a group of men training in battle sequences, while others cleaned their equipment. It appeared more like a town than a military fort, but the emissary had informed him that the men in the fort were an elite force of warriors and should not be underestimated.

"You have a very organised community here, Elisedd. Is this all your men?" asked Germanus.

"No, Lord Germanus," replied Elisedd. "We have one group on ships patrolling the coastline between here and the old Roman fort at Andredescæster. We also have another group patrolling inland, in case there are any attacks from the north or east."

"Impressive," said Germanus, and he was impressed. Elisedd and his men had clearly retained a lot of the Roman military knowledge, strategy and tactics, despite Rome's forty-year absence. He surmised that Elisedd's Romano-British heritage must have had a strong influence on him when growing up.

The group approached Elisedd's villa, which Germanus realised was originally the commanding officer's quarters of the Roman fort, called the praetorium, where Lavena was waiting to welcome Germanus to their home.

Elisedd introduced Lavena to Germanus, Severus and their emissary, who each thanked her for making room in her home for them.

Lavena then introduced each of them to a servant by name, saying, "They will show you to your rooms, and there will always be at least two servants available if there is anything you require. We will let you settle after your long journey."

As they left the servants to take their guests to their rooms, Lavena approached Elisedd and asked, "How did it go, Elisedd?"

"As well as I expected," replied Elisedd. "I am pretty sure that Germanus saw through my plan in bringing Caradoc with me to meet him, so it may not be a surprise when I broach the subject tonight. We both want something from this so, like any negotiation, we just have to make sure the terms are fair on both sides. Has there been any news from Hywel?"

"Not yet," said Lavena. "Cunedda knew you were busy, but told me that they should be arriving back tomorrow."

Cunedda was Elisedd's commander of the fort, responsible for the security and protection of the fort's inhabitants, while Hywel commanded the group of Gewisse warriors on patrol in country.

"Can I leave you to deal with our guests?" said Elisedd. "I need to find Cunedda and tell him to send out the scouts. I want a definite answer that they will be here tomorrow. This is vital."

*

That evening, a large group of people gathered in the great hall for a banquet to welcome Bishop Germanus. The attendees included the elders and their families from the nearby settlement.

At the top table, Elisedd left Lavena to charm Germanus, whilst he exchanged small talk with Severus and the emissary. At the end of the table, Arturius and Caradoc looked like they were having the most fun, laughing as they chatted with Cunedda.

Before the banquet began, Elisedd stood up and slammed his goblet down on the table to gain everyone's attention. When there was quiet, he spoke.

"Thank you all for coming tonight. We are here to give a special welcome to our guests from Gaul and the Roman Church. It is well over a generation since Rome's forces departed these shores, to deal with a significant threat to the Roman Empire. During this period, we have had to face ongoing attacks from all directions, be it the Hibernians, Scots, Picts or Saxons. We, the Gewisse, know all too well about these threats having dealt with a number of these challenges head on.

"However, tonight is about the visit to our shores of lord bishops Germanus and Severus, representatives of the Church, which is facing its own challenges. Whilst I have no doubt that any Christians living nearby are loyal to the Church of Rome, the bishops seek our help in tackling a group of heretic Christians, who are advocating something called Pelagianism. So, we offer them our hospitality, and assistance in their mission. For tonight, we welcome our guests, with good food, excellent wine and great company..."

Then turning to Caradoc, Elisedd finished with a laugh, saying, "...except for a certain young man who will be heading for bed shortly!"

Raising his goblet, Elisedd called, "To friends, both old and new!"

All the guests stood and responded, calling out, "To friends, old and new!"

Once Elisedd had sat down, Germanus stood up. When the murmuring had calmed down, he began to speak.

He said, "As a representative of the Church, I am not normally in receipt of such a friendly welcome, but if I have learned anything today it is that you must not believe what you hear. For instance, across in Gaul, it is believed that Britannia is descending into lawlessness. However, Lord Elisedd has shown me that the civil and military organisation that Rome brought to these shores over many generations is still alive and, whilst he is not yet a Christian, I cannot hold that against him."

Laughter rippled around the hall.

Germanus continued, "It has given me hope that the country could rise again, if its leaders are more like him. My task is simple, but yours is not, and I pray that God gives you strength to defend your people from the greed of others who plot to take what is yours. And I hope that one day you will see the light of his love for this country and its people."

Raising his goblet, Germanus called, "To Elisedd and Britannia!"

"Elisedd and Britannia," echoed around the hall.

Germanus sat down and, as he did so, Lavena laid her hand on his arm, saying, "Beautifully put, my lord bishop."

Shortly afterwards, Arturius helped Caradoc up and they left the hall, with Caradoc hobbling as best he could.

As if knowing their roles in a play that was just beginning, Germanus turned to Elisedd and asked, "May I ask if Caradoc's leg has been like that since birth, or the result of an accident?"

"He was born with this affliction," replied Elisedd. "Lavena went through a difficult labour while I was fighting in the north. She was living at my family's estate outside Glevum, but was not due for several more weeks. The nearest help was too far away when Caradoc decided to enter this world. The servants tried to help, but Lavena got into difficulties and they needed to get Caradoc out or else both would die. The price of both their lives was the strength in Caradoc's leg, which would appear to be a lifelong sacrifice that he is destined to bear."

Elisedd sighed, his eyes focused on something Germanus could not see, then said, "I know that there is nothing that I could have done, but I still blame myself for it and would have willingly given anything I had to give him at least an equal chance to reach his potential."

Those words alone confirmed to Germanus that Elisedd, although not a Christian, was definitely a good and decent father, who only wanted the best in life for his son.

Elisedd continued, "I know that you have performed miracles in the past and would not want to have you think less of me, but I would do anything now if you could persuade your God that Caradoc deserves a chance to grow up to become a healthy, fit and strong young leader who would replace me when my time has come."

Germanus smiled. He knew what would follow, but he did not want to press his needs in case he went too far.

"That is a dangerous statement, Lord Elisedd," he said. "I could easily demand your conversion to Christianity just for attempting to cure your son."

"I agree, Lord Bishop," replied Elisedd, "and I would, if that was the price for Caradoc's future, but it would be a flawed conversion. However, I think you are an honourable man who knows that our longer-term alliance would be more beneficial than one man's soul. I do not ask this for me, but an innocent child who did not deserve this."

Germanus nodded his head in agreement. He was going through an internal struggle. Having seen a similar condition afflicting a child in Gaul and how it was resolved, Germanus felt comfortable in being able to help Elisedd, but that could barely fall in the category of 'miracle'. Nevertheless, it would help the Church to have such an ally, and Caradoc may one day grow up to serve the Church, knowing what Germanus had done for him in God's name.

Germanus then said, "Let me pray on this, Lord Elisedd. I will give you an answer in the morning, after seeking God's guidance."

The rest of the evening went well, with excellent entertainment from local musicians and a bard, who told wonderful stories in rhyme.

Cunedda had left the banquet at some point and never returned. He had received word that a scout was returning with news about the patrol, so went to the gatehouse for an update before reporting back to Elisedd.

Later that evening, while Elisedd and Lavena were preparing for bed, Cunedda knocked on their door.

"Come," said Elisedd.

Cunedda entered, saying, "My apologies, Elisedd, but I thought you should hear the news before tomorrow."

Elisedd allowed Cunedda and his other two commanders to call him by his given name in private, as they had known each other for over two decades.

Cunedda continued, "A scout came back a little while ago. Hywel and his patrol will arrive by the time the sun sets high tomorrow. You will get your answer then."

Elisedd thanked Cunedda for the news. After Cunedda had left, Lavena reminded Elisedd that he needed to play this out very carefully if they were to get what they wanted from their visitor.

2

GERMANUS HEALS ELISEDD'S SON

Constantius of Lyon and Bede wrote that Elasius pleaded with Germanus to heal his crippled son, and he performed a miracle.

The next morning was a glorious one for Elisedd. The sun was bright, with not a cloud in the clear blue sky and a slight wisp of a breeze coming from the south, bringing the glorious smell of the sea with it.

Elisedd walked along the fort wall, acknowledging each of his warriors on sentry duty, exchanging small talk with a few of them as he passed.

He was thinking about how the day would play out. Madog, commander of Elisedd's ship patrols, was due back at port, depending on the tides, while Hywel and his patrol would be arriving back at the fort with the news he had hoped for. Finally, Germanus should be coming to see him at some point that morning, with his decision about helping Caradoc.

Elisedd met Cunedda as he was returning to the great hall.

"You have news, Cunedda?" he asked.

"Yes, but not about Hywel, Elisedd. Germanus has asked to see you in his room," replied Cunedda.

"Excellent," said Elisedd, knowing what this meant. "Thank you, my friend, I will head there after I have been to see Lavena."

Lavena and Caradoc were in Caradoc's room when Elisedd entered and told them that Germanus had asked to see him.

"That was quick," replied Lavena. "Do you think he is going to refuse you?"

"I know," said Elisedd. "I thought he would take longer to make his decision, but I doubt he will refuse. Presuming he is willing to help, I wonder why he agreed so quickly. At least we will have something to reward him with when Hywel returns. I will speak with him in private first, then let you know."

Elisedd headed to the other end of the villa, where his guests were staying. As he approached the room allocated to Germanus, the servant who was waiting in the corridor, 'on call' so to speak, stepped over and knocked on the bishop's door.

Elisedd reached the door just as Germanus said, "Enter."

Opening the door and walking straight in, Elisedd saw Severus and the emissary there too.

"Ah, Lord Elisedd, I am glad you received my message," said Germanus. "I discussed last night's conversation with my colleagues, and we have prayed for God's guidance. We would like to help young Caradoc, but it will be very painful for the boy. If we were to do this, are you and the lady Lavena prepared to put young Caradoc through a painful process when there is no guarantee of success? The result will be in God's hands."

"Of course, Lord Bishop," replied Elisedd. "We have all discussed this and any chance of a future for my boy is worth it."

"Then let us seek to try and improve God's willingness to help," said Germanus. "Could we count on you to deliver the heretics to us?"

"How could I refuse?" said Elisedd. "I will gladly find all the heretics in my region and we can then decide what happens to them."

There was an awkward pause before Germanus said, "I will need to examine Caradoc before I proceed and will have to make preparations, including having some equipment prepared, and even made if necessary. It could take a few days to prepare. Will you grant me freedom to source what I need within the fort, and I will let you know when I am ready?"

Elisedd responded, saying, "Of course. I will send Arturius, my praefectus, to help you. He handles all internal affairs and administration within the fort, and only reports to me and Cunedda. He has the authority to ensure that your needs are all met."

*

While Elisedd and Germanus were discussing healing Caradoc's leg, Cunedda was at the main gate, watching as Hywel and his group of warriors were approaching.

Hywel raised a banner bearing a gold rampant dragon on a red background, attached to a spear. This was Elisedd's banner that the Gewisse used to indicate a friendly approach and not under any duress. If there was a problem that could not be relayed, the banner would have remained in Hywel's saddlebag.

The gates remained closed until Hywel and his warriors came to a stop. Hywel waited for the gates to open, but grew frustrated when they remained closed.

This was not the first time Cunedda had done this to Hywel, but it was just Cunedda's idea of a joke. *He needs to get out and fight*, thought Hywel. This lack of battle experience was getting to Cunedda, so he was having his own fun at Hywel's expense.

"Announce yourself," shouted Cunedda from the ramparts.

Although tired from their journey, Hywel knew that he had to play Cunedda's games. He could even see Cunedda smiling on the fort wall.

"Bastard!" Hywel said under his breath, thinking that he would get Cunedda back one day for playing these games.

Hywel stepped down from his horse and approached the gates with his arms open to his sides to show that he bore no arms.

"I am Hywel, commander of the Gewisse, loyal supporter of my lord Elisedd," announced Hywel, adding, "And his best warrior", determined to get a dig in at Cunedda's expense.

"That cannot be, for I am Lord Elisedd's best warrior," replied Cunedda.

"There is only one way to settle this," was Hywel's reply. "Either let me in, or come down here and challenge me. Alternatively, ask Lord Elisedd whom he would rather have by his side in a fight. Your arse is getting fat from sitting here in fort, while we are actually out in country doing something."

"This can only be my friend Hywel," laughed Cunedda.

Their battle of words over for now, Cunedda called down to have the gates opened for the returning party, allowing Hywel and his men to enter the fort. Hywel left his horse, which was collected by one of his warriors, and he approached Cunedda, who had come down from the gate building.

"Good to see you, my friend," said Cunedda as he exchanged a forearm handshake with Hywel. "I trust your expedition was successful. Elisedd is looking for some good news to give the lord bishop. I suspect it will be needed shortly."

Meanwhile, in the villa, Elisedd entered his son's room, where Lavena and Caradoc were waiting for news.

"Germanus has agreed to help heal Caradoc's leg," announced Elisedd. "In return, I have agreed to find the Pelagian Christians wandering around the region spreading their heresy, for Germanus to punish."

Then Elisedd added, "There is one thing, Caradoc. The bishop has said that the healing process will be very painful, so you will need to show a warrior's strength when the time is right. He needs to examine you before proceeding, so Arturius may request a visit shortly."

Turning to Lavena, he said, "Can I leave this with you, my love, as I have to go and see Hywel now? I saw the gates opening up, so I am hoping he has brought the news I need from his scouting expedition."

*

Elisedd found his three commanders, Cunedda, Hywel and Madog, sharing goblets of refreshing light ale at the high table of the great hall. Madog had returned from his sea patrol along the coastline, leaving two ships to make one final trip as far as Andredescæster before returning to Portus Adurni.

"Ah, there you all are," he said as he approached the high table. "I hope that there is a goblet of ale for me too!"

"Yes, my lord, your best warrior made sure that there was one for you too," replied Hywel, offering the spare goblet to Elisedd.

"Oh no, not that again," sighed Elisedd. "How many times do I have to tell you both that I consider you equals, which is why I gave you each a specific role in my command structure, instead of choosing one commander over the others. I would hate to lose either one of you in battle, or for any other reason."

Cunedda said, "We know that, my lord. I guess we just want to know which one of us would be your champion if the situation ever arose."

"You are all great Gewisse warriors, but you should realise that each of you has his own set of skills that makes you all my champions," replied Elisedd.

He then turned to each of his commanders and addressed them individually.

"Madog, you are a great swordsman and a fantastic sailor, who would find a way to win any sea battle.

"Hywel, you are the best tracker and could find the best way out of any difficult situation if a threat of attack arose while in country.

"Cunedda, you can identify the best attack strategy given any situation, but also find a defensive solution, which is invaluable within the fort."

Then, addressing all three, Elisedd said, "And all three of you would lead your men in battle with a ferocity that would strike fear in any enemy. I would trust you all with my life and the lives of my family. However, for as long as you cannot agree with your status within the Gewisse, we are weaker, and that worries me."

Elisedd's patience was wearing thin with this constant tension, and it needed to end. Deciding that he needed to show his frustration, he raised his voice with his commanders for the first time in many years, saying, "You need to settle this, or return to Glevum."

Cunedda looked at Madog and Hywel, then spoke. "We are sorry, Elisedd. You are right as always. Whilst it started as a joke, perhaps we have taken it too far over these last few months. Perhaps we have been getting bored by the lack of action down here by the coast, when there is plenty of action to the north."

"If it is battle that you want," replied Elisedd, "I will see if King Wyrtgeorn will assign you to a force heading up north to take on the Picts and Scots, or any Saxon invaders in that region."

"No, you misunderstand, my lord," Cunedda said pleadingly. "You know that our loyalty to you, your family and the Gewisse is absolute. I am sure we will get the opportunity to fight in battle soon. We just need to be patient. We will not mention this ever again."

Elisedd accepted that these words were from all three, so said, "Good, because we may be about to face some great challenges in the coming years and need to be unified."

Satisfied that his commanders were now back to being a single command unit, he turned to Hywel and said, "Now, Hywel, what news from your expedition in country?"

Hywel gave his report, saying, "We found four distinct groups of Christian heretics within our region, around fifty of them in total. I have left scouts close by, to keep an eye on their movements until you decide what should be done."

"Excellent news," said Elisedd. "I am sure Bishop Germanus will be delighted when I tell him, after he has performed his miracle on Caradoc."

"What? He has agreed to heal Caradoc's leg?" queried Cunedda. "That is wonderful news. Worthy of a celebration."

"We must not get too far ahead of ourselves," said Elisedd. "For now, we can simply drink to a plan coming together, but there is still work to do."

*

Later that week, Elisedd and his family hosted their guests to a quieter evening meal in the dining room of the villa.

Lavena asked Germanus, "How are your preparations getting on, Lord Bishop?"

"We are progressing well, my lady," said Germanus. "I think we will be ready tomorrow morning. Arturius has been excellent in getting everything we need. We were thinking that it might be best to perform our work in Caradoc's room, so he can rest and recuperate afterwards, as it will take a lot out of him."

Lavena responded, saying, "That is wonderful news, my lord."

Meanwhile, Germanus tried to steer the conversation to other matters, asking, "Did I see both your land patrol and ships returning earlier this week, Lord Elisedd?"

"Yes, although two ships remain at sea just to check on a possible threat from sea pirates to the east," replied Elisedd. "It is an ongoing task, given our proximity to the northern coast of Gaul, which is a regular stepping stone for Saxon raiders. This is why my Gewisse warriors were sent here."

"Gewisse? That name sounds like a Saxon tribe," replied Germanus curiously.

"No, well not entirely Saxon, Lord Bishop," said Elisedd. "The name 'Gewisse' originates from a Roman auxiliary unit that was founded over one hundred years ago in the western province of Britannia."

Germanus was intrigued, so responded, "That would explain your accent, which I did not think was local. Do you know any more about their origins?"

Elisedd continued, "Yes, of course. The Roman governor set up this unit to maintain law and order in the old kingdoms of Ergyng and Ewias. They were based at an old hillfort, near a Roman town called Magnis, in the old kingdom of Ewias. This earned them the name of 'men of Ewias', or 'Gewisse', so the Roman governor bestowed the title of 'Dux Gewissorum' on Eudaf Octavius, the ruler of that region and these men.

"The unit combined local warriors with foederati soldiers, from conquered regions across the Roman Empire. You may have noticed that one of my commanders, Madog, has dark skin. His ancestors came from Africa terra and were part of the original foederati assigned to the auxiliary unit."

"Yes, I have to admit that I wondered how he became one of your commanders. Please continue," replied Germanus.

"Eudaf Octavius encouraged the warriors to share their various weapons and fighting skills with each other," said Elisedd. "Over the years, they gained a reputation as strong, powerful soldiers, who maintained peace and kept any potential invaders from the west and north at bay."

Germanus was extremely interested to hear this story, but wanted to find out where his host fitted into the picture, so asked, "How did you come to lead this Gewisse force, my lord?"

Elisedd replied, saying, "After the great withdrawal of Roman forces nearly forty years ago, the Gewisse were brought closer to Glevum, to help protect this important city, where the Romano-British noblemen attempted to maintain some sort of order. At that time, King Wyrtgeorn was ruler of the Gewisse, while my father had been chieftain of Magnis and a commander of the Gewisse.

"My wife is also related to King Wyrtgeorn's family by marriage. So, when Wyrtgeorn became High King of the Britons, he chose me, his kinsman, to take over as commander of the great warriors whom you have seen within the fort of Portus Adurni," said Elisedd, concluding his explanation.

"That is very interesting, Lord Elisedd. I am amazed that you have so much knowledge of your family's and the Gewisse history," said Germanus. "Where did you learn all this information?"

"Thank you, my lord," replied Elisedd. "My father recognised the importance of education and insisted that his sons receive the best education available, from local monks, elders and wise men he could find. He also believed that if we learned about our past, we would have the knowledge to avoid repeating those mistakes in the future. So, he made sure we learned about Magnis and the origins of the Gewisse, as well as the battles he had fought.

"His foresight has served us well, and my younger brother, Eldol, replaced my father as Consul of Glevum, while my youngest brother, Eldad, chose to become a monk and is now Bishop of Glevum."

"Ah, I have heard of Bishop Eldadus," said Germanus, using Eldad's official name as Bishop of the Roman Church. "However, I have never met him. Perhaps, I should make Glevum another destination on my visit to Britannia."

"I am sure Eldad would be delighted to meet such a famous church leader," said Elisedd. "If you want to meet with him, I will send a messenger to Glevum for a ship to come and escort your party round the coast to Glevum once your work is finished here."

Germanus appeared excited by this suggestion, so Elisedd made a mental note to organise it later.

*

The next morning, Elisedd was up early, too excited by the thought that his son could be healed today. He knew that success was not guaranteed, as Germanus had indicated as much, and cursed himself for his excitement, but the father in him was overwhelming his normal state of mind.

The day was bright and warm, but summer on the south coast was usually like this. Unfortunately, it also encouraged attacks from across the calmer sea.

Elisedd was sending Madog and his cohort out on patrol again, but was also arranging for them to meet up along the coast with the scouts who were keeping an eye on the Pelagian Christians, so they could get any updates on movements or additional converts. He wanted to be ready to act on his part of the deal once Germanus had healed Caradoc.

As he walked around the fort, Elisedd was greeted by his warriors, their families and the youths who were being trained to become Gewisse by some of his more senior warriors.

They looked to be a good group of strong young men, and he was confident they would be a great addition to his forces when they were ready. He knew that some were the sons of his own men, but there were also some boys from the local settlements.

If these boys became one of his Gewisse, like some of the others from the settlements, who were now part of his force, they would be free to choose to stay with their village should Elisedd and his Gewisse ever be given another role elsewhere by King Wyrtgeorn.

Elisedd hoped that King Wyrtgeorn would never withdraw the Gewisse from the region, given their success in protecting invaders on the south coast, but he knew that the continuing attacks from the north, west and east were beginning to make life difficult for the king.

He was aware that Wyrtgeorn had been trying to find peaceful terms with the men from the north but, knowing Wyrtgeorn as he did, the king would be up to something else without keeping Elisedd, or the other nobles, informed until the last minute.

As he approached the port gate, Elisedd saw Madog giving some last-minute instructions to the captains of the two patrol ships then boarding their ships and preparing for departure.

Elisedd liked watching the ships sail into the estuary, so he climbed the stone stairs of the port gate, which gave him access to the fort wall, and watched as both ships were rowed out into the estuary, before raising their sails and disappearing into the distance. When the ships were out of sight, Elisedd then returned to his villa and was greeted by Germanus and Severus, with Arturius.

"Good morning, Lord Elisedd," said Germanus.

"It looks to be a fine day, and God willing it will be a memorable one too."

"I hope you are right, Lord Bishop," replied Elisedd. "I trust that Arturius has been able to help you prepare everything you need. I heard that the local blacksmith and other craftsmen have been busy working on various contraptions for you."

"Yes, everyone has been most willing to help prepare. It appears that there is much love for you and your family in the area," said the bishop as he laid a hand on Elisedd's arm as if to encourage him to walk along the corridor with him.

Elisedd recognised the friendly gesture and went with Germanus as they walked away from Severus and Arturius.

Germanus spoke quietly, saying, "Arturius has just informed me that young Caradoc is up and ready to start. I hope you will allow myself, Severus and the other members of my travelling party of monks to work alone with Caradoc, but I understand if you would prefer to have yourself or Lavena in attendance.

"It will take a number of hours to complete our task, involving prayers for God's help, as well as some physical manipulation of Caradoc's body. There will be a lot of pain for Caradoc, which may not be pleasant for either of you to watch."

"I understand, and will speak with Lavena," replied Elisedd. "Arturius has asked if he could be in attendance, mostly out of a sense of involvement in the process, but also to provide moral support for Caradoc. They are good friends, and Arturius is always looking out for my son around the fort."

Something Elisedd never told anyone, other than Lavena, was that Arturius was his kinsman, the son of his uncle, who also came from Magnis. Having someone like Arturius close by meant that he had someone he could trust to protect Lavena and Caradoc, should any misfortune come to Elisedd or his commanders. That was why an excellent young warrior like Arturius remained in the fort, in an administrative role.

"Yes, of course," replied Germanus. "I have seen how they interact and I naturally assumed he would want to be there. I was more concerned that the room was going to be a little overcrowded, which is why I asked if you or Lavena also wanted to be there."

Elisedd said, "I know that Lavena would want to be there, but I will explain the situation and come up with something that will keep her distracted. However, if you know anything about women, Lord Bishop, you will know that they normally get their own way."

Both men shared a laugh, as Elisedd turned and headed out into the fort. He had to prepare something that would take Lavena's attention away from Caradoc. If ever there was an impossible mission, this was it.

Elisedd knew that Lavena would understand, but a mother's love for their child overwhelms everything. However, he knew she would trust him and, if he felt they should stay away and leave Germanus to work on Caradoc without their presence, she would accede.

When Elisedd told Lavena and Caradoc about the bishop's request, his son was afraid, but was reassured to know that Arturius was going to be there.

Elisedd told Caradoc that it was okay to be scared, but he was a brave warrior, just like his father, and he should think of the possibility that he might one day be able to walk unaided. That was surely worth any amount of pain that he might have to endure today.

Caradoc agreed and told his parents that he would make them proud.

Having given some thought to keeping Lavena occupied elsewhere for the day, Elisedd had already made arrangements with Hywel in advance. As a result, an hour later, Elisedd led Lavena, along with Hywel and his son, Gruffudd, all flanked by a protection force of twenty Gewisse warriors as they rode out of the fort, heading into the forest north of the village to spend the day boar hunting.

Elisedd knew that Lavena had enjoyed boar hunting in the past, but had not been in any mood to take part since Caradoc had been born.

Elisedd made sure that Hywel had sent a scout patrol out ahead of them to check out the area, visit the local estate and make sure that a wonderful lunch was prepared for the group.

So, while Germanus and his group were attempting to carry out a miracle on Caradoc's leg, Elisedd and Lavena were starting their first boar hunt for a long time.

It was a real challenge to kill a boar, due to their thick hides, manoeuvrability and speed, especially in the forest, but also because they could turn on their attacker. Therefore, it came as no surprise that the group had only killed one boar during their morning hunt. It was not a large boar, but you can really only kill the boars that are flushed out of the undergrowth. Perhaps they would find a big one after some lunch.

The group had lunch at a settlement called Wyke, alongside an old Roman road that forded the river. The local chieftain had a great hall that was often used as a hunting lodge and it had a reputation for wonderful barley ale.

*

Elisedd, Lavena and their party returned to the fort late in the afternoon. Their afternoon hunting had been better, as indicated by the four boars on the back of the cart. Three boars were a decent size, but the fourth was the biggest they had seen in the forest in a long time. On their way back, the group all agreed that the kitchen would have their hands full butchering the beasts, but it would make a wonderful feast for a celebration if Germanus had been successful in healing Caradoc's leg.

As soon as they entered the fort, Elisedd and Lavena split off from the rest of the group and headed straight for their villa. Their day out was now behind them, and the desperation to see their son, after his treatment by Germanus, was overwhelming.

As they reached the villa, Germanus, Severus and Arturius carried Caradoc out into the courtyard on a chair. The chair was lowered to the ground in front of Elisedd and Lavena, while Arturius came round to the front and helped Caradoc up to his feet.

Caradoc had a leather brace around his hips and a long T-shaped stick that he had placed under his arm for support. The major difference was that his weak leg was now straight down to the ground.

Caradoc started to make some tentative steps using both feet, but he started to falter after reaching ten steps. Arturius, who had been following him, quickly stepped in to catch him before he fell. He helped Caradoc over to a chair, so he could sit down and rest for a bit.

"That is magnificent!" said Elisedd and clapped enthusiastically.

Lavena rushed over to Caradoc and gave him a huge hug, saying, "That was amazing, my son."

Germanus then spoke to Elisedd and Lavena, saying, "This is just the beginning of a long journey for Caradoc. It will take several months for him to regain his strength to walk normally. Caradoc's nurse and Arturius know what needs to be done each day in terms of exercise, as well as a mixture of both hot and cold baths, that will help strengthen his leg. If he shows the same determination that he displayed during his healing, I am confident that he will grow up to be a worthy heir, my lord."

"I have no doubt, Lord Bishop," said Elisedd. "You have performed another miracle today, as promised. Tonight, we celebrate Caradoc's healing, and tomorrow, I start to repay your miracle."

And celebrate, they did!

The whole fort was invited to attend, apart from the obligatory sentries required to protect the fort. There was much merriness and speeches by Elisedd, praising

Germanus and his monks for the miracle that gave his son a future to look forward to as a Gewisse.

Caradoc even stood and, young as he was, he thanked Germanus, and Arturius, whilst joking that he now had no excuse but to start preparing to train as a Gewisse warrior, like all the other sons of the great men who protected Britannia from those who sought to destroy their way of life.

Lavena smiled all the way through, seeing the heir that she had always wanted to give Elisedd.

3

ELISEDD REPAYS
GERMANUS

Constantius of Lyon wrote that Elasius delivered
a number of Pelagian heretics into the hands of
Germanus in thanks for healing his son.

The next morning, Elisedd and Cunedda were walking around the walls of the fort, engaged in some talk about future plans, but mainly about Caradoc's miracle.

Eventually, Elisedd asked when the patrol ships were due back from their short trip along the coast to join up with the scouts who had been shadowing the Pelagian Christians.

"They should be back this afternoon, unless there has been a development that needs to be investigated further," said Cunedda.

Suddenly, there was a commotion at the fort gate.

Elisedd and Cunedda watched from the ramparts as a messenger was galloping hard on his horse down the road towards the main gate. They both rushed down to the gate as it opened and the rider entered, then pulled his horse up sharply and fell to the ground.

The horse was in some distress, having clearly been ridden very hard. One of the younger warriors stepped forward, took hold of the horse's reins and led it away to the stables for water and a rub down.

The messenger was lifted up and given a goblet of water to rehydrate himself. After catching his breath, he asked for Lord Elisedd.

"I am Lord Elisedd," responded Elisedd. "How do you know me?"

The messenger responded, saying, "My lord, I am from the old Roman fort of Durocastrum, two days' hard ride north from here. It is a place that you previously visited a few years back, when you informed us that we were now under your protection. We need your protection now."

"What happened?" asked Elisedd.

"We were attacked by a group of about forty Saxons, but managed to keep them at bay before they retired, presumably to regroup nearby. They came from the east, but we have not heard of any other attacks recently, so we have no idea where they are camped."

Hywel had been listening intently to the messenger recounting the story, then asked, "What is your name, rider?"

"I am Jemmett, son of one of the elders of Durocastrum, my lord," he replied.

Elisedd responded, saying, "I know the area you speak of, Jemmett, and it is under our protection. You will rest here for now, but help will be sent immediately."

Turning to his patrol commander, Elisedd said, "Hywel, send a horse patrol to Durocastrum straight away. We should also send scout patrols to Pontes and Lundein. For the Saxons to be so far inland without any warnings, they must have rowed a ship up the Tamesis, perhaps as far as Pontes. I cannot understand how they reached that far without drawing the attention of the king in Lundein, or his patrols there."

Elisedd then asked one of his men to take Jemmett to the barracks and give him some food and somewhere to rest up, before turning to the messenger to tell him that a second patrol would escort him back to Durocastrum when he had recovered.

Germanus had heard the commotion and arrived at the fort gate just in time to hear Elisedd's instructions. This was an unfortunate development, and he feared that this may take Elisedd's attention away from the Pelagians, given how urgent it was to suppress a Saxon attack in the region.

Elisedd noticed Germanus and, having given the necessary instructions, he escorted the bishop away from the main gate, saying, "Lord Bishop, we should discuss our next steps regarding the Pelagians, as I have a promise to fulfil."

"My lord, I understand that my mission may need to be delayed while you deal with this urgent matter," replied Germanus.

Elisedd was quick to respond, saying, "Nonsense. I have enough men to help you too. We also have a number of young warriors that we need to start embedding into our forces. I am assuming that the threat from these heretics will be minimal, so this will be an excellent opportunity to give these youngsters some experience."

"I think that sounds like an excellent plan, my lord," said Germanus.

"In fact, this afternoon, I am hoping to see the patrol ships return with some news for us about the heretics," said Elisedd. "We need to discuss what to do next, once we know where the heretics are based."

"Why do I think you have been preparing to help me since we first arrived, my lord?" replied Germanus, with a smile.

"Guilty, Lord Bishop," said Elisedd, "but I was also curious to see whether any heretics were in my region, what they were up to and whether they posed any threat to my control of the region. Let us wait to see what the patrol reports back and then we can decide on a plan."

This did not surprise Germanus at all. He had quickly learned that Elisedd was a man who was always planning ahead, to ensure he was prepared for anything.

*

That afternoon, Madog and all three of his patrol ships returned to port as expected, watched eagerly by both Elisedd and Germanus as they slowly manoeuvred up against the pier.

Madog stepped off the first ship, with two scouts following in his wake, and walked towards Elisedd.

"What news, Madog?" asked Elisedd.

Madog gave Elisedd his report, saying, "The scouts have reported back that there are four separate groups of Pelagians slowly moving across the region to the east, spreading their heresy and converting some locals. Each of the four groups has one preacher and four supporters."

Turning to Elisedd, Germanus said, "My lord, I think that if we made an example of the key members of each group, that is twenty in total, the recently converted may be more likely to return to their former beliefs. Might I suggest that we capture them and crucify them where they are staying, which is presumably in a small settlement?"

"Are you sure that you want to make it public?" said Elisedd. "Instead of striking fear, or putting any potential converts off, you may turn these Pelagians into martyrs. A small community might spread the word and a trickle of an idea could become a tidal wave of new converts."

After considering Elisedd's words, Germanus said, "You are right, of course, Lord Elisedd. I also appreciate that you probably know your people better. However, we need to make the Church's voice clear on this matter. Pelagian Christianity is an abhorrence and cannot be allowed to continue. Anyone who even considers anything but the pure form of Christianity preached by the Church must know that the punishment will be felt both in life and death."

It was Elisedd's turn to consider the bishop's words. He understood that Germanus and his Church needed to stop the movement, but he would be putting his weight behind the Christian Church. He needed time to consider all the ramifications.

Finally, he said, "Perhaps we can discuss this later, Lord Bishop. In the meantime, Madog, I think you should restock the ships and prepare for departure on tomorrow's tide."

Madog withdrew, then Elisedd turned and walked away, leaving Germanus stunned by this sudden hesitation from Elisedd.

Germanus knew that Elisedd would not backtrack on his promise, so felt he needed to give the ruler some time to reach his decision, whatever it was that was going through his mind. He decided to take a walk around the fort, taking any opportunities to speak with the families living there, before gathering his group together to pray for God's strength to help Elisedd reach his decision.

Elisedd did not want to make any rash decision that would affect his relationship with the people living under his protection. He knew that Lavena would be able to offer some useful advice, and he valued her opinion. He found Lavena in the villa and they discussed the situation in private.

Lavena was supportive of both viewpoints, but reminded Elisedd of his debt. She then suggested that, if Elisedd's men captured the Pelagians and brought them back to the fort, Germanus could determine their fate in private. He could then tour all the settlements in the region affected and preach his Church's stance in a sermon.

"Excellent idea, my love," said Elisedd. "I think I can sell that to Germanus."

*

Later that evening, Elisedd invited Germanus and Severus to have a private evening meal with him, Lavena and Caradoc. It was important that they had the privacy of being alone when Elisedd told Germanus of his decision.

After they had enjoyed their meal, Elisedd said, "I am sure you have been anticipating my decision since this afternoon, Lord Bishop. I want you to know that I have never contemplated doing nothing. I just needed to ensure that my authority in the region remained after you had left. Your determination to reinforce the pure word of your Church will be upheld. However, I just cannot sanction a public punishment of the people under my protection."

Elisedd watched Germanus take in his words to see if he was crossing any lines, before continuing, "I will order my men to capture the twenty Pelagians we have already identified and bring them back here. My proposal is that your own people take them back to Gaul, where your Church can deal with them as you wish. Meanwhile, you can tour the settlements where the Pelagians have been active, and you can preach the true word of God, countering the heretic message of the Pelagians."

After a pause, hoping that Germanus understood his position, Elisedd said, "I trust you will see that this option is a fair compromise that means everyone achieves their objectives. I do not expect you to give your answer now. Sleep and pray on this, and we can discuss it in the morning."

Germanus, who had been listening intently to Elisedd's proposals, agreed that they should all sleep on it, but he thought he had heard a plan that he could live with.

Germanus then changed the discussions to the attack at Durocastrum, as he sought to understand what was happening around the region.

*

After an excellent night's sleep, Germanus awoke early for prayers with his group of monks, with a sense of significant progress in his mission. There was nothing in the plan that he felt he could reasonably object to, and accepting the plan would cement his alliance with Elisedd.

Severus was equally happy with the overall plan, but suggested that he would escort the heretic prisoners back to Gaul. He was confident that Germanus and Constantius, his chronicler on this trip, could handle the sermons while he was away.

Germanus decided to talk to Elisedd after their morning meal and found him at the main gate, talking with Hywel and Cunedda.

Hywel was preparing to lead another group of warriors to follow the first group that left for Durocastrum yesterday. Jemmett was with them and looked much more refreshed after his long ride to Portus Adurni.

Germanus listened as Elisedd told Hywel that he wanted every Saxon found, and killed. Their ship should also be found and destroyed.

When Elisedd noticed Germanus, he wished Hywel good fortune and walked towards the bishop, asking him, "How are you feeling this morning, Lord Bishop?"

"As always, my lord, I am happy to be doing God's work," replied Germanus. "I am also appreciative of the efforts you have taken to help us. Your proposal last night is an acceptable compromise, considering that I am just a visitor to this region, and you need to rule the people and rely on their support long after I am gone."

"Excellent," said Elisedd. "I will send Madog out on

the next tide, to meet up with our scouts, arrange the capture of the Pelagians and bring them back here. Then, once your ship has departed for Gaul with the prisoners, Madog can take you back along the coast and will provide protection while you undertake your tour of the affected region."

"While I am waiting," said Germanus, "perhaps I could spend some time exploring the area around the fort, preaching to your community?"

Elisedd responded, saying, "You are free to go wherever you wish, Lord Bishop. If you wish, a small protection guard, as well as some locals, who can act as your guides, can be arranged. Just let Cunedda know what you want to do and he will make the necessary arrangements."

Elisedd turned and headed back to the villa. He was keen to see Caradoc trying his daily exercises. Seeing his son walking more naturally brought a huge smile to Elisedd's face.

It had also brought him closer with Lavena, knowing that they had a son who could now grow up as a potential ruler of the Gewisse. It was the greatest wish of every British nobleman for their heir to grow up to succeed them and even build on their legacy.

*

A few days later, Madog returned from along the coast, with twenty prisoners on board his ship. They were brought into the fort but, having never taken prisoners in the past, Cunedda did not have a dedicated secure building to hold them. They settled on guarding the prisoners in the stable that Hywel's patrol normally used, since it was empty at the moment.

Germanus and his entourage went down to the stables to see their captives and questioned each man separately, seeking to reassure themselves that the prisoners were indeed Pelagians and not just evangelistic Christians in Elisedd's region. Germanus also tried to find out if there were any others in the region, but also if any of their group had left the region to preach their heretic beliefs elsewhere.

While Germanus was satisfying himself that the threat in this region had been eliminated, Severus was working with their ships' master, to prepare a secure section on their ship to hold the prisoners for the trip overseas, when they were ready to sail back to Gaul.

After two days, Severus and several monks followed as Elisedd's men took the captive Pelagians out the port gate to Germanus's ship, secured them in the cargo hold, and then all set off as the tide turned and the winds would help take the ships back to Gaul.

Meanwhile, Germanus and Constantius boarded another ship with Madog, the scouts who had been following the Pelagians and forty of Elisedd's men. They would be undertaking the tour of the affected region, where Germanus would preach to the people about the true word of God's church.

Elisedd knew the bishop's mission would take around a week, which allowed him to focus on the Saxon attack on Durocastrum.

He had also received word from his brother, Eldol, in Glevum, after inviting him to visit Portus Adurni by ship to escort Germanus back to Glevum once his work was done in the region.

Eldol would be arriving in a few days, which would give Elisedd a chance to catch up with his brother and discuss current politics, including what King Wyrtgeorn was up to.

Elisedd found Cunedda with Arturius in the great hall, and they discussed the Saxon threat in the north of the region. They were expecting word back from Durocastrum, to let them know what Hywel had found when he arrived there, plus confirmation that the second patrol had also arrived.

Elisedd was worried about the ease with which the Saxons had been able to sail up the river Tamesis to get deep into his region. They had no reason to be that far upriver, so he wondered what was going on in Lundein. The returning scouts should help him decide his next steps.

A few hours later, a scout patrol arrived at the fort with mixed news. Elisedd's Gewisse forces had secured the fort at Durocastrum, found the Saxon camp at Pontes, killed the Saxons and burned the ship to the ground. Elisedd's men had suffered a few losses, with another four injured, although not severely. This was not unexpected whenever a force met with the brutality of the Saxons. The Gewisse would remain in Durocastrum for a few more days, before returning to Portus Adurni.

The bad news came from the scouts who had checked out what was going on in Lundein and how the Saxons safely sailed up the river past the city to attack Durocastrum. There was another Saxon ship docked there, and the news was that the king had held a banquet with the Saxon leaders, in an attempt to secure peace in that region. No one knew what had happened to the second ship.

For Elisedd, this confirmed what he already thought. King Wyrtgeorn was so consumed with being ruler and remaining in power, that he was unable to perceive any real threat from the Saxons.

"That man will be the death of us all," cursed Elisedd under his breath. His brother's arrival could not come too soon.

*

Five days later, a ship appeared on the horizon, prompting an alert around the fort. However, once it was identified as being Eldol's ship, from Glevum, alert turned to excitement, especially in Elisedd's family, with Lavena keen to hear news from Glevum, Caradoc eager to show his uncle how well he was able to walk after his miracle healing, and Elisedd looking for Eldol's insight and advice on what they could do about the Saxons and King Wyrtgeorn.

Elisedd decided that Lavena and Caradoc needed to have time with Eldol first, as Hywel's group were due back in fort and he wanted a briefing from his commander before talking to Eldol.

The two brothers exchanged greetings at the port gate, and shared small talk as they walked to the villa where

Lavena and Caradoc were waiting. As they reached the villa, they could see Lavena and Caradoc outside waiting.

Caradoc, still wearing the brace around his hip, was now walking with the help of the support poles created by Germanus and his monks.

When Eldol was close enough, Caradoc started walking towards his uncle. It was clear that there was some discomfort, but the smile on Caradoc's face was infectious for the others too.

When they met, Eldol hugged his nephew, saying, "What a glorious sight to see my nephew smiling, and walking. I am sure you will soon be running around the fort, giving your father sleepless nights as he tries to keep up!"

Everyone laughed.

"That would indeed be a wonderful sight to see," replied Lavena.

Eldol turned to Lavena. "Sister-in-law, it is pleasing to see you looking as beautiful and as happy as you were when I first met you many years ago. I can see that Caradoc's miracle has taken a heavy weight off your mind. That is worth this trip alone."

Elisedd told them all that he would see them later at their evening meal as he had business to deal with and wanted them to have time to catch up.

Greetings out of the way, Elisedd headed for the main gate as Eldol, Lavena and Caradoc moved into the villa.

*

That evening, Elisedd and Eldol had the opportunity to catch up on developments in their respective regions.

Eldol told Elisedd that, in the west, they had been busy repelling attacks from the Gaels of Hibernia, who had been sailing up the river Hafren, as well as coming across country, attacking villages and attempting to take Glevum. The Britons had kept them at bay for now, but the outlying settlements had suffered badly.

Glevum had also been badly affected by the attacks, leading many families to relocate further west, which they perceived would offer protection from future attacks. Most were heading to Corinium, as well as other smaller communities to the north and east of Glevum.

"That brings me to our next problem," said Eldol. "Although it is not affecting Glevum, the king has lost many men defending numerous invasions to the north of the kingdom, from the Picts and Scots, coming down the west coast and attacking the fortified towns from Deva Victrix as far south as Letocetum. He even sent a request to Rome for support, especially as there are a lot of Romano-British noble families under threat. I was informed that Rome's response left him in no doubt that we were on our own."

After taking all this in, Elisedd said, "That is certainly troubling news. I am surprised that King Wyrtgeorn did not recall the Gewisse back to defend his powerbase."

"He has seriously considered it, my brother," said Eldol. "He is spending more time in Lundein right now, but I think that is mostly because it is safer there than it is in Glevum. I was one of the consuls of Glevum who said that if we pulled you from the south, we would end up facing constant attacks on all fronts. In the meantime, I am trying to build up another force of warriors, like the Gewisse, to defend Glevum and the surrounding areas, including Corinium."

Elisedd said, "Yes, it would have been a mistake to withdraw us from this region right now. Although we had to deal with almost weekly attacks when I first arrived, things are calmer here now, thanks to expanded sea patrols, plus an early warning system of pyres set up along the coast, so we can receive an alert whenever there is an attack by sea. We also send out regular patrols of the kingdoms to deal with any land-based attacks."

Elisedd then watched his brother closely to see his immediate response when he said, "However, we recently had to deal with an unusual attack by a Saxon ship that sailed up the Tamesis, past Lundein, to attack a settlement called Durocastrum."

Eldol nearly choked on his drink when he heard this news.

"What!" he said. "The king has been in Lundein for the past month. How did the Saxons get upriver, past Lundein?"

"I hope you are ready for the next part of this story then," said Elisedd. "While the Saxon ship was attacking Durocastrum, another Saxon ship was berthed in Lundein, and its commanders were reported to have been guests at a banquet held by the king. I have been told that he discussed a peace pact with these Saxons, while their brethren were killing my people."

Eldol was silent.

"Did you hear what I said, Eldol?" asked Elisedd.

Eldol put down his goblet and said, "Yes, I heard you clearly, brother. I am just trying to comprehend what on earth Wyrtgeorn is up to. There is clearly something else going on, some sort of plan that the king is keeping close to his chest. If it has anything to do with the Saxons, I fear for all of us."

"That was exactly my first thought, too," said Elisedd. "Why is he keeping his nobles in the dark? Does he fear that we would rebel against it and wants to present us with some sort of Saxon treaty that we cannot stop without having to face him and the Saxons?"

"I would not put that past him," muttered Eldol in frustration. "There are too many questions and no way to get the answers. I need to think on this overnight. We should discuss this in the morning, with fresh eyes."

"Agreed," said Elisedd.

*

The next morning brought no answers for either Elisedd or Eldol. They could not go against the king on their own, and they did not really know what the king was planning, even if they believed the Saxons were involved somehow.

Eldol also had his own challenges at home, forming a defensive force to protect Glevum and the surrounding areas against invaders from the north and west. He felt that, if King Wyrtgeorn was going to spend more time in Lundein, then life in Glevum might be more bearable.

The brothers agreed to concentrate on their own regions for now, but would keep in touch more regularly and especially if there were any new developments.

As they concluded their discussions, a horn blew from the port gate to signal the sight of a ship entering the estuary.

By the time Elisedd and Eldol had arrived at the port gate, the gold rampant dragon on the red flag waving atop Madog's ship mast revealed that Germanus was returning from his mission.

Severus had already returned from Gaul, so there would be nothing to stop Germanus and his party from departing for Glevum as soon as he wished.

Eldol turned to Elisedd and said, "I will have my ship's master prepare the ship for departure on the first tide tomorrow. Whilst I would love to stay a little while longer, I should return to Glevum as soon as possible."

Elisedd was quietly delighted. Whilst it had been a wonderful and fortuitous event to receive the bishop on these isles, and give Caradoc a brighter future, he found religious diplomacy tiring and would rather get back to focusing on the menace of invading Saxons. He told his brother that he would introduce him to Germanus, and they would share a family meal together that evening.

Before their evening meal, Bishop Germanus blessed Elisedd, his family and the Gewisse, who were protecting these shores from the scourge of the heathens. He also prayed for Caradoc's health and a future at Elisedd's side, growing up to be a worthy ruler like his father.

The following day, Elisedd, Lavena and Caradoc

watched as the two ships left Portus Adurni, bound for Glevum.

Caradoc's walking was improving greatly, although he was still using the stick for support, but he had managed to walk down to the pier by himself to wave his healer on his journey.

Meanwhile, Elisedd's mind was already turning back to the increasing Saxon threat and the unknown plans of King Wyrtgeorn.

4

THE KING'S
SAXON ALLIANCE

In AD 449, the *Anglo-Saxon Chronicle* records that
King Wyrtgeorn invites Saxon mercenaries to Britannia
and "directed them to fight against the Picts".

The next two years ended up being relatively quiet for
Elisedd, his family and the Gewisse. After defeating
the Saxon invaders near Durocastrum, the Tamesis
valley did not suffer from any further attacks. However,
Elisedd had to deal with an increasing number of 'sea
pirates', looking suspiciously like the Saxons, attacking the
southern coastlines, from Cantia to Ordinges.

Elisedd sensed that they were probing for weaknesses
in the defences, as they never really engaged in any
fighting, choosing to withdraw when Elisedd's Gewisse
warriors came close.

Elisedd was also pleased that Caradoc had been
extremely dedicated to his daily exercises and was now
walking without the stick, although he still favoured
his other leg. Caradoc was even starting to run further,
especially around the fort.

The most significant development was that Lavena
was with child again and appeared to be in good health,
despite morning sickness in the early stages.

Naturally, Elisedd was concerned for Lavena and the baby's health, so he found the best healers, midwives and servants to look after her. This had caused some frustrated outbursts from Lavena, but she eventually realised that Elisedd meant it for the best reasons. He was simply trying to ensure that they had a healthy baby and safe delivery for Lavena.

*

One afternoon, as he was watching the Gewisse training with the younger warriors, Elisedd heard the horn from the port gate, announcing that there was a ship approaching the fort from the estuary.

By the time Elisedd reached the port gate, he could tell from the ship's flag, showing a red dragon on a white background, which was flapping strongly in the wind from the top of the mast, that it was his brother's ship.

On becoming ruler of this southern region, Elisedd had chosen to have a different flag on his ships, preferring a gold dragon on a red background instead.

Elisedd was eager to speak with Eldol, as he had learned from his scouts that Saxons had been regular visitors to Lundein over the past two years. They reported that two Saxon brothers, called Hengest and Horsa, who were leading this group of Saxon mercenaries, had been regular visitors with the king.

Once Eldol had disembarked from his ship, Elisedd stepped forward and greeted him with a hug, saying, "Good to see you again, Eldol."

"You too, brother," was Eldol's reply.

"So, what news from Glevum?" asked Elisedd as they walked into the fort.

Eldol replied, saying, "Not good, brother. We have a defensive guard protecting as much of the city and surroundings as we can, but the Hibernians are a devilish lot. Once they realised that we had our own militia, they started raiding in smaller numbers on the outlying settlements, taunting us to come out and tackle them. Whilst we have had a number of victories over them, their raids continue."

"You are right, brother," said Elisedd. "That does not sound good."

Eldol continued, "It gets worse. With the increasing numbers of families leaving for a safer life inland, my forces cannot be easily replenished. The city elders sent a messenger to King Wyrtgeorn, informing him of these developments. His response was that he had no free warriors as they were up north fighting the Picts, so I am hoping that you will give me some good news."

Elisedd said nothing as he took in this news.

"Oh no," said Eldol. "Your silence says more than enough. Do we have time now, or will we leave the worse news until after seeing your family has cheered me up?"

"Later, come and see Lavena and Caradoc first," replied Elisedd. He could sense pieces of a puzzle starting to fit together and needed more time to process the latest piece from his brother.

"I am jealous of you, Elisedd. You have a beautiful wife, who has blessed you with one son and possibly another on the way. I have yet to meet anyone who would give me half as much pleasure as it appears that you enjoy with Lavena."

"What can I say, brother," said Elisedd, smiling. "I guess I have stolen the best woman that Glevum had to offer."

The following morning, Eldol and Elisedd spent some time walking along the ramparts of Portus Adurni, when Eldol asked, "So, brother, what is your bad news?"

Elisedd then told Eldol about the report from his scouts in Lundein, saying, "I think you have already surmised what the king is up to, but I can fill in the details for you, and it is not good. I suspect that we will hear it officially soon, but the facts are these.

"For the past two years, King Wyrtgeorn has been involved in negotiations in Lundein, with a band of Saxon mercenaries, behind the backs of the regional chieftains and noble families. He has been seen regularly with two Saxon brothers, called Hengest and Horsa, who are leaders of these Saxons, although their forces consist of Angles and Jutes too.

"While this is going on, I suspect that these Saxons are applying pressure, by invading eastern coastlines north of Lundein, as well as the southern coastlines, posing as sea pirates, just close enough for word to reach the king of an increasing threat to his power.

"I think he is about to announce that he has reached an agreement for these Saxons to provide protection to Britannia. The question is, at what cost, and where is he going to find the funds to pay for it?"

Eldol sat quietly for a few minutes pondering everything that Elisedd had just said. He was trying to calculate all the implications of this, both for the country and for him as *de facto* ruler of Glevum. When Eldol eventually spoke, it was quietly, but clearly and concisely, so that Lavena could also understand what he was saying.

"Elisedd, my brother, my advice to you would be to prepare an exit plan for you, your family and the Gewisse," he said. "I fear that this deal with the Saxons will not last long and, given your proximity to Lundein, it could place you all in danger, including King Wyrtgeorn, although I do not yet know how. Call it a gut feeling, but I am genuinely concerned."

"Returning to Glevum would be our best option," replied Elisedd. "However, I should have a backup if Glevum is at risk. I could establish a landholding over in Armorica, round the peninsula, in the western region of the old Veneti. We could establish a merchant business and keep in touch with Britannia, using our ships to trade with Dumnonia and Glevum as a cover."

"Do not reveal these plans to anyone, other than those you trust to help with your preparations without arousing any suspicion," replied Eldol.

Eldol then told Elisedd that, after he left Portus Adurni, he was heading over to Armorica, to meet with some nobles already living in exile over there. He suggested taking someone from Elisedd's command unit with him, as part of a scouting mission.

Elisedd quickly agreed, suggesting that Madog

accompany Eldol, under the cover of looking to establish a base for a new merchant business.

Elisedd then suddenly had another thought, adding, "I think I will also send Arturius with Madog. I would like to get him more involved in a command role, especially as he is kin and sworn to protect us. This could be a good first step, even if nothing comes of it."

Eldol agreed with his brother's plan.

"I will discuss it with Madog and Arturius straight away," said Elisedd. "In the meantime, we must await news of whatever deal our king agrees with these Saxons, to answer the questions that evade us for now."

Eldol then added, "You know, it is in times like these that I envy our brother, Eldad. He remains immune to such politicking and deception, but his church calling was something that evaded me, just like a good wife!"

And so it was that Madog and Arturius boarded Eldol's ship the following morning, and Elisedd watched as it headed out into the estuary, bound for Armorica.

Elisedd had told Madog and Arturius the cover story before they left, but had asked Eldol to brief them thoroughly during the journey to Armorica. Whilst they were away, Elisedd had told Cunedda and Hywel what was being planned. All four Gewisse commanders were sworn to secrecy.

It was clear that they had an understanding of the implications for the future for Elisedd, his family and the Gewisse arising from the developments with the king, and agreed with Elisedd's plan if Portus Adurni came under threat from the Saxons. They knew their leader was no coward, so this must be serious for such a plan to become necessary.

*

A week later, Eldol's ship returned to Portus Adurni with Madog and Arturius.

Elisedd greeted his brother, saying, "Welcome back, Eldol. I trust your trip was fruitful. How did you get on with Madog and Arturius?"

"They were natural communicators and built some excellent relationships that I think will be useful going forward," replied Eldol.

"That is great news, brother, but we can discuss the trip in more detail later," said Elisedd. "While you were away, messengers arrived from Lundein. The king has commanded our presence in Lundein in three days' time, to hear news of a treaty with the Saxon mercenaries. The same message has been sent to all noblemen and rulers throughout the land."

"Well, I might as well head there straight from here. And we have our ships," replied Eldol.

"I am wary of taking a ship, just in case there is an attack along the coast while we are occupied in Lundein," said Elisedd. "I think an overland trip would be safer, especially if I bring a protective guard, sufficiently large to put off any attack on us. However, we would need to prepare to depart first thing tomorrow. Are you happy with that?"

Eldol responded, "I trust your knowledge of this region and wariness of a sea attack whilst the nobles are in Lundein, so I accept your assessment of the most favourable route to and from Lundein."

"Excellent," said Elisedd. "In the meantime, a room has been prepared for you in the villa. Go and rest up for now. I will finalise the details of a journey by land with Hywel, so he can send out an advance party of scouts to check out our route and also prepare overnight camps. We have a long journey ahead of us."

*

Three days later, Elisedd and Eldol arrived in Lundein with 200 Gewisse warriors as their protection guard. Hywel had secured an encampment just outside the walls, to the west, giving them options should a quick departure be necessary.

During the journey, Eldol told Elisedd about the trip to Armorica. They had travelled as far as Darioritum, where the local chieftain had welcomed them, treating Madog and Arturius with great respect, especially when he heard that they were Gewisse. It turned out that he originally hailed from Cantia and knew of the Gewisse.

Madog and Arturius had proven to be talented negotiators, and there was a port-side warehouse available if they wanted to start up a genuine merchant business. Arturius had suggested that it would be worth starting it up now, on a small scale, so it could be expanded quickly at a later date.

The next day, Elisedd and Eldol ventured into the city to attend the pronouncement by the king at the old

Roman governor's palace. This was one of the few Roman buildings to survive when the Romans left Lundein and was used by King Wyrtgeorn as his official residence.

Elisedd and Eldol entered the great hall that was part of the palace complex and found a seat midway down a long table on the side that was closest to the doorway they had just entered.

Whilst their seniority merited a seat near the top table, their decision to sit amongst more junior nobles might make other nobles wonder what they knew. However, there was a risk that King Wyrtgeorn might notice this deliberate move by two senior nobles, and realise that they were already aware of his plans and did not approve. If he did notice, he might call them out on it, but that was a risk they were prepared to take.

Servants began filling goblets with ale for all the nobles as they took their seats, and continued to fill empty goblets for those with a thirst.

As far as Elisedd could see, the only absentee amongst the attending nobles and rulers was King Erbin of Dumnonia, who clearly felt immune to Wyrtgeorn's rule or commands, which surprised nobody.

Eventually, a steward called for silence and announced the king. Everyone stood up as King Wyrtgeorn entered, accompanied by the Saxon leaders, Hengest and Horsa, and a young woman, who sat next to the king. The four of them sat down at the top of the table, alongside the king's three sons. The king signalled for everyone else to take their seats.

As Elisedd and Eldol sat down, they turned to look at each other. The appearance of the Saxons at the meeting and their closeness with the king was unexpected, proving that this pronouncement was not up for any discussion. But their big question was, who was this woman?

King Wyrtgeorn stood and addressed his nobles.

"For many years now, our kingdoms have been envied by our neighbours, who saw wealthy lands, without the protection of Rome, as an easy target. While Lord Elisedd and his Gewisse warriors have kept our southern shores relatively secure from attack by sea pirates, they simply moved round to our eastern coastline and have been ravaging our lands to the east."

Elisedd noticed the emphasis on the danger being sea pirates, not the very Saxons who had attacked his lands. He was also sure he saw the king looking around the room for him after mentioning his name, before he continued speaking.

"We also have the Hibernians and the Picts making incursions from the west and north and, while we have managed to keep them at bay for now, there have been significant losses, making these lands susceptible to being over-run in the near future.

"I approached the Roman Emperor, appealing for help, but Rome refused our pleas, as it has bigger issues to deal with closer to home right now. This left me with only one alternative. I needed to recruit a force of mercenaries to help protect us where we are weakest.

"My first challenge was to find a suitable band of warriors who would be willing, and able, to help us defend these lands. I sent scouts overseas to Gaul to find anyone who would meet our needs. It took over a year, but they came back with reports of a group of mercenaries, led by Hengest and Horsa, who you see seated with me here.

"I have spent the last few months negotiating with Hengest and Horsa to reach a mutually beneficial agreement, which is why I have commanded your presence here today."

Elisedd and Eldol both turned to look at each other after hearing the king claim that he had only been talking with these 'mercenaries' for a few months. They both knew that was a blatant lie, but they may be the only ones who knew it.

The king continued his speech, saying, "Hengest and Horsa have agreed to bring three ships of their mercenaries to defend our lands to the east and north from the Hibernians, Picts and sea pirates who have blighted these lands.

"In exchange for their service, I have promised to pay Hengest and Horsa the sum of 20,000 pounds of gold weight, and I expect the ruler of each region to pay a share of the gold weight as a tax, depending on their region's hidage. I have also granted the territory of Tanat's Island in Cantia to Hengest and Horsa, for their men to build a community there.

"Finally, I have one further announcement. In order to cement our new alliance, Hengest has agreed that his daughter, Rowena, whom you see here, will become my wife. You all know that I have been without a queen since my wife, Sevira, died several years past. I am delighted that Rowena has agreed to wed me and become your new queen.

"I am sure you will all agree that this treaty will help secure our kingdom's safety for the foreseeable future. And, I cannot complain about having a new queen to share my bed!

"So, raise your goblets and toast our new allies… Hengest and Horsa."

The nobles all raised their glasses high, shouting, "Hengest and Horsa."

Feeling smug with himself, and having been able to tell all the nobles about his new young bride, Wyrtgeorn sat down.

The murmurs began to rise amongst the nobles until Wyrtgeorn's eldest son, Gwerthefyr, stood up and spoke.

"My lord, I am sure your nobles will all support the decisions you have taken for the good of the kingdom. And, as your son, I welcome Rowena into our family. I am sure she will make you very happy and will make a wonderful queen. So, we should celebrate the king and his new bride with a toast."

Gwerthefyr then raised his goblet and shouted, "King Wyrtgeorn and Queen Rowena!"

The nobles then responded, repeating Gwerthefyr's toast.

Gwerthefyr sat down next to his brothers, knowing that no one would question the king's decision, especially if his heir supported this treaty.

Elisedd turned to Eldol and raised his eyebrows. He thought it would be unwise to speak freely in this company, and his brother would know what his facial expression meant, especially as they already had an inkling what King Wyrtgeorn had been planning. The tax on their regions was not unexpected, but the granting of lands in Cantia was a surprise. However, it was the marriage to a young woman that astonished them the most, especially given the massive age difference.

As food was brought out by the servants, and they all enjoyed the celebration banquet, the two brothers simply exchanged small talk with each other and their nearest guests, carefully avoiding giving away their true positions on the king's announcement.

After the banquet, Elisedd and Eldol returned to their encampment and spent the rest of the evening discussing the implications of the day's pronouncement.

"How on earth can he see that this is a good decision?" asked Elisedd.

"I do not agree with it any more than you do," said Eldol. "However, who else was going to come to our aid?"

"Yes, I can see that," Elisedd responded. "However, these Saxons cannot be trusted, even if he has been generous in giving them gold and lands to settle with their families. My biggest concern is that they are going to be based on my doorstep. Why not base them further north, so they are between the enemy and the lands they are meant to protect? Now, I am going to have to spend more time watching the border with Cantia, to make sure these Saxons remain within their own lands."

"What did you think of Gwerthefyr's support for his father's treaty at the end?" asked Eldol. "Was it genuine, or did he utter it out of duty and loyalty to his father?"

"I am not sure," said Elisedd. "If the Saxons do attack in any force, I doubt the king will be inclined to take up arms against his wife's father. However, Gwerthefyr might be convinced to rise up against them if he believed that Hengest would seek to usurp him in the event of the king's death."

"That is an interesting point," considered Eldol. "I will try to see what I can do when we return to Glevum. If the king remains in Lundein, Gwerthefyr will probably head back to Glevum with his brothers, before they proceed on to their own kingdoms further west. I could assess his real feelings towards the treaty. I also wonder if he knows that they are the very Saxons who have been attacking our shores."

"Be careful, brother," suggested Elisedd. "We do not know how much Gwerthefyr was involved in his father's treaty."

Changing the subject, Elisedd then asked, "Did you notice the young nobleman called Ambrosius Aurelianus, a Romano-Briton like us, at today's gathering? He has recently been installed by the king as ruler of the lands to the west of me."

"Yes, I saw him," said Eldol. "I have heard that he was found as a young boy by King Wyrtgeorn and has been brought up by him, like a son. Strangely, he bears a striking resemblance to the former Emperor Constantine, whose death allowed Wyrtgeorn to become king. If he is Constantine's son, we might be able to persuade him to join us in an alliance to protect the southern lands from these Saxons. Would you be able to work on him?"

"Definitely," said Elisedd. "I will arrange to pay him a visit as a neighbouring ruler looking for peaceful relations.

I can gauge his level of support for the king and, if he is wavering, I will start to bring him round to our way of thinking, assuming he is not just a weak puppet put in place by Wyrtgeorn to spy on me!"

After finishing his goblet of ale, Elisedd said, "We should get some sleep. We have an early start and I want to get back to Portus Adurni to start making plans to increase patrols on my eastern lands, as well as finding 6,000 pounds of gold, which I presume is the amount I will be expected to pay to have these Saxons on my doorstep."

"Yes," said Eldol. "We can talk further in the morning on our return journey."

They retired to their tents, but sleep would elude them for most of the night. They both knew that a storm was coming.

Their journey back to Portus Adurni was quiet, with Elisedd and Eldol both considering the challenges ahead of them. Their discussions did not lead to any new revelations, so the plans they made the night before remained for now.

After arriving back at Portus Adurni, Eldol left on the very next tide, to make sure he was back in Glevum before Gwerthefyr and his brothers arrived there.

*

A few weeks later, Elisedd heard from his own scouts that Hengest and Horsa had returned to Britannia with nearly 150 Saxon mercenaries, on three ships. They had landed at Wippidsfleet in Cantia.

For Elisedd, it could have been worse, but the proximity of the Saxon base to the estuary leading up to Lundein was concerning. It meant that the king was closer to these Saxons than he was to his powerbase in Glevum.

It also meant that they had a base to attack the southern coastlines more often, assuming they were part of the same group that had previously attacked the region. That could help Elisedd convince Ambrosius Aurelianus of the need to establish an alliance with him against an increased threat from the Saxons on his region. It would be a good starting position, at the very least.

5 ANOTHER SON FOR ELISEDD

Elisedd and Lavena are blessed with the birth of
a healthy son, but the Saxon threat increases in
southern Britannia.

Six months later, Elisedd and Lavena were blessed with
the birth of their second son, and the best news was
that both mother and baby were healthy.

It was a time of joyous celebration for the whole family,
prompting a return to Portus Adurni for Eldol, this time
accompanied by his brother Eldad, the Bishop of Glevum.

Elisedd and Caradoc greeted them at the port gate,
with both uncles showing their delight to see that Caradoc's
walking was much improved, to the point where he no
longer needed a stick to help him.

It was the first time that Eldad had seen Caradoc in
years, so the bishop was the first to speak as they walked
into the fort, towards the villa.

"I cannot believe this is my young nephew standing
before me," he said. "It is indeed a miracle! Praise our lord
for bringing Bishop Germanus into our lives and giving
Caradoc the chance to grow up and be a great warrior like
his father."

"Thank you, uncle," said Caradoc. "My leg is getting stronger and stronger. I can run and jump now. Father says it will not be long until I start learning how to fight like a Gewisse warrior."

Right on cue, they all heard crying from the villa.

"I hear that my baby son is awake," said Elisedd. "I am sure that Lavena will be bringing him down shortly, especially once she hears that you have arrived."

"Have you chosen a name yet?" asked Eldol.

"We have," said Elisedd.

"We have called him Ceredig," shouted Caradoc excitedly, revealing his joy at having a baby brother.

"Ceredig?" said Eldad. "That is a fine name."

"It means 'cherished' in the old language," said Elisedd. "After everything that Lavena has been through over the past few years, this is another miracle and Elisedd will truly be cherished."

"I am sure he will be cherished, brother," said Eldad.

At that point, Lavena joined them in the garden of the villa, carrying their new baby, Ceredig, who immediately became the centre of everyone's attention.

Later that evening, with Ceredig and Caradoc both asleep and Eldad spending time with Lavena, Elisedd and Eldol were alone in the great hall, enjoying a goblet of light ale.

"So, brother, what news from Glevum?" asked Elisedd.

Eldol responded, saying, "I was able to talk with Gwerthefyr and his brothers back in Glevum after the treaty announcement. They were unaware of the Saxons' subterfuge and surprised that the king had been in talks with them for over two years. They also share our concerns about the deal, and it seems that their father is infatuated with Rowena. On a more positive note, I have been able to build a good relationship with Gwerthefyr and his brothers, and we have been working more closely together, joining forces to take on any attacks from Hibernia."

"That is at least some good news," said Elisedd. "However, Gwerthefyr is probably oblivious to the fact that the Saxons have also been exerting their authority across Cantia. There has also been another arrival of ships at Wippidsfleet, with more Saxon mercenaries."

"How have you been able to find that out?" asked Eldol.

"You know I never trusted them," replied Elisedd. "So I have had scouts checking on them. They have expanded beyond Tanat's Island and now have control over Durovernum. A large number of Cantia nobles appealed to the king for help, but when he ignored them, they fled from the region, heading overseas to Armorica, while some of their people have sought safety and work in my region."

Elisedd could see that Eldol was shocked at the sudden and unopposed expansion by the Saxons, so continued with his news.

"If all of Cantia falls under their control, I am pretty sure that the Saxons could turn their attention to the southern coastline and the old Roman fort at Portus Lemanis. From there, Andredescæster comes under threat, which will put us at odds with them. They also control the route to

Lundein up Watling Street, and the estuary, so Lundein is effectively under their control too."

Eldol asked, "That is very concerning, Elisedd. What can you do?"

"Well, I am not going to let them walk into my lands unopposed," said Elisedd. "As you had suggested, Hywel has been recruiting more fighters from across the lands for a secondary militia force. They would be based up and down the border with Cantia, with each patrol under the command of one of my Gewisse warriors. We have also instituted a series of fire beacons at each settlement along the coast as an early warning system, in case they come by sea."

Eldol responded, saying, "Well, at least you have a plan ready to deal with them if they make their move."

"Yes," said Elisedd. "However, if they continue to bring more forces from overseas to bulk up their numbers, I will need help from elsewhere. I do not expect help from the king in Lundein, so Gwerthefyr could be crucial to any defence against these Saxons."

"What about Ambrosius Aurelianus, ruler of the Durotriges to the west?" asked Eldol. "Have you had a chance to meet him?"

"Yes, I visited Durnovaria during a ship patrol and met with him there," said Elisedd. "He comes across as an excellent leader and is also concerned about these Saxons. He has agreed to provide support to me, if required, especially as my sea patrols now venture as far west as his region, so he is benefiting from this. He has over 300 trained warriors, mostly locals, but includes some sons of

Romans with excellent training. That will help for now, but if Hengest brings even more mercenaries to Britannia, that still may not be enough."

Eldol responded, saying, "I will raise this with Gwerthefyr when I get back to Glevum. I am sure he will understand, especially as it reinforces his own concerns."

"That would be a great help, brother," said Elisedd. "Now, enough politics. Let us toast my new son."

They raised their goblets and said, in unison, "To Ceredig!"

*

After celebrating the birth of Ceredig, Elisedd's brothers returned to Glevum, and life settled down again at Portus Adurni.

Caradoc's leg had improved to the point where he was regularly seen running the circuit of the fort, with Arturius joining in, whenever he had time.

Ceredig was growing fast and was a delightful baby, giving Elisedd and Lavena peaceful nights, which was a stark difference to Caradoc's early years.

Lavena was enjoying having two healthy children and enjoyed seeing Elisedd's happiness visibly showing too. She knew things had been tense since he had returned from Lundein and he had told her about the escape routes they had planned if the Saxons became a threat to Portus Adurni.

Elisedd was happy with his family situation and tried to take time to be with them more often. However, he was very good at keeping his concerns about the threat that the Saxons posed away from his children. As far as he was concerned, they deserved peace for now. Elisedd knew it would not be long before he had to lead his men into battle against the Saxons, so the current peace was welcome.

A small number of incursions along the coastline by sea pirates, looking suspiciously like Saxons, kept Madog and his men busy. Meanwhile, Hywel and his regular patrols now included a tour of the border units, and any incursions into Elisedd's lands from the north were small and easily dealt with. However, Elisedd knew these were just initial probes by the Saxons to identify any weaknesses in his forces.

Cunedda had asked Arturius to get more involved in training the younger warriors, as he wanted Arturius to gain as much experience in the various aspects of commanding the Gewisse.

Elisedd had noticed this increase in Arturius's activities, and approved. He could see that Cunedda was mentoring the young man, developing his skills to take command in some capacity going forward.

Elisedd liked Cunedda's foresight that the Saxon threat needed warriors ready to step up in the event of losses at command level. He was also aware that Hywel was involving his son, Gruffudd, in his regular patrols, so thought he should speak with Hywel, Cunedda and Madog with a view to setting up a varied range of command experience for any other Gewisse warriors who had shown potential for command roles.

However, Elisedd knew that this relative peace would not last. He was proven right when Gewisse scouts arrived back at the fort one day, to report that a band of forty Saxons had found a way through the marshes that formed a natural boundary between Cantia and the lands of the Regni. They had attacked a small settlement, killing the men there, and slaughtered cattle and taken the meat as well as a couple of young women with them back across the marshes. They had escaped before a local patrol had even heard the news.

This new development had come earlier than he thought. It was clearly a sign of restlessness amongst the Saxons. They had won several battles in the north against both the Picts and the Hibernians, with the number of invasions reducing to the point of being handled easily by a force of Saxons who had remained in the north. This would have been perfect for Elisedd, but the expanded numbers of Saxons now living in Cantia had left a large number of them without a reason to spend their time fighting in the north.

And, as far as Elisedd was concerned, a restless Saxon is a dangerous Saxon. There were now over 1,000 Saxons in Cantia. They had families, lands of their own to manage, but that was still not enough. Just as Elisedd and Eldol had predicted, they had set their sights on controlling a larger region.

Now they were starting to encroach into his lands, Elisedd knew it would not be long before he had to lead his forces into battle against these Saxons.

*

The summer harvest stopped any further attacks by Saxons, and the winter was particularly cold, wet and windy, which helped keep the peace. However, when spring came, the attacks increased and the local patrols had their first battle against the Saxons. There were losses on both sides, but the Saxons retreated back through the marshes.

A month later, another group of Saxons attacked estates in the forests of Andredeslea, but their tactics changed. This time, there were larger numbers of Saxons and they stayed on the lands they had attacked. They killed the local families, keeping the livestock for their own use.

One of Elisedd's patrols tried to take them on, but this time they were completely wiped out.

For Elisedd, this was the final straw, so he immediately ordered a large force of his warriors to prepare to leave to take on these Saxons. He also decided that this was the time to lead from the front, but he also wanted to make a statement that Hengest and Horsa, the Saxon leaders, would hear, which was "keep out of my lands".

Leading 300 men for the first time in years brought back happy memories for Elisedd, but Hywel was a great commander and made it easier for him.

The Gewisse warriors were also slightly awed by having Elisedd lead them once again, after so long. Some of the older warriors remembered being at Elisedd's sides in the early days when he had just taken over as ruler of the Gewisse and they had journeyed down to Portus

Adurni to take control of the region. The stories of past battles could be heard around the camp the night before they were going to face the Saxons for the first time.

However, Elisedd, Hywel and the three leaders in the patrol command group, including Gruffudd, were busy discussing their tactics. Hywel's scouts had reported that around 150 Saxons were camped together at one estate and appeared to be anticipating an attack.

Elisedd's local patrol groups had also been brought together and had camped to the north, ready to support the attack on the Saxons. His instructions were clear. The local patrol group were to circle round behind the Saxons, to prevent any escape, while Elisedd's warriors would attack, using overwhelming force to destroy these Saxons.

Elisedd knew that a message needed to be sent, and the journey had given him a chance to consider an appropriate one. He commanded that no mercy be given to any of these invaders, until they were down to the last man.

As dawn broke the next morning, Elisedd's men commenced their march towards the Saxon camp. Within a mile of the Saxons, Hywel gave the order to start making as much noise as they could, both shouting and hitting the front of their shields with their axes.

Elisedd enjoyed the feel of carrying his shield for the first time in a long while. It was a Roman cavalry-style oval shield, with a gold rampant dragon on a red background, similar to his banner. Eldol had commissioned the shield as a gift for his brother after Elisedd had become ruler of the Gewisse.

As the farm estate came into sight, Hywel ordered Elisedd's men to stop moving but continue making as much noise as possible, designed to build up the tension of the impending battle. They waited in full view of the Saxons, who could be seen preparing for battle.

Then Hywel ordered the men to stop the noise. There was no point in continuing making a huge noise when it had served its purpose. This would normally signal an impending attack. Yet, Elisedd's men still waited. Both Elisedd and Hywel's eyes were focused on the distance, waiting for a signal that the local patrol warriors were in position.

When a column of smoke rose above trees behind the farm estate, Hywel blew his horn three times, as a signal for the Gewisse to start their march towards the Saxons.

Suddenly, bursting out of trees to the Saxons' left and right came mounted Gewisse warriors, led by Gruffudd, galloping at full force towards the Saxons' flanks. The Saxons were confused by this, unable to decide which was the greater threat.

The horse riders were faster and attacked the Saxons, first from the left and then from the right. This attack was not intended to kill, simply disrupt the Saxons, allowing the Gewisse force to reach them while they were in disarray after the second wave of riders had passed.

Now running towards the Saxons, Elisedd and his men had timed their run perfectly and hit the Saxons just as the mounted warriors dispersed.

The battle was short, with Elisedd's plan working perfectly, thanks to the overwhelming numbers of Gewisse.

The mounted Gewisse took out any Saxons attempting to flee the battlefield.

After an hour of fighting, there were only a handful of Saxons left, backed up against the wall of a farm building, surrounded by the Gewisse.

Elisedd, Hywel and Arturius stepped forward into the space between their men and the cornered Saxons. Sensing their impending death, the five remaining Saxons chose to charge the leaders all at once, thinking that they could possibly take them out before being killed themselves, knowing that was the inevitable conclusion to this battle.

Hywel and Arturius stepped forward, taking two men each and killing them with ease.

The sole Saxon who attacked Elisedd sensed his opportunity, but did not realise how skilled a fighter he was taking on. Elisedd quickly assessed the skill of his opponent and was able to toy with him, letting him make all the attacks, parrying them away. After a while, the Saxon was clearly tiring, so Elisedd swatted away his opponent's next attack, disarming him of his axe and knocking him to the ground.

"Please, my lord, let me die with my axe in hand," the Saxon pleaded as he lay on the ground.

"Be thankful that it is not your destiny to die today, Saxon," replied Elisedd. "I need you to deliver a message to Hengest and Horsa. As the last Saxon standing, you get to be my messenger. Will you take my message back to your rulers?"

"Yes, my lord," said the Saxon, accepting that he had no other option.

Elisedd then told him, "I need to you to listen to my

message clearly and deliver it to your leaders. Tell them that Lord Elisedd of the Gewisse does not care if the Saxons control the whole of Cantia. I am ruler of this region and will defend these lands against any and all invaders, even if it means the end of all Saxons in Britannia. The next time I find Saxon invaders in my lands, I will kill every single man, then pile them up high in a ship, sail it round to Wippidsfleet and, when it is in sight of the port, I will set this ship alight and send it into port."

After giving the Saxon some time to absorb his message, Elisedd asked him, "Do you understand what I have said?"

"Yes, my lord," replied the Saxon.

"Excellent," said Elisedd.

Whilst Elisedd had been talking to the Saxon, Hywel had set about a task he had discussed with Elisedd the night before. He returned and nodded to Elisedd, to signal that all the preparations had been made.

"Now, Saxon, I cannot allow you to ever take up arms against us again, and I need Hengest and Horsa to take my message seriously," said Elisedd.

He then nodded and two of his men stepped forward, dragging the Saxon to his feet as Elisedd stepped forward to remove the Saxon's seax long knife from its sheath.

"You will get your seax back when you are allowed to leave," Elisedd said.

The Saxon was taken round the building into the farmyard area, where a fire had been lit. There was a table and bench near the fire, to which the Saxon was taken and forced to sit on the bench.

"You fight with your right hand," said Elisedd.

It was not a question. Elisedd had watched him fight with his axe in his right hand. This was a signal to the men controlling the Saxon to grab the Saxon's right arm and force it down onto the table.

Almost immediately, Hywel swung an axe and severed the Saxon's right hand from his arm.

The Saxon screamed so loud that Elisedd hoped it would be heard in Cantia.

Arturius, who was standing by the fire, picked up an implement from the fire, approached the Saxon and pressed the hard, hot surface of the blacksmith's tool against the wound, cauterising it, which stopped the bleeding immediately.

Another man stepped forward and wrapped the Saxon's arm stump in cloth, to protect the wound from infection while it healed.

Almost immediately, two more Gewisse warriors stepped forward and helped the Saxon's two handlers lift the Saxon up and laid him down on the table, holding him down tightly, as Arturius returned from the fire with another implement.

When he realised what was about to happen, the Saxon screamed "No!" and started to struggle, trying to turn his head away from Arturius.

Hywel grabbed the Saxon's head and held it steady, facing upwards, as Arturius took the hot poker and pressed it against the left eye of the Saxon, who screamed as the poker sizzled while blinding him.

Another man came with a cloth to wrap around the Saxon's head, covering the injured eye.

Elisedd then told the Saxon, "That will ensure you are unable to fight ever again, but will allow you to hold your seax in the event of your death at some point in the future. Now, do you still remember my message for your leaders, or do I need to repeat it?"

The Saxon was almost bent double holding his right wrist from the severe pain, but nodded to confirm that he understood Elisedd. He then shouted an obscenity as the effect of nodding impacted on his eye wound.

"Good," said Elisedd, who approached the Saxon and placed the seax back in the Saxon's sheath, confident that the Saxon had no means to use it.

The Saxon was taken over to a horse and helped to mount it, before Elisedd said, "This horse will help you get back to your own lands faster, so your message reaches Hengest and Horsa before they make another stupid mistake in thinking that we Britons are helpless."

Elisedd then slapped the hindquarters of the horse and it started to trot away, carrying Elisedd's Saxon messenger on its back.

*

For the next year, Elisedd's scouts did not report any incursions by the Saxons into his territory. He concluded that Hengest and Horsa had received his message and understood the ramifications of challenging him, at least for now. However, these scouts informed Elisedd that the Saxons had extended their control over most of Cantia and that another three ships had arrived in Wippidsfleet with more Saxon mercenaries.

With the numbers that Hengest and Horsa now had at their disposal, Elisedd knew he would definitely need reinforcements of his own, in case the Saxons chose to attack in larger numbers.

Elisedd's alliance with Ambrosius Aurelianus would increase his numbers by up to 300 men, but that would not be enough against a full Saxon attack.

Elisedd had kept his brother and the king's sons informed of the Saxon's expansion plans. Meanwhile, Gwerthefyr had sent his own messenger to Portus Adurni to confirm his support for Elisedd against the Saxons expanding their territory beyond Cantia, offering to bring a force of 500 warriors if needed.

Gwerthefyr had appealed to his father, King Wyrtgeorn, to intervene and get the Saxons to stay within their own lands, which was now generally accepted as being the whole of Cantia, only leaving when they were needed to deal with northern invasions.

However, the king had taken Hengest's side, saying that he had only been dealing with invaders around Cantia. This convinced Gwerthefyr that Rowena had bewitched the king to the point where he was simply repeating what Hengest told him.

The following spring brought news that Elisedd did not want to hear, having hoped that Hengest and Horsa would have taken his previous threats seriously.

King Wyrtgeorn's decision to support them over his own son, as well as their increased numbers, had given Hengest and Horsa enough confidence to take on Elisedd. As a result, a large force of Saxons, led by Horsa, had travelled on ships, landing near Andredescæster, and attacked the old Roman fort and settlement there.

Luckily for the inhabitants, Hywel had been visiting Andredescæster as part of his regular patrols, so there had been a sizeable contingent of Gewisse warriors in the fort, who had successfully repelled the Saxons' initial attacks. Hywel also had scouts in the area and, having seen the attacks, they quickly returned to Portus Adurni for reinforcements.

On hearing the news, Elisedd immediately ordered Madog to prepare the four ships now in their fleet, and they headed out on the next tide, with a full complement of men. The scouts accompanied Madog on his ships and would disembark at a natural harbour round the coast from Andredescæster, where Madog and his ships would remain out of sight.

Elisedd and Arturius took most of the remaining Gewisse in fort and headed out on horseback at their best speed, leaving Cunedda and Gruffudd with sufficient numbers to defend the fort from attack.

When Elisedd and his warriors met Madog at their prearranged meeting point, the scouts had also returned, reporting that Hywel and his men in the old fort were holding their ground against the Saxons. The scouts had also come across Saxon scouts, killing four and capturing one, whom they had brought with them for questioning.

They discovered from their captive that there were 500 Saxons in the initial attack, although they had suffered some losses and injuries. There were ten Saxon ships beached on the shoreline, south of the fort, manned by limited numbers of guards.

There was no easy way to approach the Saxon ships without being seen, but they would not be able to move while the tide was out. If the Saxons were expecting a response from Elisedd, it was by land. Elisedd's concern was whether Horsa knew how many men he would be bringing.

The scouts advised that Elisedd's men could sweep round Andredescæster and come from the north. There were woods up to within 400 yards of the fort. That had been where Elisedd's scouts had found the Saxon scouts, so it was clear the Saxons had expected an attack from that direction, but the Gewisse scouts were there to warn them in advance. That would be to Elisedd's advantage.

A plan had formed in Elisedd's head, so he told them what he envisaged could be done, to confirm with Madog and the scouts whether it would work.

They concurred with his plan, so the scouts headed inland to ensure their attack point was secure, while Elisedd and his warriors waited until it was the right time, and Madog prepared his ships.

Several hours later, by the light of the midnight moon, Elisedd and Arturius led the horsemen inland, heading up into the hills for the forest of Andredeslea, before turning round to come south towards Andredescæster.

Meanwhile, Madog and his ships slowly headed out into deeper waters. They wanted to approach the beached ships from the south under the cover of darkness and while the tide was out.

After another two hours, Madog's ships approached the beach from the south. They could see that the tide was starting to climb up the beach, so the timing of his task would be crucial.

At the stern of each ship, a fire had been established, but protected by a wooden barrier so it would not be seen from land. The centre aisle had been cleared of any equipment and as many spears as they could find had been adapted with some cloth wrapping around the tip end. There were four men standing around each fire, the strongest spear throwers amongst Elisedd's men.

When Madog's ships were close enough to the Saxon ships, each thrower picked up a spear, placed it in the fire and, once the cloth was burning, they raised the spear and ran down the centre aisle, launching their spear towards the beached Saxon ships. After a couple of attempts from each ship, the throwers' aim improved and hit their targets, setting the Saxon ships alight.

The Saxons, alerted to the attack by sea and realising that their ships were lost, left their siege of the castle and began to form up in preparation for an attack from Elisedd's ships as they approached the beach.

Meanwhile, Elisedd and his men had watched the blazing Saxon ships lighting up the horizon and started to march out of the forest to the north, heading towards the Saxons, but hidden from view by the fort.

From the ramparts inside the fort, Hywel had watched events taking place on the beach. He was then informed that another group of warriors had appeared from the woods to the north and were carrying Elisedd's banner.

Hywel called for his men to form up into attack formation and ordered the fort gate to be opened. He led his men out of the fort, to join up with Elisedd and his men as they reached the fort, and the larger force headed down to the flat land near the beach, where the Saxons had set up their defences.

The Saxons were too focused on the events taking place at the beach to realise what was happening at the fort, until one of the Saxon commanders noticed the large force of men heading towards them from the north, and called for his men to form up and prepare to meet this more imminent threat.

A large bloody battle followed over the next three hours. It was obvious to both sides that the Saxons were suffering more losses than Elisedd's Gewisse and were being pushed back towards the beach.

Horsa ordered his men to pivot round to the east along the beach looking for an escape route. Elisedd, sensing victory, called for one final push for his men to overwhelm the Saxons. Horsa also sensed imminent victory for the Britons, so called for his men to retreat eastward by land.

Elisedd let them flee. He had made his point, and perhaps Horsa would now convince his brother that Elisedd was in total control of his lands, so it was pointless making any further incursions into Elisedd's region.

Although he had won, Elisedd found out that just over fifty of his men had died and that some had suffered various injuries, mostly minor.

However, Elisedd was completely stunned when he

learned that one of his men killed in battle was Hywel, his commander and friend, who had been struck down by Horsa during the battle.

In the chaos of battle, fighters can get knocked over by others falling in the attack. On this occasion, Hywel had been fighting with Horsa, when he was knocked from the back and lost his balance.

He managed to avoid falling completely, by taking a knee for balance, but this left him below Horsa, who took the opportunity to swing his axe down on Hywel's shoulder with such force that it sliced through his shoulder blade, killing him immediately.

Hywel's death hit Elisedd hard. He knew grief would come, but for now, he was angry and wanted revenge. There had been some Saxons severely injured still lying on the battlefield, so Elisedd ordered his men to kill them all without remorse. After all, Elisedd had made a promise to the Saxons that he intended to keep.

Elisedd had a final task to complete before returning to Portus Adurni, so issued his commands to his men to move all the dead Saxons from the battlefield onto the one remaining Saxon ship that had not been destroyed by Madog's men. Elisedd then joined Madog on his ship and they pulled the Saxon ship out into deeper waters.

Without Hywel, Arturius took charge of the remaining Gewisse warriors and organised carts to take their dead and injured back to Portus Adurni.

*

Two hours later, Madog's ship approached Wippidsfleet, with the Saxon ship, containing the pile of dead Saxon bodies, coming alongside.

Madog's men on board the Saxon ship fixed the sail and rudder in position to take the ship into the harbour, while Madog's ship held it steady using ropes. When everything was in place, Madog's men set the pile of Saxon bodies on fire, returned to his ship and released the ropes on the Saxon ship, so it started to drift towards the port.

Madog ordered his ship to row back out into the channel, and they all watched as the Saxon ship approached the port. The ship was now fully alight, with a large column of smoke rising up into the sky and being blown by the wind that was also taking the tide and ship towards Wippidsfleet. Elisedd could also see activity in the port as the Saxons spotted the flaming ship heading towards the port and hurriedly began boarding their remaining ships.

Elisedd was not concerned that the Saxons were planning to attack his ships. He knew they were going to attempt to stop the burning ship from entering the port and damaging the other ships. He also knew that Hengest and Horsa would get the message, so decided it was time to leave. Madog gave the signal to the other Gewisse ships and they began their return journey to Portus Adurni.

On the return journey, Elisedd and Madog took the time to consider their next steps. They both knew that the Saxons were unlikely to take this lying down. There would be consequences to this day's events. When they returned to Portus Adurni, the general mood changed as the Gewisse all mourned the loss of Hywel.

*

A few days later, after Hywel's burial outside the fort, Elisedd, Cunedda and Madog got back down to business in the great hall. First, they needed a new patrol commander, and Cunedda was quick to put himself forward for this role. He felt he needed a new challenge after being stuck in fort for so long, with little opportunity to join in battle. He pre-empted Elisedd by suggesting that Arturius be promoted to fort commander, which would also allow him to protect Elisedd's family and oversee Caradoc's training. Elisedd quickly agreed with Cunedda's proposal.

Madog then asked what they should do about Hywel's son, Gruffudd, who had been deputising for his father as a patrol leader. Elisedd had already singled him out as a future Gewisse commander, but said he was concerned about Gruffudd's likely reaction to his father's death.

Elisedd told Cunedda and Madog that he wanted to keep Gruffudd away from any action for now, in case he lost his head in battle. However, it would be useful to give him some experience of fort command, especially if he appointed Arturius as fort commander. After his commanders agreed, Elisedd said it would only be right to see what Arturius thought about having Gruffudd as his second-in-command, although he did not expect that would be a problem for either man.

Elisedd then informed Cunedda and Madog that he would need to arrange a meeting with Eldol, Ambrosius and Gwerthefyr to prepare them for the next battle with the Saxons.

Hengest and Horsa would be seething after Horsa's defeat, so Elisedd expected that they would recruit more mercenaries from overseas with a view to a new attack, sometime within the next two years.

They then called for Arturius and Gruffudd to be brought to the great hall to confirm their new appointments, which delighted both young commanders. Their attitude pleased Elisedd and he expected great things from both of them.

*

A few months later, Elisedd met with Eldol, Ambrosius and Gwerthefyr during the annual festival of Baal, which celebrated the end of spring and start of summer at the ancient temple of Cor Gawr, located in the lands of Ambrosius Aurelianus.

The meeting took place in the great hall of the local hillfort, at Vespasian's Camp, with the permission of the local chieftain, who was delighted to host such great leaders.

Elisedd hoped that hosting the meeting with the king's son would help persuade Ambrosius to commit his men to the large battle that would surely come.

At the start of their meeting, Elisedd explained what had happened at Andredescæster, and his justification for believing that the escalation of events would surely lead to a greater battle the following year.

Gwerthefyr agreed with Elisedd's assessment, but felt it would be better to take the battle to the Saxons rather than having to wait and then react to a Saxon attack. He suggested that they prepare for a battle the following year, in the springtime, taking a large force into Cantia to face Hengest and Horsa on their own lands. This would give everyone a year to prepare, make enough weapons and train their men as much as possible.

When Elisedd asked how the king would react to Britons attacking the very men he had brought to Britannia to protect it, Gwerthefyr said that he would head to Lundein to discuss the Saxon situation with his father, in an effort to persuade him to tell Hengest and Horsa to back down and stick to the terms of the original treaty agreed just four years ago.

If the king did not support his son for a second time, despite the evidence against the Saxons, then Gwerthefyr would consider it his responsibility to put the Saxons in their place.

They agreed to another meet again later in the year, at the same location, to review their progress and, if necessary, finalise the plan of attack on the Saxons in Cantia.

*

Sadly, when the rulers met again in the autumn, Gwerthefyr looked depressed. His meeting with King Wyrtgeorn in Lundein had gone badly.

Whenever he tried to discuss the situation with his father, Rowena was constantly by the king's side. She openly berated Gwerthefyr for believing Elisedd's lies about what the Saxons were doing. The king took Rowena's side, leading to raised voices between father and son.

Gwerthefyr said he had to walk away, accepting that his father was now under the complete control of Rowena and her father. He also pointed out that he clearly heard her father's words when Rowena blamed Elisedd for any enmity between Britons and Saxons. Horsa's defeat at Andredescæster had clearly hurt the Saxons, but also embarrassed them.

The group accepted that a battle with the Saxons was inevitable, so they agreed that preparations would be stepped up over the winter and made plans to meet at Calleva in the spring before heading westwards to Durovernum.

*

On a cold spring morning the following year, Gwerthefyr was leading a large force of Britons across the fields of Cantia towards Æglesthrep. There were over 1,000 warriors, under the command of Eldol, Ambrosius, Elisedd and Gwerthefyr's brother, Cadeyrn, who had also joined the Britons, bringing men from his kingdom of Pagenses.

Alongside Elisedd were Cunedda and Gruffudd, who had persuaded Elisedd that he was ready to fight in battle against the Saxons and would not let his ruler down.

In the distance, Elisedd could see the hillfort of Æglesthrep, but it was the large force of Saxons in front of the fort that drew his attention. Over a mile away, but still clearly visible, the Saxons had somehow managed to increase their forces significantly over the past year themselves. Elisedd estimated that their numbers were similar to the Britons'.

Elisedd's scouts had also confirmed that there were no other Saxon warriors hiding elsewhere to the north, south or behind them. This would be an even fight, coming down to the brute force of battle and the strength of their fighters.

Elisedd was disappointed that Gwerthefyr had not considered any battle strategy with the other leaders. Elisedd had put forward a battle plan, but Gwerthefyr felt that there was no need to make things complicated.

There was little point in delaying the fight in a battle like this. This view was shared by both sides, so an almost co-ordinated decision was taken by both leaders to signal attack at the same time.

The battle was bloody, brutal and ferocious. No quarter was given and many excellent warriors died that day. The Britons and Saxons were so evenly matched that neither side was gaining an advantage. After several hours, each side had lost at least a quarter of their men.

Eventually, both sides withdrew from the battlefield, primarily to rest and recover from their exertions, while the leaders discussed whether there was any tactic that would achieve any significant step forward against the other side.

Gwerthefyr was still insistent that the Britons could win in the end, so a little while later, the battle lines reformed and another attack began.

As before, it was a merciless battle, with more good men losing their lives. After an hour, the fighting at the centre of the battlefield suddenly stopped. Slowly, the other fighting stopped as everyone realised that a significant event had occurred. As the sides withdrew, the reason emerged.

Hengest was kneeling down, holding the limp body of his brother, Horsa, while Gwerthefyr was holding the body of his dead brother, Cadeyrn.

It turned out that they had been fighting each other and, as Horsa had swung down his axe onto Cadeyrn's torso, Cadeyrn had been bringing his sword up towards Horsa's unprotected chin. They had hit each other at exactly the same moment, killing each other.

It was such a freak accident in battle that everyone around them simply stared in disbelief. It was this temporary truce that rippled out from the centre of the battle, to end the fighting.

Slowly, each side withdrew further apart, as Hengest and Gwerthefyr carried their brothers' dead bodies off the battlefield. The battle was over for now. Neither side would fight until they had mourned the loss of one of their leaders properly.

The Saxon forces withdrew towards the hillfort, while the Britons brought carts onto the field, lifted their dead and injured warriors onto them, and slowly marched eastward towards Elisedd's lands.

Elisedd ordered his scouts to keep an eye on the Saxons as the Britons headed away, just to make sure the Saxons remained in Æglesthrep, which they did, collecting their own dead and injured before returning to the hillfort.

As the retiring Britons were camped that night in the forest of Andredeslea, close to the border with Cantia, there was a large unit of sentries protecting the camp, and Elisedd's scouts were patrolling further out, making sure that the Saxons were not considering a night-time assault.

The leaders and commanders sat together eating in silence when, suddenly, Gwerthefyr spoke up, saying, "I need to inform my father that Cadeyrn is dead, and who killed him. I will take his body north to Lundein, to show my father what he has allowed to happen. He must act now!"

Elisedd knew there was no point in arguing, so he said, "My lord, if you must insist, I will arrange to provide some of my scouts to aid you in your journey to Lundein, just in case the Saxons predict that you would head there."

"Thank you, Lord Elisedd," said Gwerthefyr. "I will ensure they return to you with news of my discussion with my father."

The next morning, Gwerthefyr led his men north to Lundein. Meanwhile, Elisedd, Eldol and Ambrosius led their men onward to Calleva, before heading towards their own regional bases. They all had men to bury and mourn. The leaders would have to consider what happened next.

*

Elisedd's scouts returned to Portus Adurni a week later, informing him that Gwerthefyr had informed his father of Cadeyrn's death, and the king had returned with Gwerthefyr to Glevum for his burial.

Elisedd hoped that getting King Wyrtgeorn away from Lundein might help Gwerthefyr convince him of the need to take action against the Saxons. However, Eldol arrived in Portus Adurni a few weeks after that, with devastating news.

Gwerthefyr was dead!

According to Eldol, he had died suddenly overnight without any explanation. There was no proof, but Eldol blamed Rowena, believing that she had poisoned Gwerthefyr as revenge for her uncle's death.

For King Wyrtgeorn, it meant he had to bury two sons in less than a month. He was devastated and inconsolable, but he surprised everyone by returning to Lundein with Rowena to mourn, rather than stay with his youngest son, Pascent.

Elisedd was equally devastated, having lost the one major ally he could have relied on to provide sufficient numbers to take on the Saxons in battle, as the kingdom of Guenta was now leaderless, leaving the chieftains to fight amongst themselves. He was seriously worried about what would happen next, for him, his family and the Gewisse.

6
TREACHERY OF THE LONG KNIVES

In his *Historia Brittonum* chronicle, Nennius states
that Saxon leader Hengest plotted his revenge against
the Britons he held responsible for the death of his
brother, Horsa.

For the next year, barring a number of small attacks that
the local patrols had been able to deal with, the Saxons
had generally remained in Cantia, and Elisedd's lands had
experienced a period of relative peace.

Caradoc, now in his mid-teens, was fully recovered
and training with the other prospective Gewisse warriors,
with Arturius spending any spare time he had helping
him, especially with his swordsmanship.

Young Ceredig was becoming a real handful for
Lavena and the house servants. He had also taken a shine
to Arturius and could often be seen following him around
the fort.

For his fifth birthday, Elisedd had arranged for a local
carpenter to make wooden replicas of his own sword and
shield, albeit on a smaller scale for his son. The shield had
also been painted to look like Elisedd's, including the gold
rampant dragon.

Ceredig loved playing with his sword and shield around the fort, pretending to be his father, the ruler of the Gewisse, especially with the other children of the Gewisse. His status gave him confidence to be the leader of all their play activities, and the other boys sought to have their own, simpler swords, so they could play as Gewisse warriors too.

Caradoc and Ceredig were being educated by local monks, learning to read and write in several languages. Their father took it upon himself to teach them about their heritage and the history of the Gewisse, dating back to their origins in the western province of Britannia. Meanwhile, Cunedda, Madog and Hywel would tell them stories of the battles of the Gewisse, although they both loved to hear similar stories from their father whenever the opportunity arose.

One afternoon, Cunedda was telling them both about their father's first battle as ruler of the Gewisse, when a messenger arrived from Lundein with a message for Elisedd from the king.

King Wyrtgeorn had been negotiating with Hengest to agree a peaceful settlement between the Britons and the Saxons, and this was an invitation to all of Britannia's regional rulers, chieftains and nobility to attend a meeting to finalise a peace treaty with the Saxons.

Given his lack of interest in interceding when his own son had pleaded with him, Elisedd was astounded that the king had made any effort. However, the loss of two of his sons may have prompted the king into action. On that basis, Elisedd was prepared to give him the benefit of the doubt.

King Wyrtgeorn and Hengest would present the terms of the treaty to all Britons and Saxons invited to attend, with a view to reaching consensus to avoid further bloodshed and, ultimately, achieving peace in Britannia.

The final part of the invitation stated that, since it was to be a peace treaty, all attendees were to be unarmed, as an act of good faith.

The meeting was to take place in a month's time, at the old hillfort known as Vespasian's Camp. This was the same hillfort where Elisedd, Eldol, Ambrosius and, the now deceased, Gwerthefyr had met the previous year.

It coincided with the festival of Baal, at the nearby temple of Cor Gawr, when there would be many Britons in the area to celebrate the start of summer. This meant that there would be large numbers of unfamiliar people in the area, making security extremely difficult to maintain.

The location and timing of this meeting concerned Elisedd. It meant there would be many Saxons given free movement across his lands to attend. He would definitely be taking a large unit of bodyguards, under Cunedda's command, to protect him and any local landowners who had been invited.

*

Three weeks later, Eldol's ship arrived into port at Portus Adurni. He had decided to sail round to stay with Elisedd in advance of making the trip to the peace treaty meeting with the king and the Saxons. He had left the noblemen of

Glevum to travel under the protection of the local militia when the time came.

The kingdoms to the west of Glevum were in disarray, having lost their rulers in quick succession, with local chieftains having to deal with their own problems.

Elisedd greeted his brother as he disembarked from his ship, saying, "Welcome, brother. I am so glad you have come to stay, even if the circumstances are not ideal."

"Me too," said Eldol. "I am concerned about this meeting with the Saxons being so close to your lands, so we need to prepare a plan to deal with them after the meeting too. I am also keen to hear what Lord Ambrosius has to say."

"Then you are going to be disappointed," said Elisedd, as they entered the fort gate and walked towards the villa.

"What? Why?" asked Eldol.

Elisedd explained, "I have just heard that he has fled to Armorica after a major disagreement with the king, who threatened to strip him of his lands and titles. It appears that he decided to pre-empt this action by the king and fled with a group of loyal warriors."

"Well, that explains why the king has chosen Vespasian's Camp for the location of the meeting," replied Eldol.

"So, you see an ulterior motive in this meeting?" asked Elisedd.

Eldol said, "Well, I cannot help but think the king has been under Saxon control since his marriage to Rowena, a deliberate ploy by Hengest to neutralise the king. Therefore, whatever peace treaty we are being invited to discuss will probably lean towards the Saxons. My guess is that you will have to give up your lands close to Cantia, and the Saxons will undertake to never encroach on this new boundary."

"Until, that is, they decide they want more land, and we start all over again," Elisedd replied.

Eldol said, "That may be the good news, brother. The king could order you and your Gewisse warriors back to the western province, leaving the whole southern region under Saxon control."

"Thanks for that, brother," said Elisedd. "I had hoped that you coming here might cheer me up!"

*

When the time came to leave for the peace treaty meeting, Elisedd told Lavena that he would be taking Caradoc with him and Eldol to the meeting. Elisedd felt that, at fifteen years of age, Caradoc was ready to start learning about the politics involved in ruling a region.

Lavena was unhappy and made her feelings known to Elisedd the night before they departed. She knew this day had to come, but she was aware of her husband and Eldol's concerns about the motives of the Saxons, and she did not want Caradoc put at any risk before he came of age.

Elisedd reassured her that he would keep Caradoc by his side throughout, and Cunedda would also attend the meeting with them to advise and protect Caradoc.

Since Elisedd was taking Caradoc, six-year-old Ceredig said he also wanted to go with his father to meet the king, but Lavena explained that she needed her brave young warrior to remain in Portus Adurni and protect her from the nasty Saxons.

Reassured that he had an important role to play, Ceredig told his mother that he would be her Gewisse protector and kill any Saxons who came near Portus Adurni while his father was away.

Disaster averted, a sad Lavena and an excited Ceredig waved as Elisedd, Caradoc, Eldol and Cunedda left the fort, along with a group of local landowners and chieftains from the region, and a force of one hundred Gewisse warriors for protection.

*

Vespasian's Camp was already very busy when Elisedd and his group arrived three days later. They made camp to the south of the hillfort, across the river, which gave them easy access to an old Roman army road heading south to the old hillfort of Searobyrg, then east to Portus Adurni, the route they had travelled from Portus Adurni.

The meeting was to take place the next day, so they had time to settle into their camp and establish a sentry perimeter.

Elisedd's scouts arrived in camp an hour later, with news of the Saxon contingent that they had been following all the way from Cantia, through Elisedd's lands. The Saxons had been peaceful throughout their journey and had immediately entered the hillfort, along with the king and Rowena. They were staying there at the king's pleasure.

The next day, Elisedd, Eldol, Caradoc and Cunedda, along with the other nobles who had camped with them, made their way across the old Roman bridge into the hillfort. As instructed, they were all unarmed.

Elisedd's men would remain outside the hillfort for the duration of the meeting. They were joined by Eldol's militia unit from Glevum, who had fought with Elisedd's men at Æglesthrep, so the two groups waited together until the meeting ended.

Elisedd's full complement of scouts had departed in the early hours for a sweep of the area, to ensure there would not be any late Saxon arrivals.

Inside the hillfort, it was extremely busy with all the Britons waiting in groups because the door to the hall was closed. Elisedd, Eldol, Caradoc and Cunedda found a spot to wait with the other Britons.

When the sun was at its height, the door to the great hall opened and King Wyrtgeorn came out, with Hengest by his side.

"Britons," Wyrtgeorn shouted, "welcome to Vespasian's Camp. The great hall will be very busy with nearly 500 Britons and Saxons. Since it is a meeting about peace, I have agreed with Lord Hengest that we will sit together, Briton next to Saxon, next to Briton, next to Saxon and so on, instead of two separate groups facing each other. Now, enter the hall and find a place next to a Saxon, who are already seated."

Eldol turned to Elisedd and said, "Only Wyrtgeorn could think that this was a good idea. At least Rowena is not by his side this time. I wonder why she has stayed away?

After all, she probably helped him in his negotiations with her father."

"What do I do about Caradoc?" asked Elisedd. "He is not yet fifteen and does not have enough experience to handle this."

"Get him out of here," replied Eldol.

Elisedd grabbed hold of Caradoc's arm and turned to escort him out of the hillfort, so he could remain with the Gewisse warriors, but he found the gate of the hillfort closed and guarded by the local chieftain's men.

As Elisedd and Caradoc approached the gate, the guards told them they had instructions that no one was to leave.

"I am not trying to leave," said Elisedd. "I just want my young son to join my warriors outside now that I am about to enter the peace treaty meeting."

The main guard responded, saying, "Sorry, my lord. No exceptions, by the king's command. I suggest that you and your son head into the hall and hope you can get a spot near each other."

Elisedd put his arm around Caradoc and told him that it would be alright. When they returned to the great hall, Eldol had ensured that there were alternate spaces next to each other for him, Elisedd and Caradoc, with Cunedda on the next alternate seat.

Once everyone was seated, the banquet started as the hall's servants brought in food and served ale to everyone. The atmosphere was rather tense, with little conversation taking place between Britons and Saxons.

Elisedd and his group had no idea whether the Saxons amongst them had taken part in the previous year's battle at Æglesthrep, so tried to avoid any discussion in that area. In fact, most of the conversation was with a fellow Briton across the table from them.

Once the banquet was complete, the tables were cleared and servants replenished everyone's goblets with ale. Then, King Wyrtgeorn stood up and banged his fist on the table to bring everyone to order.

When the hall was quiet, Wyrtgeorn said, "This ongoing feud between Britons and Saxons has been extremely disappointing, especially when we are supposed to be trying to stop invaders like the Picts from the north, or the attacks from Hibernia. If we spend most of our time fighting and killing each other, there will be fewer warriors to deal with the greater threat. I want an end to the bloodshed. That being said, it is now clear to me that the Saxons need more land to build better lives for themselves and their families. I have, therefore, decided to grant Hengest more lands to the west of Cantia, in the region of the Regni, as far as Alfoldean and Ordinges."

Elisedd looked over at Eldol after that comment. It looked like his brother was spot on with his assessment that the Saxons would end up right on his doorstep.

The king continued, "In exchange, Hengest has given me his reassurance that this would be sufficient for them to settle and the Saxons would not seek to increase their lands beyond this new border. However, battles between Britons and Saxons must cease. Does anyone have any objection to these terms of peace?"

At that point one of the Regni chieftains whose lands would now fall under Saxon control spoke up.

"My king, whilst I recognise that peace often comes at a price, what happens to chieftains, like myself, whose Regni lands are being given to the Saxons? Are our lands now forfeit? Do we receive compensation?"

The king's response was quick and concise. "Yes, your lands are forfeit and you have a month to leave. No, you will not be compensated, unless Lord Elisedd chooses to help you."

It was clear that no one was expected to object to the terms of the peace treaty. There was now a tense atmosphere around the hall that you could cut with a knife.

"Excellent," said the king, then turned to Hengest, saying, "Since everyone agrees with the terms of this new peace treaty, I believe, Lord Hengest, that you wanted to make a statement."

Hengest stood up and said, "Yes, Lord Wyrtgeorn, I do."

Elisedd wondered if anyone else noticed that Hengest had not referred to the king by his title. Instead, he chose a term equal to Hengest's own given title. That showed how the relationship between the two had changed, into one of parity. *Very curious*, he thought.

Hengest looked around the room, taking in the scene before him. Two hundred and fifty Britons sitting next to 250 Saxons. He was amazed that King Wyrtgeorn had accepted his seating suggestion, as well as agreeing that all attendees come unarmed to a peace treaty meeting.

What neither the king nor any of the Britons knew was that Hengest had taken the death of his brother Horsa very badly. He had allowed his brother to take command of the Saxons in the battle against the Britons that led to his death, because Hengest was too distracted thinking about how to persuade King Wyrtgeorn to allow the Saxons to have control over more land to the west of Cantia, more specifically, the lands of the Regni, from Lord Elisedd.

Hengest felt guilty that he had been there when Horsa died, thinking that, somehow, he should have been able to prevent his brother's death. His only consolation was that his brother had died a warrior's death and would now be in Valhalla. That did not calm his angry heart, though, and he wanted revenge!

The night before the peace treaty meeting, Hengest had instructed his Saxons to hide their seaxes somewhere on their bodies before entering the hillfort in the morning. He told them about the seating arrangement that the king had agreed to set up and said that, when he shouted "*Nimed eure Saxes!*", they were to withdraw their traditional Saxon long knives and kill the unarmed Britons sitting either side of them, then kill any others near them who may have survived the initial attack.

As he looked around the great hall, Hengest felt a heavy weight lifted from him as he was just about to avenge his brother and deal a final blow to any British resistance to Saxon rule. He raised his goblet as if to make a toast to celebrate the agreement, then shouted, "*Nimed eure Saxes!*"

As soon as Hengest had shouted his command, every Saxon did as they had been instructed, removing their hidden seaxes from the bindings of their footwear, pulling them down their sleeve or from under the back of their jacket. They all turned to the Britons next to them and started the massacre.

The Britons were momentarily stunned, which helped the Saxons in killing a large number of them before they could react.

Elisedd sat paralysed in disbelief, watching as Cunedda was killed first, then Caradoc, his son, who had overcome such a great liability in his early life, only to have it cut short so easily by these treacherous Saxons.

As Caradoc collapsed in a heap, Elisedd was an easy target for the Saxons either side of him, as they both turned and stabbed him multiple times in the chest. Elisedd cursed the king as he slumped down and breathed his last. The last thing he saw was Eldol deflecting the initial stabs of the Saxon next to him.

Hengest's plan worked to perfection. He had extracted his seax and placed it at the king's throat, saying, "Just remain where you are, Wyrtgeorn. We need a king to rule the Britons, but we have no need of warriors and leaders who might rise up against us."

Hengest forced King Wyrtgeorn to watch the scene before him, as the Saxons were massacring the Britons, but Hengest could not resist uttering "Yes" in seeing Elisedd being killed by his men.

Of all the Britons, Elisedd was the one ruler that Hengest feared. Lord Elisedd had shown great ability in fighting and defeating the Saxons, and was responsible for hundreds of his countrymen being killed.

In the meantime, a small number of British nobles had survived the first onslaught by the Saxons and had even managed to disarm and kill some of their attackers.

Eldol was one of them. He had reacted instinctively,

mostly to the tone of Hengest's command to attack. When the slightly older Saxon seated next to him responded more slowly to Hengest's order, Eldol knocked the knife out of his hand and jumped out of his seat. He grabbed a pole that had held a banner against the wall behind him and hit the Saxon with it, then pushed the broken end into the Saxon's body, killing him instantly.

Eldol was furious at the deceit by the Saxons, the foolishness of the king and the sight of his brother and nephew being killed. He grabbed hold of the head of another Saxon and hammered it against the table, before taking his seax and killing him.

Eldol ran for the door of the great hall and barged through it, closely followed by the few other Britons who had somehow survived the onslaught. They all looked for potential weapons or shields, grabbing anything that lay nearby which they could use to defend themselves.

Eldol and the other Britons turned to face fifty Saxons, who had exited the great hall, brandishing their seaxes. The Saxons attacked in unison, hoping their overwhelming numbers would suffice to take care of the survivors. It had been Hengest's command that no Briton was to be allowed to leave the hillfort alive.

The sentries guarding the gates to the hillfort did not know what to do. They had been commanded by the king to guard the gate, so leaving their post was not an option, even though they could see their fellow Britons in serious trouble. They were confused about what to do, and could only watch as the fight between the Britons and the Saxons took place.

Eldol and his fellow nobles were initially successful in killing half of the Saxons who attacked, but then the Saxons changed tactics, recognising that Eldol's side of the Britons were stronger.

While some Saxons attacked Eldol and the small group of Britons beside him, most of the other Saxons focused on the other Britons and killed them with relative ease. Then they turned their attention to the other Britons next to Eldol.

Eventually, Eldol was the sole surviving Briton, against ten remaining Saxons. Eldol did not like his odds, but then another group of Saxons exited the great hall. Now he really was in trouble!

Outside the gate, Elisedd's men had heard the distinctive sounds of metal clashing with metal and the screams of death. They began to hammer at the gate, but the bar on the other side was too strong and would not break.

The gate guards had watched in horror at the brutality of the attacks by the Saxons on the Britons. Ultimately, it became too much for them. They knew that this was a massacre and, if they stayed, they were likely to suffer the same outcome.

The guards quickly lifted the bar across the gate and, as they ran out of the hillfort, in rushed Elisedd's men. When they saw Eldol, they quickly ran to his side, bearing axes, swords and shields, forming a shield wall. They considered attacking the Saxons, but more of their number were exiting the hall, reducing their odds of success.

Eldol turned to the Gewisse warriors and said, "Lord Elisedd, Caradoc, Cunedda, everyone. They are all dead and we cannot help them now. Get me out of here."

Eldol and the Gewisse retreated outside the fort, shouting as loud as they could, to everyone they could see, saying, "The Saxons have killed the nobles. Flee for your lives."

The Gewisse then quickly escorted Eldol back to their camp, mounted their horses and galloped off at speed, leaving everything but their weapons as they headed south.

*

As Eldol and the Gewisse rode south past the hillfort of Searobyrg, two of the warriors peeled off and rode up to the hillfort gate to relay the earlier events to the local chieftain. They would then head straight for Portus Adurni, joining up with the rest of the Gewisse.

Eldol and the remaining Gewisse turned left and charged along the old Roman road towards Ventacæster, where another two warriors left to warn the people living in the hillfort there. The main group continued galloping on towards Portus Adurni.

One of the Gewisse horse riders had the sense to increase his speed and raise Elisedd's banner on a spear above his head, as they galloped towards the gate at Portus Adurni.

The wall sentries spotted Elisedd's banner, as well as the speed of the horses, and sensed the urgency. One called for the gatekeepers to open the gates, while the other blew a horn to alert the rest of the fort to an emergency.

As Eldol and the other horsemen rode at speed through the gate, the gates began to close quickly behind them, but there was confusion amongst the gate's sentries, as they could not see Elisedd, Caradoc or Cunedda.

Eldol was dismounting his horse as Arturius arrived at the main gate. He quickly relayed the events that had taken place earlier, telling Arturius that he needed to see Lavena immediately, and they rushed towards the villa, where they found Lavena with Ceredig playing in the garden area.

"Eldol, Arturius," she said. "What has happened? I heard the noises from the gate. Where are Elisedd and Caradoc?"

"I am sorry, Lavena," said Eldol as he approached her and hugged her closely, and then told her about the brutal massacre of her husband and son.

Lavena screamed in anguish, raising her hands to her face, and began sobbing uncontrollably as she took in everything that Eldol had said. Her maid immediately came over and comforted Lavena, while one of the servants took a very confused-looking Ceredig inside the villa, away from his mother's grief.

Eldol and Arturius told Lavena to take some time to absorb the day's events, and they would come and see her in a little while.

Madog and Gruffudd had also heard the news and just arrived at the villa. The four men quickly agreed that this was now a state of emergency, but before they decided what to do, they needed to consider the whole picture.

Eldol turned to Arturius, Madog and Gruffudd and led them to the great hall, where they were given goblets of ale by servants, whom they dismissed. The discussions that would follow needed to be done in private and without prying eyes or ears.

Eldol started by relaying the day's events, from their entry into the hillfort that morning, the king's speech about the strange seating arrangement, then Elisedd's failed attempt to get Caradoc to safety out of the hillfort. He gave the details of the peace treaty that gave a large portion of Elisedd's lands to the Saxons, before Hengest, the Saxon leader, stood up and gave his men a pre-planned order to use their hidden long knives to kill the unarmed Britons.

Then Eldol told them about Cunedda's quick death, then Caradoc, followed by Elisedd. Eldol explained how he managed to disarm a Saxon next to him, and how he and other Britons escaped into the yard, fighting the Saxons until only Eldol remained, and his escape, thanks to Elisedd's warriors making entry into the hillfort.

Elisedd's commanders listened in disbelief at the massacre of their leader, but also of their fellow countrymen.

After Eldol had finished his story, Arturius said, "We cannot take on the full might of the Saxon forces, especially if they decide to head to Portus Adurni first. If so, they are most likely to reach here in the morning. We could only defend this fort against the Saxons for maybe a month, and we know that there are no reinforcements coming to help us. What happened to the militia unit from Glevum, Lord Eldol?"

"We told everyone outside the hillfort to flee," replied Eldol. "Therefore, I would imagine that the militia unit has rushed back to Glevum, to warn everyone there and prepare to defend the civitas if the Saxons head west. I doubt whether there would be any willingness to leave Glevum to help us, especially as the Saxons have taken the king hostage."

After a few moments' silence as they all considered their options, Madog spoke.

"Our leader is dead, and our control over these lands is at an end," he said. "Like Arturius, I am convinced that the Saxons will seek to consolidate their control over the southern region by heading straight for Portus Adurni, if not immediately, then certainly within the next week. Once they have control over Portus Adurni, their ships will be able to travel between here and Cantia unhindered. In fact, they may even have prepared their ships for a two-pronged attack, by land and sea, especially as they had planned to kill the nobles, so they may be sending ships along the south coast in the next day or two. Therefore, we should make plans to leave the fort on the next tide, in the morning. It is simply a case of where we go."

Eldol then said, "We should travel to Glevum. The Gewisse would be a welcome enhancement to the city's militia, and some, if not most, of your older warriors may still have family in the region. Lavena and Ceredig would be welcome to live with me in my estate."

Madog said that he would take the Gewisse ships to Armorica, along with as many men that were willing, to continue the merchant business they had established as an escape route if it became necessary.

They all knew that Elisedd and Madog had been working on this project as a potential route, if the Saxons overwhelmed Elisedd's lands, so agreed that Madog should continue to develop the business in Darioritum.

"I could also take a unit of Gewisse warriors to help recruit and train a new generation of our forces, with a view to returning to take on the Saxons when the time is right," Madog said. "We would make regular trading trips to Glevum to keep in contact with you, Lavena and Ceredig. This would continue to provide you with an escape route if the Saxons make Glevum a target for their expansion."

Arturius then spoke, saying, "As his kinsman, Elisedd charged me with protecting his family, especially Ceredig, his son and now future ruler of the Gewisse, so I will go with them and Eldol to Glevum."

"You are welcome to live with us at my estate outside Glevum, Arturius," said Eldol. "It would be useful to have a small protective guard on the estate, given the likely ongoing threat from the Saxons."

Gruffudd said that, if Arturius were to protect Lavena and Ceredig, he would be willing to command the remaining Gewisse warriors as part of Glevum's militia unit.

With a plan agreed, Eldol said he would discuss it with Lavena, to make sure she was happy with their proposals. In the meantime, he charged Arturius, Madog and Gruffudd with making the necessary preparations for the Gewisse to evacuate the fort early in the morning, for whichever destination each group was heading.

Arturius also told them he would send half the Gewisse scouts out to all the major settlements in the region and inform the locals about the Saxon threat that was coming, so they could choose whether to remain and hope for the best, or flee to a safer region.

Eldol found Lavena and told her about the plan to evacuate Portus Adurni and relocate to his estate near Glevum. Although it was clear she was still grieving her loss, she was able to maintain a clear head to tell him that she understood the threat to her, Ceredig and the Gewisse, so agreed with the urgent need to leave the region.

*

The next morning, the whole fort was a scene of great activity. Down by the port gate, Madog's four Gewisse ships and Eldol's ship were having their cargo holds filled with the bare essentials that the families were permitted to take with them.

Arturius had been concerned about protecting the security of their evacuation, so he had established a perimeter of scouts at all access points to Portus Adurni, to alert the fort if the Saxons arrived in the area before they had departed.

Ceredig appeared bemused by the flurry of people rushing around the fort, paying him no attention, especially Arturius, who seemed more intense than usual and brushed off Ceredig's attempts to get him to play.

Eventually, Ceredig gave up and headed into the villa to be with his mother.

It had been agreed that the families of the Gewisse headed for Glevum would travel on two ships, while the warriors, including the scouts, would remain until the ships had all left the estuary. They would then travel west by land, following the coastline through Durnovaria, then north via Aquaesulis to Glevum.

The other two Gewisse ships would head for Darioritum in Armorica under Madog's command, taking Gewisse warriors who had no family in Glevum. The ships bound for Glevum would join up with Madog in Darioritum after dropping off their passengers.

By mid-afternoon, the ships were all loaded and ready to leave. The tide was about to turn, aiding their departure out of the estuary into open sea.

Arturius and Eldol escorted Lavena and Ceredig down to Eldol's ship. As they approached the port gate, Arturius and Lavena turned and looked into the fort that had been their home for the past fifteen years.

Arturius had been a young warrior when he arrived there, as part of Lavena's escort to Portus Adurni, after Elisedd had sent word for his wife and eldest son to join him. Now, Arturius was a commander leading a retreat from that very home back to Glevum. He had grown to love the fort as the Gewisse's home, but wondered if he would ever see Portus Adurni again.

He turned to young Ceredig and said, "Remember this day, Ceredig. This is your home. You were born here, the son of a great ruler. These are your family's lands, and the

Saxons murdered your father and brother to get them. One day, you will return and avenge their deaths, reclaim these lands and become the king that was your father's destiny."

Ceredig looked at Arturius and said, "I will, Arturius, but I need you to make me the best warrior ever, so that I can become ruler of the Gewisse and come back to chase these Saxons from my lands."

"I promise to help you do just that," said Arturius.

"Good. When do we start?" asked Ceredig, who was still holding the wooden sword and oval shield his father had given him.

"As soon as we reach a safe place to stay," replied Arturius, unable to believe the strength of determination in this little boy. He had no doubt that he would follow him into battle one day.

They turned back and walked out onto the pier, then Arturius lifted Ceredig and they boarded their ship, just after Lavena.

Arturius could see that Lavena was holding back tears, presumably for Ceredig's sake, but he knew she must be full of grief for her lost husband and son. He knew she would keep it together until they reached Glevum, but was sure the floodgates would surely open when they were all safe.

Madog gave the signal, and all five ships headed out into the estuary, first using the power of men rowing and then under sail.

Once the ships were out of sight, Gruffudd turned and mounted his horse, then led the Gewisse warriors out of the fort gate, wondering if he would ever see his childhood home again.

7 | CEREDIG GROWS UP IN EXILE

While the Saxons were expanding their control across Britannia, many Britons, like Ceredig, had fled from their threat to live in exile over the sea in Armorica.

Seven years later, Lavena and Ceredig had settled into life on Eldol's estate, which was built on the side of a hill to the east of Glevum, with beautiful views looking east across the valley towards the old Roman road of Ermin Way between Glevum and Corinium.

Ceredig, now thirteen years old, had grown fast over the past few years and was now taller than his mother. He resembled his father in looks, with his long oval face, dark brown hair, brown eyes and strong jawline, which was a constant reminder to Lavena of the husband she had lost.

Ceredig had shown an aptitude for learning, with the support of his uncles, including Bishop Eldad and monks from the abbey. However, he had no real friends of his own age living nearby, so spent most of his time practising with Arturius to become a Gewisse warrior, including the various battle tactics used by the Gewisse to deal with different scenarios. With nothing to distract him, Ceredig put everything into this and was a fast learner.

In an effort to provide variety in Ceredig's education, Eldol had also begun taking him into Glevum with him on official business, so Ceredig could see what was involved in running the administration of the Roman civitas.

Meanwhile, over in Armorica, Madog had established quite a profitable merchant business, increasing the number of ships under his control to ten, and his ships had become regular visitors to Glevum, primarily for trading purposes, but also to meet up with Eldol, Gruffudd and Arturius to discuss the latest developments on either side of the sea. On his most recent visit, he informed them that a large number of Britons had fled to Armorica as a direct result of the Saxons' expansion across the southern region of Britannia.

King Wyrtgeorn had died in Lundein a few years earlier, whilst under Saxon 'protection'. Rumours suggested that Rowena, his queen, had poisoned him slowly over time, but there was no evidence to support this.

The Saxons now ruled the eastern, central and southern regions of Britannia. After hearing that Elisedd's family and the Gewisse warriors had escaped over the sea to Armorica, Hengest was furious and ordered his men to raze Portus Adurni to the ground, leaving only the fort walls standing.

It had now been two years since the Saxons had ventured beyond their now enlarged territories, but Eldol and Ambrosius were not being complacent. It would not be long before the Saxons pushed their boundaries once more.

After hearing of Wyrtgeorn's death, Ambrosius had returned from Armorica and made an alliance with King Erbin of Dumnonia, who had become more involved in the political affairs of Britannia since the massacre. They had begun regular discussions with Eldol and the other rulers in the western province to consider their options when, not if, the Saxons pushed beyond their lands once more.

A few months later, their concerns proved to be correct, when news reached Glevum that Hengest, the Saxon leader, and his son, Æsc, had attacked Durocornovium, just two days' march from Glevum. The Saxons had not retreated back to their lands after the attack. They remained in Durocornovium to taunt the Britons. It looked like they were spoiling for a fight with the Britons, again.

Gruffudd sent Gewisse scouts to gauge the Saxons' numbers. Meanwhile, Eldol and Ambrosius were already gathering as many fighters from the region and beyond, including the kingdoms of Guenta, Pagenses and Glywysing, and word had also been sent to King Erbin, of Dumnonia, for fighters.

After hearing the latest news from Eldol, one morning, as they were training in the courtyard of Eldol's villa, Ceredig asked Arturius, "What are we going to do, Arturius?"

"I do not know, this time, Ceredig," replied Arturius. "You are too young and not ready to join this battle. My duty is to remain here and protect you and your mother, and Lord Eldol accepts this. I know that he and Ambrosius are excellent leaders. Depending on the numbers they are facing, this could be an opportunity to defeat, and maybe kill, Hengest and his Saxon forces."

*

Ten days later, a force of 500 Britons approached the settlement of Durocornovium. King Erbin of Dumnonia had sent one hundred warriors, but did not lead them himself. Instead, he sent his son, Gereint, to lead his forces.

Durocornovium's defences comprised a ditch and a rampart with wooden palisade instead of defensive stone walls, because it had the added protection of marshland around the town.

Gruffudd's scouts had reported back that there were approximately 300 Saxons, so the Britons' leadership felt confident, having brought nearly twice that number.

The Britons approached from the south. Since the Roman road called Ermin Street ran straight down from Glevum, through Corinium, to Durocornovium, this route would result in a battle over the town's notorious marshes. Therefore, after Corinium, the Britons turned south across open field, before turning east to the deserted hillfort at Badonbyrg.

As they marched north, up towards Durocornovium, the open land in front of them would be ideal for any battle to take place. They were just south of Durocornovium when the Britons stopped and waited for the Saxons to come forward to face them in battle. After an hour, there was still no sign of the 300 Saxons leaving the town.

The Gewisse scouts returned saying that the Saxons were still there, but they seemed to be waiting on something. This news caused great concern for Eldol, Ambrosius, Gruffudd and Gereint. There was only one thing the Saxons would wait for instead of going into battle, and that was reinforcements. How many more men were they expecting and from what direction?

The answers to these questions arrived soon after, when more scouts arrived at haste, reporting that another force of nearly 300 Saxons was approaching from the south.

They must have been waiting in Cunetio for their own scouts to report that the Britons had arrived near Durocornovium. They had anticipated the route that the Britons would come to avoid the marshes. This allowed them to set up a pincer movement, and the Britons were now caught in the middle.

Ambrosius had suggested this tactic himself for the Britons to use against the Saxons at Durocornovium, but the marshes would have worked against their northern forces. Now it was being used against them.

The Britons would need to split their forces to deal with each Saxon front and would be fighting with fewer numbers on both flanks.

Eldol and Gruffudd, with the Gewisse warriors, would take on the Saxons from Durocornovium. Their numbers came to just under 250 men. Their task would be to keep the Saxons occupied and unable to join up with their reinforcements.

Meanwhile, Ambrosius would take his warriors with Gereint and the Dumnonians, giving them just under

300 men to face the Saxon forces coming from the south. Those were better odds to win against the South Saxons.

The Saxons in Durocornovium had watched the Britons splitting their forces, with nearly half heading south as a sign that their Saxon reinforcements were approaching, so they left their defensive position to take on the Britons in front of the town.

The battle outside Durocornovium was a typically bloody face-to-face battle over three hours, with neither side making any significant gains, despite losing around half their men each. These Saxons were battle-hardened and fought with a fury that Eldol and Gruffudd had never seen before.

Eldol and Gruffudd had no idea what was happening to the south, but hoped that their comrades might be winning their battle against the other Saxons and would be sending reinforcements soon.

However, no reinforcements were coming, at least not the way they were expecting. Ambrosius and Gereint had suffered greater losses and were now greatly outnumbered by this Saxon force. Sensing imminent defeat and death, many of their fighters were fleeing the field of battle.

Gereint led his forces from Dumnonia to the west, then south towards the safety of their kingdom. Ambrosius was left with no choice but to withdraw his warriors, but sent a messenger north, as fast as he could ride, to let Eldol and Gruffudd know of their defeat and retreat. The message told them that Ambrosius and his remaining forces would congregate at Corinium, just in case the Saxons decided to follow the retreating Britons.

The messenger arrived just in time for Eldol and Gruffudd, and they immediately ordered their warriors to retreat. There would be no collecting the dead or severely injured from the battlefield that day. They would remain where they lay.

When the Britons retreated to the west, Hengest had a decision to make. He could follow them and face the possibility of a larger force waiting for them at Corinium or Glevum. It was tempting, but Hengest could not know how many Britons awaited them, so decided that this would be too risky.

Another option was to remain in control of Durocornovium and Cunetio and bring more Saxons to establish a permanent presence there, but it was just too close to the Britons and too far to quickly send reinforcements if there was an attack from a much larger force of Britons from Glevum and Dumnonia.

Hengest felt that this was too risky as well, so he ordered his men to withdraw to the safety of their own lands, which they could easily defend.

They would also be taking a large treasure trove from their battles with the Britons back with them. In terms of battle plunder, it had been a fruitful venture. The Saxons had their pick of the weapons, equipment and horses left behind by both groups of Britons in their retreat.

Having retreated to Corinium, the western Britons were on a battle footing, preparing for the possibility of a Saxon force turning up, flush with success after their recent victory.

Eventually, scouts had reported back to Eldol,

Ambrosius and Gruffudd in Corinium with news that the Saxons had withdrawn from Durocornovium and Cunetio, and headed back to their own lands. Eldol immediately sent a messenger to Glevum with this news, and Corinium stood down from its state of alert.

Eldol, Ambrosius and Gruffudd, along with their remaining forces, remained in Corinium for another day before heading back to Glevum. Humiliated by their defeat, and angry that they had not brought a larger force, they decided that they would not underestimate the Saxons again.

*

When Eldol returned to his estate in the hills two days later, he gathered Arturius, Lavena and Ceredig together for a serious discussion about the future.

"The heavy defeat to the Saxons was chastening," he said. "Hengest now has enough Saxon numbers to see the crown as High King of the Britons within his grasp. Lord Ambrosius is in favour of taking the fight to the Saxons, using small militia groups to raid Saxon settlements in Cantia and the southerly kingdoms, killing any Saxons who raise their weapons against him and his men. This will bring retaliation from the Saxons, with more battles against them and further losses."

After listening to Eldol's assessment, Arturius turned to Lavena and said, "The threat to you and Ceredig is significantly greater. It is now time to relocate to Armorica, where you would be safe under Madog's protection. There are many former Gewisse warriors in Armorica, so we could build the Gewisse into a force again. When the time is right, we can plan your return to Britannia."

Lavena turned to Ceredig and said, "I have to agree with your uncle and Arturius, my son. These Saxons saw no issue with killing your brother when he was only a few years older than you. And it would not harm your education to spend a few years in Armorica."

Ceredig felt the weight of expectation, coupled with an unexpected sense of achievement. This was the first time that his mother, uncle and best friend were waiting for him to agree with their proposal. He did not feel like an adult, but they were treating him as one.

Naturally, he agreed with their proposals, simply because the case presented by his uncle and Arturius made a lot of sense, but also because he wanted his mother to be safe, and she would accompany him overseas.

"Good, that is settled," said Eldól. "Madog should be arriving in Glevum with a trading ship in the next few days. We should prepare for your departure when he returns to Armorica."

*

A week later, Ceredig, Lavena and Arturius were on Madog's trading ship, heading for a new life in Armorica.

Madog spent the journey overseas telling Ceredig stories of Armorica, the successful trading business he had established and the estate that he had acquired in the hills above the citadel of Darioritum, big enough to house over 200 Gewisse warriors, with space for many more than that.

He also spoke of the chieftain of Darioritum, who had embraced the Gewisse warriors into the community after Madog had promised their support in protecting the region. Madog told Ceredig of the chieftain's two children, a girl around Ceredig's age and her younger brother, whom he thought Ceredig would like to meet.

Ceredig and Lavena watched as land appeared on the horizon, although the ship continued to sail south. Madog pointed out that these lands were the western coast of Armorica, but they had two more days of sailing to reach their destination. Eventually, the ship turned east, close to land, sailed round a peninsula and headed towards an estuary.

Ceredig expected the port to appear soon, but they were in a large sea lake and still sailing through the middle of it, manoeuvring round various islands. His first impression was that their destination appeared so well hidden that any potential invaders would struggle to find the port, unless they had been there before, or had a local sailor to guide them. Ceredig thought this made it easy to set up an early warning system to alert the citadel of any impending sea attack.

Finally, after they had passed between an island and the mainland, a city appeared and the ship quickly approached the port filled with many trading ships. Elisedd noticed that nine of the ships were flying a flag that looked suspiciously like his father's banner, a gold rampant dragon on a red background. He looked up and noticed that Madog's ship carried the same flag. How did he not notice that before?

Madog saw Ceredig looking at these ships and said, "Yes, Ceredig, these are your ships. I thought it would honour your father for his banner to appear on all our ships, especially as they will be yours one day."

After the ship docked against the harbour wall, Madog, Ceredig, Lavena and Arturius disembarked and mounted horses that Madog had arranged for them, before Madog led them through the city and up into the hills to the north.

After about thirty minutes, they approached an estate entrance. It looked very similar to Eldol's estate near Glevum, built by the Romans before their departure from Armorica. However, the big difference was that this estate was much larger and with many more buildings.

"Is this your estate, Madog?" asked Ceredig. "It is enormous."

"No, it is yours, Lord Ceredig," was Madog's calm response.

It was just beginning to sink in to Ceredig that these men were granting him the same authority that they had given his father. They saw Ceredig as their leader, in waiting, at the very least.

A cart arrived at the estate an hour later with the personal belongings that Ceredig, Lavena and Arturius had brought with them. Madog insisted that they all stay in the main villa, which was more than big enough to accommodate them.

Over the next few days, Ceredig got to know all the

Gewisse warriors living in the estate. They had not seen him since they fled from Portus Adurni, but everyone treated Ceredig with great warmth and respect.

Ceredig also discovered that his education was not yet finished. Madog had made arrangements for a local group of monks to continue his education. The first thing they taught Ceredig was about Armorica, how the kings of Dumnonia claimed overlordship over the kingdom, with local chieftains responsible for maintaining control. The local language was similar to the language of the Gewisse, which he had learned in Portus Adurni and Glevum, so he was quick to pick it up.

Ceredig also noticed that a large number of those living and working in Darioritum were also exiles from Britannia, mostly from Cantia. Some had arrived within the past few years, whilst the more established residents were second generation Armoricans.

*

The next six years passed peacefully for everyone in Darioritum, but they were kept informed on the latest developments from Britannia through Madog's trading trips to Glevum.

Madog informed them that Ambrosius had established small militia units who carried out raids on Saxon communities across their lands. This had worked against the Saxons for the first five years. However, in the sixth year, the Saxons had finally tired of these raids, so targeted Ambrosius as leader of the Britons. Over the following year, the Saxons learned to anticipate the attacks, resulting in significant losses for the Britons.

After one significant defeat to the Saxons, Ambrosius had retreated to Dumnonia where he had made an alliance with King Erbin. As a reward for saving his son, Gereint, in battle, King Erbin had granted Ambrosius overlordship of Armorica. For the past two years, Ambrosius had been based in Namnates, south from Darioritum, where the locals called him 'Riothamus', or 'high king', because his rule was considered absolute.

Whilst he was ruling Armorica, King Erbin had charged Ambrosius with forming an army of exiled Britons to return to Britannia and, once and for all, defeat the Saxons so badly that they returned from where they came.

Ambrosius had yet to travel beyond Namnates, as he had been busy forming the beginnings of a great army there. However, Ceredig hoped that Ambrosius would venture up to Darioritum at some point, as he had heard great stories of Ambrosius's exploits in Britannia, and knew that Madog and Arturius would also be interested to meet with him.

Now nineteen years old, Ceredig had grown into a tall and powerful warrior, causing problems for Arturius, who was finding it more of a challenge during their practices.

Ceredig looked even more like his father now, especially in build, thanks to his regular training with Arturius. His hair was shorter than his mentor's, because Ceredig had found long hair annoying when training, but it still reached down to his shoulders, and he now had a beard, although he kept that short for practical reasons.

While Madog had begun showing Ceredig how the shipping business worked, increasingly taking him on trading missions, Ceredig did not join Madog on trips to Britannia. That journey was considered too dangerous for now.

Ceredig had also developed a great friendship over his nine years in Darioritum with the chieftain's children, Ophelia and Flavius. With no one else his own age for company, he spent all his free time with them, either at the chieftain's palace or on his own estate.

He had enjoyed having these friends to grow up with, compared to his complete isolation when he lived in Glevum. Even Lavena had noticed that Ceredig was much happier since leaving Glevum.

The chieftain and his family were originally from Britannia too, but had left their lands in Cantia over twenty years ago, when the Saxons had been granted lands there by King Wyrtgeorn. Like Ceredig, they had fled to Armorica and their father had become the largest landholder within the region around Darioritum, eventually taking over as chieftain.

Lavena also thought she saw an attraction between Ceredig and Ophelia, but they rarely spent any time alone for anything to develop, mostly thanks to Flavius looking upon Ceredig as a big brother he could look up to.

*

A few months later, a scout arrived at the estate to inform Madog, Arturius and Ceredig that King Ambrosius and fifty of his men would shortly be arriving at the estate and wished to meet with them.

Lavena and Arturius had immediately set about preparing to receive their guest, while Ceredig headed down to the stables to spend some time with the horses. He was learning to ride, so the master of the horses encouraged him to take a horse out riding across the estate.

Later that afternoon, Ceredig had just arrived back at the stables when he heard a commotion coming from the gates of the estate. He returned his horse to the stable, washed himself in the trough outside the stables and then headed up to the villa. He arrived just in time to see Lavena and Arturius finish greeting Lord Ambrosius, dressed in all his battle finery. Ceredig stepped forward to greet the great warrior.

Ambrosius took a split second to take in the sight of the young man before him, then said, "Ceredig? Look at how you have grown, and you look just like your father. The resemblance is uncanny. He was a great warrior and leader of men, so I am looking forward to seeing if you can reach the same heights he did."

He turned to Arturius, saying, "I take it we have you to thank for turning this young boy into the warrior I see before me, Arturius?"

"I cannot take all the credit, my lord," replied Arturius. "Ceredig is a very determined student, which made my job easier."

Then they returned to the conversation that they had been having before Ceredig arrived, with Arturius saying, "Madog is due back at the villa later, so I trust that we can discuss the matters at hand then. While you wait, one of the servants can take you to your room, so you can freshen up and rest until food is ready, although, I would be delighted to give you a tour of the estate if you would prefer."

"Thank you, Arturius, that is most kind," he said. "I would also like to talk with Ceredig about his life in Armorica before we eat, just in case I do not get the opportunity in the morning, as I need to leave early."

After an hour's rest, Ambrosius left the villa and found Ceredig practising with Arturius in the horse training ring, which also proved to be useful as a sword training ring.

Ambrosius watched as they engaged in their training session. He thought Ceredig handled his sword well and gave Arturius as good as he got. After ten minutes of parrying with each other, swords clashing, metal on metal, Ceredig appeared to be just as strong as he was at the start.

Ambrosius admired the strength of youth, but realised that age brought wisdom, which more than compensated for any loss of power that the years brought.

When they took a break, Lord Ambrosius stepped forward and said, "How about a different challenge for Ceredig. After years practising together, he probably anticipates your moves by now, Arturius."

Arturius agreed and stepped out of the ring as Ambrosius withdrew his sword.

"Are you ready, young warrior?" he said.

"Yes, always, Lord Ambrosius," said Ceredig, raising his sword to meet the challenge.

Lord Ambrosius was not gentle on Ceredig, who deflected the attacks that kept coming. To the casual observer, it looked like Ceredig was struggling to contain the strength and variety of moves from his opponent, but that was not the case. Ceredig was watching and learning, and doing it quickly.

After ten minutes, Ceredig began retaliating with attacks of his own. He deliberately made them obvious, knowing that Ambrosius would be able to defend them quite easily. It was how he defended them that Ceredig was watching. It was clear that his opponent was a skilled swordsman, but his style was traditional, designed to use his strength to overwhelm.

Arturius had taught Ceredig this style, but had also taught him how to use his body as a weapon to turn defence into attack when the time was right.

Ambrosius was also older, around fifty years by Ceredig's reckoning. This meant that his strength in wielding his sword in a fight would eventually drop, albeit slightly. That was when Ceredig would strike.

When he was ready, Ceredig deflected the next attack, swivelled round behind Ambrosius and ducked in anticipation of a slice from his opponent. When it came, Ambrosius turned to reset his position, giving Ceredig the opportunity to step forward and place the sword at Ambrosius's chest.

"Outstanding," said Ambrosius. "You are an excellent teacher, Arturius. And you are a worthy Gewisse warrior,

Ceredig, just like your father. If you are done with training, can we talk?"

"Yes, my lord," replied Ceredig.

They both sheathed their swords and Arturius walked away, knowing the conversation was not for his ears.

As they walked through the estate, Ceredig told Ambrosius about his education from the local monks and the local language being similar to the one used by the Gewisse, to which Ambrosius said that the Dumnonians also used a similar dialect. Ceredig also told Ambrosius about the local chieftain and his two children, who were Ceredig's friends. He then provided information about their shipping business that traded up and down the coast, as well as across to Britannia, but never with the Saxons in Britannia or in northern Gaul.

Ambrosius then told Ceredig about the militia attacks on the Saxons, their change in tactics and his escape via Dumnonia to Namnates. He knew that the only way to rid Britannia of the Saxons was to destroy them in battle and, for that, he would need as large a force of Britons as he could muster, including any fighters living in Armorica.

"So, you are not looking to live and rule over Armorica with such an army?" asked Ceredig.

"No," was the immediate reply from Ambrosius. "I want to return home to Britannia, defeat the Saxons and get my lands back. What about you?"

"I also want to return to Britannia and claim back the lands that my father had once ruled," said Ceredig. "I want to kill Hengest, or whoever rules them now, to avenge my father and brother. And I want to return to Portus Adurni, the place of my birth, to live out the rest of my days."

"That last wish might be a problem," said Ambrosius. "I presume the news has not reached you that the Saxons destroyed Portus Adurni, leaving no buildings standing. It is useless as a stronghold now. However, if you and your Gewisse warriors join me, we could achieve everything else that we both want."

Ceredig replied, saying, "I am not commander of the Gewisse warriors, my lord. One day maybe, but not yet. We are a divergent group of mercenaries right now, trying to make a living until the time is right to return to Britannia, but have no single leader yet."

"I have a feeling that may change soon, Ceredig. From what I have seen, you are ready to succeed your father and become ruler of the Gewisse," said Ambrosius. "And when you do, I have a feeling that you will be an excellent leader, just like your father."

Whilst Ambrosius did believe that Ceredig would make a great leader one day, at this point in time he was an inexperienced young warrior, who was susceptible to flattery. Ceredig did not realise that Ambrosius had let him win their sword fight earlier. It was a good move, but an experienced sword fighter would have seen that move coming and dealt with it. However, Ambrosius could see Ceredig becoming leader of the Gewisse in the near future and knew it would be useful to have Ceredig and the Gewisse as an ally.

That evening, Ambrosius, Madog, Arturius, Lavena and Ceredig shared a light meal in the villa's dining room.

It was an enjoyable evening, with excellent food and wine, the latter being something for which Ceredig had recently developed a taste, especially the apple wine produced from their own orchards.

After their meal, they discussed Ambrosius's mission to establish a great army of Britons in Armorica, that would travel back to Britannia to join up with Eldol's forces from Glevum and the western province of Britannia, as well as an army from Dumnonia.

This large force would then travel towards Cantia, to take on Hengest and the Saxons in a great battle, which they aimed to win by virtue of sheer numbers. No mercy would be given and, if any Saxons fled from the field of battle, they would be pursued and killed. The Britons would then travel north to take on the Angles, who had come to Britannia and settled to the north of Lundein. Again, these forces would face the same fate as the Saxons.

There was general consensus with the overall plan, although Madog and Arturius asked a few questions about how many men Ambrosius planned to take from Armorica to Britannia, where they would get the hundreds of ships that they would need to get over the sea to Britannia and where they were planning to land.

Ambrosius laughed.

"I should have expected the Gewisse to be so well organised that a detailed plan would be needed," he said. "I am going to need over 10,000 men. So far, I have only identified 500 battle-hardened fighters in Namnates. If Darioritum can match this number, I would be happy.

However, if the Gewisse joined us, they would be worth double that."

He continued, "In terms of ships, I will be seeking to commission all the trading ships up and down the kingdom. King Erbin of Dumnonia will provide me with sufficient gold weight to pay for these ships.

"Finally, the best place to land would be the coastline close to Durnovaria. From there, they can travel northeastward with Dumnonia's forces to meet Eldol's army at Calleva, having taken care of any Saxons we find on your father's lands on the way. From there, we can travel as one large force into Cantia."

After listening to this, Ceredig said, "If all this comes together, we can finally rid ourselves of these murderers, but it sounds like there is a lot that could go wrong. However, this is an opportunity that must not be ignored, even if it takes longer to happen. I am sure I speak for everyone here when I say that the Gewisse would want to be part of any plan that involves avenging my father and brother's deaths, and reclaiming my father's lands from the Saxons."

Ambrosius, Madog and Arturius agreed with Ceredig's stance, so they all settled back to enjoy more wine.

With his work done in Darioritum, Lord Ambrosius and his men left early the next morning, heading north on the next stage of his mission, with a promise to visit again on his return journey.

8

CEREDIG, RULER OF THE GEWISSE

Sixth-century historian Jordanes wrote of the Goths' victory in AD 470 over Riothamus and a large Armorican force of 12,000 men in battle in the region of the Bituriges.

A few months after the visit from Ambrosius, Lavena took Ceredig down to the stables, under the guise of taking the horses out for a ride on the estate. However, as they arrived at the horse ring, Ceredig was surprised to see Madog and Arturius already there, along with other commanders and about forty of the Gewisse.

"What is going on?" he asked.

Madog stepped forward and said, "Ceredig, you have demonstrated great skill and determination in your education and Gewisse training, so Arturius has asked that we should consider whether you are ready to become our leader.

"Normally, the simple vote of the commanders would suffice to elect you as their leader, but your age and lack of battle experience left a few concerned at placing the lives of the Gewisse in the hands of such a young man. Since you have never fought in battle, you have yet to face the test of an unknown situation and overcome it.

"If you are willing to face a series of challenges that have been set for you by the Gewisse, the commanders have agreed that you would be recognised as our ruler. Do you accept the challenge?"

"Yes," said Ceredig immediately.

He did not think he could turn down an opportunity that Arturius and the Gewisse already thought he was ready to face. If he had even hesitated, it would place further doubt in their minds, which could make him a liability if they ever went into battle.

"Excellent," said Madog. "Inside the stable is a full battle outfit befitting a Gewisse warrior, which you need to wear to face your challenge. Get dressed and return to the horse training ring."

Ceredig entered the stables and dressed in the standard Gewisse battle outfit, including a sword, dagger and axe. It felt a little heavy wearing a full battle outfit for the first time, but it also felt comfortable, so he knew it would not affect his movement. He would just have to fight against any tiredness from carrying the extra weight during the challenge. He left the stables and returned to the ring. He also noticed that the sword had been blunted, which he knew would be relevant later.

"There is a path laid out across the estate, which you must follow," said Madog. "The first challenge is horse-based. As you head down the path, you will come across several obstacles, which you must overcome. At the end of the path, you will be met by the stable master, who will take your horse from you. You then follow the path down to the orchard. As you follow the path through the orchard, you will come across further challenges. Once these are completed, you will find your horse waiting for you. You then need to ride your horse back here to the training ring, where you will face one final challenge. When you are ready, mount your horse and pick up a spear."

Ceredig knew the spear must relate to his first challenge. If not, it would be a hindrance. He mounted his horse and used his spear to tap the horse's hindquarters and get it moving. He then squeezed his legs against its body to speed it up. He left the ring and followed the path that had been laid out for him with spears bearing his father's banner.

He saw the first challenge quite early. It was a barrier that he could not jump. On the other side of the barrier was a thick prickly bush, with five apples strategically placed where only the spear could reach them, but would need careful horse management to avoid the horse being pricked by the sharp prickles.

Ceredig carefully manoeuvred his horse as he used his spear to pierce each apple and remove it from the bush. A Gewisse warrior then pointed beyond the bush where Ceredig saw a wooden boar shape, leaning against a tree nearby. The warrior told Ceredig that he would have to hit the boar with his spear from his horse. Ceredig took his time trying to steady his horse before throwing the spear straight into the wooden shape of the boar.

Obstacle one completed, thought Ceredig.

The Gewisse warrior opened a gate to Ceredig's left and sent him on his way. Ceredig immediately saw a high barrier blocking his way. He knew he would have to jump it, so he kicked his legs, making the horse speed up to a gallop and gain momentum to get over the fence. He made it over.

Obstacle two completed.

As Ceredig slowed the horse down to a canter, two groups of men bearing shields suddenly appeared on either side of the path, making a shield wall. They started to close the gap.

This must be the third obstacle, thought Ceredig, and he needed to pass.

The men were wearing their full armour, but bore no weapons as far as Ceredig could see. So, he pulled out his blunted sword and prepared to push through the gap. As he met the two shield walls, he made his horse fishtail side-to-side, to disrupt the shield wall. Ceredig also used his sword to find gaps through the shield wall, to hit any vulnerable areas he could. As each warrior was hit with the sword, they withdrew. The horse fishtailing also helped put some of the men off balance, which sent some to the ground, although they returned to the shield wall. Finally, Ceredig broke through the shield wall and continued down the path at a canter.

With obstacle three completed, Ceredig then saw the horse master, so stopped and dismounted, leaving the horse master to take the horse.

Ceredig saw another Gewisse warrior, holding three spears, who pointed out across the orchard to a shield that was propped up and informed Ceredig that his next challenge was about accuracy of spear over a distance. He told Ceredig that at least two spears out of three must hit the target.

Ceredig's first throw was close, but landed just to the right and about three feet short of the shield. That was a sighter for him, but the next two needed to hit the target.

Ceredig's next throw then clipped the edge of the shield. He looked at the warrior, who nodded his agreement that this counted as a hit. Ceredig breathed a sigh of relief and picked up the third spear.

His final throw hit the shield full on, remaining stuck in it. He had overcome another obstacle, but knew he now had two more to go in the orchard.

The warrior then pointed Ceredig in the direction of his next challenge, which he could now see across the other side of the path through the orchard. It was a wooden man-shaped structure, bearing the outfit of a warrior, with an axe attached to an outstretched limb and a shield attached to the other.

An axe challenge, thought Ceredig. He withdrew his axe and sliced at the axe of the 'man' in front of him. He was surprised when the body swivelled round and the shield swung towards him, forcing him to duck to avoid being hit by it.

Okay, thought Ceredig. This was not going to be as easy a challenge as he first thought.

The body was still swinging round from the momentum of Ceredig's first attack, so he waited for the opportunity to step into the arc of the swinging arms and quickly slice down, removing the axe arm at the wrist and pulling out before the shield came round to hit him. Ceredig then sliced down, cutting off the shield arm, then the head of the 'man'.

Another challenge completed. Only one more to go, he thought as he returned to the path and continued down it towards the end of the orchard.

He then saw seven men, bearing shields, who were blocking his path in a loose shield wall. He also saw a shield leaning against a tree, suggesting that he would need to use only his shield to break through this shield wall.

As Ceredig approached them, he sized up each man before deciding on his tactics. Taking a firm grip of his shield, he began walking towards the men, as if to try to simply push through the centre. When he got within ten feet of the shield wall, and the men prepared for a push, Ceredig suddenly started to run at them, with the shield pressed out in front of him.

At the last minute, Ceredig veered slightly to hit the join between shields two and three, just off centre, before they could get the shield wall tight enough to withstand such force. It was the point where the youngest warriors were positioned. He had gambled that they did not have much experience using a shield wall in battle, only training, and would not have expected Ceredig's speed and force. It worked. He broke through quite easily.

A group of men who had been watching this started cheering at Ceredig's achievement and also the ease with which he overcame the shield wall.

Ceredig then saw the horse master waiting with his horse, who handed the reins to Ceredig and told him to make his way up to the horse training ring, adding that there would be no further obstacles between here and there.

Ceredig mounted his horse and headed back up to the stables. As he approached the stables, there was a large crowd of men around the training ring. Arturius stepped forward and took the reins of the horse, allowing Ceredig to dismount.

"You have one final challenge left," said Arturius. "Inside the ring is the best Gewisse swordsman we have. It is Madog and he will find out if I have trained you well enough. Trust me, he has sword skills that I do not."

Arturius handed Ceredig his sword in exchange for the blunt one and ushered him towards the ring. Ceredig saw Madog waiting for him in the centre, holding his sword in one hand and his shield in the other.

Ceredig had not trained with a shield very often, but saw one lying on the floor of the ring, so he approached it and reached to pick it up. Almost immediately Madog stepped forward and used his own shield to push Ceredig off balance.

"Lesson one," Madog said. "Always get your weapon out first."

Suitably chastened, Ceredig stood up, removed his sword, then his shield and prepared to fight.

Ceredig wished he had used a shield more during his training with Arturius, as it felt unusual having to fight with the shield in his left hand as an extra weight. He adjusted his stance and approached Madog, waiting for him to attack since it was his objective to defeat Ceredig.

Madog watched Ceredig take his stance and then attacked with a wide swing that knocked Ceredig to the side as Madog's sword hit Ceredig's shield with real force.

Madog was strong, thanks to constantly working on the ship.

Ceredig realised that this fight would be tougher than anything he had faced before. There were no rules and Madog was not going to make it easy, so Ceredig would have to find his weakness.

After fifteen minutes of each attacking the other, Ceredig had still not seen an opportunity or a weakness. However, he would not be rushed into a careless move, even despite Madog's attempts to rile him with insults about his swordplay. The crowd, though, were enjoying every minute, whooping and cheering each attack.

Ceredig tried to put Madog's words and the crowd out of his mind. He needed to focus on the fight. He decided to try one of the tactics that had worked earlier in one of his challenges. He opened his sword arm as if he were about to swing again but, this time, he pushed off with his rear foot and used his shield to push into Madog.

It caught Madog off guard for a second, but he managed to keep himself upright and get his balance again. However, Ceredig then brought down the sword onto Madog's shield, and knocked it out of his hand and onto the ground.

Madog immediately swung his sword, but Ceredig had his shield back in position and was able to defend it. Ceredig then stepped forward as if to repeat the move, but Madog backed off to avoid another hit.

Now without a shield, Madog changed his stance to rebalance his weight. Ceredig threw his shield to the ground and did likewise. The crowd gasped in disbelief that Ceredig had given up an advantage.

As far as Ceredig was concerned, this was now a straight sword fight, which he had trained for every day since he could hold a sword.

Another fifteen minutes of sword fighting went by, without any body hits. Ceredig was closely watching Madog's stance, sword strokes and micro-movements for any sign of weakness. He realised that Arturius had been right. Madog was the best swordsman he had ever fought.

Ceredig considered a similar move to the one he used on Lord Ambrosius, but then realised that Arturius had probably told everyone how he had bested such a great warrior, so Madog would probably anticipate such a move.

Ceredig then thought, *Why not make him think I am about to try it, but give it a different ending.* Therefore, he waited on Madog to make a right swing with his sword, then deflected it with his sword and made a feint to swing round to his right.

Madog had clearly anticipated such a move, so was prepared for it, as Ceredig had thought. As Madog continued to turn, instead of stopping to swing his sword back towards where he was supposed to think Ceredig was going, Ceredig pivoted back to where he had been.

Madog finished his turn and swung his sword, only to find that Ceredig was not where he should be and was now behind him, swinging his sword against Madog's shoulder, just below the bare neckline, hitting him with the flat of the sword.

Ceredig had won!

A massive cheer rose up from the men who had been watching the fight.

Madog turned round to face Ceredig and said, "That was an excellent fight and worthy of your father's son. I knew Arturius was an excellent teacher, but you have been an exceptional student, with a natural aptitude for sword fighting. You have natural skills that cannot be taught, which is a valuable asset in a leader. I would be honoured to fight at your side, my lord."

He turned to everyone who had watched the fight and proclaimed Ceredig as worthy to become ruler of the Gewisse, asking whether anyone objected.

When there was complete silence from the crowd, Madog raised his sword to the sky and shouted, "Ceredig!"

Then everyone responded, shouting, "Ceredig!"

At that point, Lavena stepped forward, holding something over her arm. It was a sword lying on a bright scarlet red Roman cloak, similar to the one that his father had worn. Attached to the cloak was a large round gold brooch. It bore a Celtic design around the outside, with small red rubies inset in the centre.

"Is that Father's sword and cloak?" he asked, somewhat confused. "How?"

"Sadly, no," said Lavena. "After the Saxon massacre, Gruffudd had sent out some scouts to see if they could recover the bodies of your father, brother and Cunedda, but when they arrived at the hillfort over a week later, the bodies were missing and no sign of your father's cloak. We still do not know where the bodies were taken."

"Where did these come from then?" said Ceredig, pointing at the sword and cloak.

"We arranged to have new ones made here," replied Lavena, handing the sword to Ceredig. "We had your father's sword, but there was too much damage, so Madog and Arturius had a new one made to look just like it, using some of the old sword elements. This is your sword."

Lavena handed the cloak to Madog, who went behind Ceredig and wrapped it around his shoulders, while Lavena fastened the brooch to the cloak, then knelt down in front of her son and bowed, saying, "My lord Ceredig."

Ceredig turned round to face the men of the Gewisse as they all knelt down and proclaimed in unison, "Lord Ceredig, ruler of the Gewisse."

That night, there was a huge banquet on the estate to celebrate the elevation of Ceredig as ruler of the Gewisse. For most of the Gewisse, as well as Lavena, it was tinged with sadness that Elisedd had to die for Ceredig to succeed him, remembering Ceredig as the little boy running around the fort at Portus Adurni, playing with his wooden sword, pretending to be a Gewisse ruler, just like his father.

Ceredig celebrated too, but his mind was drawn back to the day he left Portus Adurni and his conversation with Arturius. He was now ruler of the Gewisse, just as Arturius had foreseen. He was one step closer to avenging his father and brother, and reclaiming his family's rightful lands.

*

Ambrosius returned to the estate a few weeks later. He had been informed that Ceredig had become ruler of the Gewisse and was quick to congratulate him, saying that he knew when they had last met that Ceredig was ready to assume his father's mantle as ruler of the Gewisse.

Once the congratulations were complete, Ambrosius informed Ceredig that the Wesi Goths from Hispania were posing an imminent threat to Armorica. Their new king, Euric, had been expanding north into Gallia Aquitania, with great success, and now controlled most of that region. The continuing collapse of the Western Roman Empire had made their expansion much easier, and the Goths were now in a position to push further north towards Armorica.

As a result, Ambrosius now had a more urgent mission than retaking Britannia from the Saxons. He urgently needed to build as big an Armorican army as he could, so he could take on the Goths in the last region of Gaul that stood between them and Armorica.

Ambrosius had received support from Anthemius, ruler of the Western Roman Empire, who had granted the Goths land in the southwestern region a few years earlier, in an attempt to broker peace. Just like the Saxons, the Goths had broken the peace, so Emperor Anthemius had promised warriors to Lord Ambrosius to take on the Goths.

Ambrosius was now in Darioritum seeking a commitment from the Gewisse to join this large force of warriors, which was now estimated to be over 10,000. He had discussed the present situation with the chieftains from

Darioritum and Namnates, who had agreed that Ceredig and the Gewisse should lead their combined forces, while he would lead the rest of the northern Armorican forces.

Ceredig knew he would have the battle experience of the chieftains of Darioritum and Namnates, as well as Arturius and Madog in his command group, and could only learn more about the reality of battle with a great warrior and leader like Ambrosius Aurelianus. How could Ceredig refuse the opportunity to command the southern Armorican forces in battle?

*

A few months later, Ambrosius and Ceredig were leading a force of nearly 12,000 men of Armorica towards battle against the Goths. They had congregated at Namnates, then marched over ten days south along the coast, arriving just north of the river, near Burdigala, where the Gewisse scouts had reported that the Goths were encamped.

Ambrosius had expected to have a much larger army, after Emperor Anthemius had reassured him that he would have another 10,000 men. However, the emperor and his Gauls had tried to defeat the Goths on their own in battle the week before, at a place north-east of Burdigala. The Gauls lost heavily, with Anthemius's men fleeing for their lives. As a result, the Armorican army were on their own against the Goths.

The Armoricans set up camp just outside a citadel called Bourg, at a fork in the river. The citadel had suffered from an earlier attack by the Goths and been left deserted, although some locals, who had fled from the approaching Goths, had returned to Bourg after they had established their base in Burdigala.

These locals said Bourg had once been the estate of a Roman consul, who had fortified the estate at some point, but had been taken over by the locals after the Roman withdrawal.

The next morning, a small group of seven Goths rode towards the Armorican camp. They waited a sufficient distance away for them not to be considered a threat. Ambrosius sent Ceredig, Arturius, Madog and an Armorican, who could act as translator if needed, out to meet the Goth entourage.

When the two groups met, the Goth in the middle of the group spoke in Latin, saying, "I am Euric, King of the Wesi Goths."

Ceredig was fluent in Latin, so understood Euric's introduction. He responded for the Armoricans, introducing himself as "Ceredig, ruler of the Gewisse, from Darioritum", then announcing his fellow Armoricans to King Euric.

"Splendid," said Euric. "I think it always good for warriors to know who they may be fighting. I am assuming that is why you are here with so many men?"

"That depends, Lord Euric," replied Ceredig. "If we receive reassurances that you and your people will return to your own lands and stay there, leaving Western Gaul and Armorica to live in peace, then we can avoid any violence."

"I wish that I could make that promise, Lord Ceredig," said Euric. "Unfortunately, these lands now belong to the

Goths and we will not be leaving. I did not have any plans to expand into Armorica, but if you insist on battle, then you will be placing your own lands at risk."

"Very well, I will pass on your response to Ambrosius Aurelianus, Riothamus of Armorica," responded Ceredig. "Do you wish to wait for his answer?"

"What? You are not in command of these men. Why is this Riothamus not here making these demands himself?" said Euric in a raised voice.

"We did not anticipate that the king would be the one to come to face us. It is normal for us to send senior commanders for discussions and relay them back to our leaders," said Ceredig.

"Well, Lord Ceredig," said Euric, who was now frustrated, "you may relay my conditions to your leader, Riothamus. Tell him that, if your warriors are still here tomorrow afternoon, I will have my answer, and my men will meet you in battle on the fields to the west of here on the following day."

With their meeting concluded, King Euric and his men turned and rode away on their horses.

Ceredig and his companions turned and headed back into camp, where Ceredig informed Lord Ambrosius of his conversation with King Euric, and the terms given if the Armoricans wanted to remain and fight.

After much discussion between Ambrosius, Ceredig and the chieftains of each region, it was agreed that they needed to take on these Goths in battle, because they would certainly come for Armorica if they ran away from battle.

With the decision made, they settled in for the night. Battle tactics would be discussed in the morning, in preparation for battle the following day, assuming the Goths did not withdraw.

*

Two days later, Ceredig's scouts came back and reported that a very large force of nearly 20,000 Goths had moved out of the walled town of Burdigala, crossed the river and were heading to the west of the Armoricans' position. The Armoricans were heavily outnumbered.

Ceredig said, "Well, that settles it. There will be battle today."

During their wait for the Goths to choose whether to fight or retreat, Ceredig, Ambrosius and the commanders had settled on a three-pronged attack. They had hoped to draw the Goths towards them on foot, with the plan of having a mounted group of warriors to swing round and come in from the north and rear.

Arturius had led a third of their men out of the Armorican camp in the early hours, heading up the coast, as if returning to Armorica. Gewisse scouts had gone out earlier to ensure that no Goth scouts were able to return to Burdigala to let King Euric know that Arturius's men were swinging around to the north of the anticipated battleground.

Ceredig had cautioned against this manoeuvre, but Ambrosius had made the final decision to proceed. Ceredig knew that Arturius was an excellent battle tactician, so trusted that Arturius would see the larger Goth numbers and realise that they would need to join the battle earlier than originally planned.

At around midday, the Goth forces started to march towards the Armoricans.

The Armoricans were in position to the east of the citadel of Bourg, but wanted to draw the Goths towards them and further away from their horses.

As he watched the Goths approaching, Ceredig suddenly felt a pang of nerves. This would be his first real battle and he was leading his Gewisse into the fight. Whilst they were well trained and should operate as a cohesive unit, all their lives rested on decisions he would need to make.

As if sensing his leader's nervousness, Madog put his arm around Ceredig's shoulder and said, "Do not worry, Ceredig. You are a Gewisse, and you are Elisedd's son. Battle is in your blood and your men will follow you anywhere without question. Once you make your first kill, you will realise that fighting is about luck, but battles are about tactics. Look around for opportunities to change the focus of battle, target any weakness you see in the opposition, or simply put them on the back foot."

"Thank you, Madog," replied Ceredig. "My father was wise to have chosen you as a commander."

Ceredig then looked over the battle site and noticed that the land was extremely flat, and any on-field manoeuvre would likely be seen by the Goths. After a few minutes' thought, Ceredig suggested something to Ambrosius, who agreed it was worth a shot.

He issued instructions to Madog, who retreated with a group of men back to their camp. They mounted their horses and headed back to the Armorican forces, trying to keep themselves as low as possible. As they approached their own group, they suddenly sat up proud on their horses and increased their speed to a gallop. Instead of heading towards the Goths, they headed to the southern end of the Goth forces, towards the river, as if to flank them.

Ceredig had hoped that the Goths would react to this, at the very least, splitting their forces, which they did, but by using their own group of horsemen, who had been walking behind the main force with their horses held by their reins. The Goths mounted their horses and headed round the south flank of their group to take on Madog and his mounted force.

It seemed as if whatever tactic Ambrosius or his commanders came up with, the Goths had been planning for it themselves. There was no other option but to take on the Goths in a straight fight, warrior against warrior. Ambrosius gave the command for the Armorican forces to commence marching towards the enemy and prepare to fight.

As both sides increased their pace towards each other, 4,000 Armorican horsemen appeared out of the woodland to the north and headed straight for the Goths. Ceredig knew that Arturius must have been watching from his elevated position and realised that his forces were needed now.

Arturius and his forces rode down towards the rear of the Goths, aiming to take out any stragglers, but, at the very least, forcing them to turn to face this third front.

Meanwhile, Madog and his horsemen were now engaging the Goths on horseback in a battle by the river. It appeared to be an even fight, from Ceredig's viewpoint, with men falling on both sides. He just hoped that Madog would emerge from this alive and well.

Ceredig now turned to focus on the oncoming Goths that the Armoricans were about to take on in battle, using various weapons, depending on preference.

The Goths favoured swords and spears, so Ceredig expected an onslaught of spears heading his way shortly. Luckily, the Armoricans also favoured spears, so the Goths would also have to face a similar attack before they met in hand-to-hand combat. Ceredig readied his spear.

Ambrosius hoped that making their attack first, they would take out men holding spears before they could be thrown. On his command, the Armoricans let rip with their spears towards the Goths. The Goths reacted straight away and their spears began heading towards the Armoricans, so both sides needed to take shelter under their shields.

Ceredig and his Gewisse formed a tight shield wall to deflect the Goth spears, but some of the other Armoricans were not so lucky, with quite a few losses. Ceredig and his Gewisse then withdrew their swords and ran into battle. Side by side, they fought against the Goths, killing many, injuring even more.

Madog had been right. Once Ceredig had killed a Goth, he suddenly felt as if he was where he should be. He was fighting with his kinsmen for something they believed was right, and they had trained for this.

The Gewisse excelled themselves in this battle, only suffering a few losses amongst their most inexperienced warriors. However, the rest of the Armoricans had little battle experience, so, against the Goths who had been gaining experience in battle all the way up through Gaul from Hispania, they were outclassed and out-fought. The Armoricans were decimated.

Arturius and his forces continued to attack the Goths from the rear and were quite successful at first. However, the Goths had greater numbers, so were able to divert a significant number to taking these men on directly.

It was an exhausting battle and, when he had the opportunity to take stock of how the battle was developing, Ambrosius could see that the Goths were winning. He ordered the Armoricans to withdraw and, seeing this move, the Goths also withdrew.

After a short while, King Euric and the same six men, who had come to talk to Ceredig and his men two days before, approached the Armoricans with their weapons in their sheaths. Ambrosius joined Ceredig, Arturius and Madog as they rode out to meet the Goths.

Euric addressed Ambrosius directly, saying, "My lord, I am Euric, King of the Wesi Goths. Am I correct in presuming that you are Riothamus, leader of this army?"

"Yes, I am Ambrosius Aurelianus, ruler of Armorica," said Ambrosius.

"You and your forces have fought well, my lord," said Euric. "I commend your tactics and fighting skills. This has been our toughest battle to date. However, I am sure you can see that you are outnumbered and losing."

"That may be your assessment of the situation, my lord," replied Ambrosius. "However, a battle is never over until both sides agree it is."

Euric responded, saying, "I estimate that we now have three men to your one. I do not wish to kill such excellent fighters, unless I have to. And, I am sure that you do not wish to lose men when it is unnecessary. I offer you the opportunity to withdraw, with dignity and no further loss of life. Your men can return to their families and lands and live the rest of their lives in peace. All I ask is that you and your leaders swear an oath of fealty to me and offer reassurances that Armorica will never take up arms against me for as long as I rule."

After hearing these terms, Ambrosius said, "I will consider your offer along with the chieftains of Armorica. If you set up camp, we will come to you once we have made our decision."

"While you are conferring with your leaders, it is a good time to gather the dead and injured from the battlefield," said Euric. "No harm will come to any men while we are in this period of truce, but do not take too long to decide your future, or I will make it for you."

With their discussions over, Euric and his men turned and rode back to their camp.

Ambrosius, Ceredig, Arturius and Madog returned to the Armorican camp, and issued instructions to collect the fallen from the field of battle.

As the commanders met up in Ambrosius's tent, Ceredig learned that the chieftain of Darioritum had been killed in battle. He imagined a difficult conversation with his friend, the chieftain's son, Flavius, who was too young to have participated in this battle, when he got home.

Ambrosius explained the terms that King Euric had offered to the other regional chieftains, then said, "Every man of Armorica here today has proven themselves in battle against a formidable opponent with greater numbers. It is their bravery that has given the Goth king pause for thought and has been instrumental in his offering such favourable terms for peace."

The regional chieftains nodded in agreement.

Ambrosius continued, "Euric could easily continue the battle, resulting in the death of most, if not all, of us. After that, he could march into Armorica and install one of his own as ruler. If we accept his terms, you can return to your homes in Armorica, and you will never be able to take up arms for or against King Euric's Goths for as long as he lives. On that basis, I recommend we accept his terms, but you all have to agree."

There was a lot of murmuring, but little dissent from the regional chieftains. Ambrosius took this as a consensus and said, "Since we are all in agreement, I will send a messenger to the Goths with our decision. We will then go together to accept King Euric's terms of surrender."

An hour later, Ambrosius, Ceredig and the other regional chieftains arrived at the camp of King Euric, where they waited, before one of Euric's commanders, whom they recognised from the previous negotiations, came out to meet them. They followed him into the Goths' camp, where several of Euric's men took the reins of the Armoricans' horses and held them while they dismounted.

As the Armoricans entered a large tent, King Euric was seated in a chair at the top table, eating food. A man standing behind him leaned forward and whispered something in his ear. Euric stopped eating and looked up.

"Ah, welcome, my lords," he said. "I understand that you all agree to my terms for peace?"

"Yes, my lord. We have considered your peace offer and agree with your terms," replied Ambrosius.

"Excellent," said Euric. "Then I ask you to line up in a row and kneel down before me. I will then present my hand for you to swear fealty to me for the rest of my days, and then you will sign or place your mark on the two peace treaty documents lying on the table."

Ceredig smiled at the confidence this king had in already having drafted the two documents while Ambrosius was still discussing the terms with the chieftains of Armorica. He had to admire this king's honour, self-assurance and respect for peace, with violence seen as a last resort.

The Armorican leaders all took a knee in a row in front of King Euric, who stood up and came round from the table.

He approached Ambrosius first, who pledged his fealty to the king for as long as he lived. Euric then missed the next chieftain in the line to come to Ceredig next. It was a clear sign of the hierarchy that the king held towards Ceredig in terms of respect. After Ceredig had pledged his fealty, Euric returned to the chieftain he had missed, then moved on to the other chieftains.

Once they had all sworn fealty to Euric, the Armorican leaders stepped over to the table and each man reviewed then signed the two documents. Euric then handed over one of the copies of the charter to Ambrosius and turned to each man and gave them a forearm handshake, out of respect for these opponents, before returning to the table, where enough goblets had subsequently been laid out.

He picked up a jug and poured wine into each goblet, handing them out to the Armoricans, before taking one for himself. He raised his goblet up and said, "To peace!", then drank from his goblet.

Having seen the king drink from the same wine they had been given, the Armoricans followed Euric's lead, raising their goblets and saying, "Peace!"

Euric turned and went back to his chair, before saying, "It is late, so you can remain in your camp tonight, before returning to Armorica tomorrow. We will remain in Burdigala for the summer, before returning south."

When Euric sat down, his commander came forward and escorted the Armorican leaders out of the hall. They mounted their horses and left the Goths' camp, heading towards their own camp, feeling somewhat satisfied that, having proved themselves in battle, they had achieved their primary objective of stopping the Goths from marching into Armorica and taking control.

The next morning, Ambrosius and Ceredig led the Armoricans away from Bourg, north towards Namnates.

9

CEREDIG THE
CHIEFTAIN

After defeat to the Goths in AD 470, Ceredig became
vassal ruler of Darioritum, under the overlordship of
the Goth king, Euric.

On their journey back to Namnates, Ambrosius
informed Ceredig that he was returning to Britannia
straight away. He argued that there was no need for a high
king with the kingdom under the overlordship of the
Goths. Therefore, he would return to Britannia with as
many men as he could persuade to join him and undertake
another campaign against the Saxons, using small militia
groups to attack them again.

Ambrosius also told Ceredig that he wanted him to
take over as chieftain of Darioritum. The chieftain's son,
Flavius, was too young to assume his father's mantle, so
Ceredig was the natural successor, especially as he had
now proven himself in battle. Ambrosius also reminded
him that even King Euric thought him worthy by asking
for his fealty immediately after Ambrosius had given his.

Ceredig discussed this with Arturius and Madog on
the journey, asking them whether the Gewisse should
return to Britannia with Lord Ambrosius. Although they

both said that they would follow Ceredig if he chose to do so, Madog advised that he felt it was not the right time, especially after they had just suffered some losses in battle against the Goths.

Arturius suggested that they spend the next few years trying to build up their numbers again, aiming to recruit 1,000 Gewisse warriors before even considering a return to Britannia. Madog added that he should also use this time to build up their shipping business, so they had a fleet of ships with the capacity to take these 1,000 Gewisse warriors to Britannia.

Ceredig recognised the wisdom of their advice. He also acknowledged that he had pledged fealty to King Euric, so he felt that he was bound by honour to live up to that agreement, regardless of Ambrosius's attitude towards it.

Ceredig reminded Arturius and Madog that he was now the effective ruler of Darioritum as a result of the chieftain's death. Ceredig knew he faced a difficult conversation with Flavius and Ophelia when he got home.

When Flavius and Ophelia heard the news about their father's death, Ceredig's friends were naturally distraught. Then Ceredig informed them that he was now chieftain of Darioritum, but they told him that they understood the need for strong leadership, especially Flavius, who knew that he was too young to succeed his father, so they were happy that it was their friend who would be chieftain.

Ceredig reassured Flavius and Ophelia that their family would not lose any of their status while he was chieftain, and that he would ensure that, when the time was right, Flavius would replace him as chieftain.

*

The next three years brought peace to the region, making Ceredig's role as ruler of Darioritum much easier than anticipated.

King Euric had stuck to his word and left Burdigala later that summer, returning to Hispania. This meant that Ceredig was able to focus on working with Madog to increase the size of their shipping fleet, in terms of numbers, but also in terms of size. If they had any realistic chance of taking a force of 1,000 warriors across the sea to Britannia, Madog would need a larger fleet of ships.

The standard trading ship that Madog had used for sea patrols, under Ceredig's father, only held around twenty men with horses. That would mean fifty ships like these would be required for the crossing to Britannia. That was practically a navy.

Madog suggested that they needed a ship that was capable of holding at least 300 men, horses and equipment. He remembered a very large Roman-style merchant ship that could hold 400 men and horses, but the last time he had seen one was in port at Dumnonia around twenty years ago.

Therefore, while Madog and his men were away on trading routes, they had another task to find the largest ship they could that would meet Ceredig's requirements. Their trading routes were focused mostly on Britannia and the mainland of Gaul, using the large river systems that took them far inland. The northern coast of Gaul was out of bounds, mostly because of the Saxons and Franks controlling this region, and the Vandals held control over Africa terra and the southern sea. However, Ceredig had taken advantage of his fealty to King Euric of the Goths to request trading rights with the Goths down the coast in Hispania, which Euric had granted.

There was one significant development for Ceredig. With sixteen-year-old Flavius now having to focus on looking after his family's estates, Ceredig and Ophelia spent more time together on their own, and their friendship developed much further, very much encouraged by Ceredig's mother, Lavena, who rationalised that, as chieftain, Ceredig should be thinking about his family's future.

Since the two families held the same status, it was considered a good match for Ceredig and Ophelia to marry, and Flavius gave their marriage his blessing.

Within a year, Ceredig and Ophelia were married on Ceredig's estate. Unknown to Ceredig, Madog had informed Eldol of the upcoming wedding whilst in Glevum on a trading mission. As a result, Eldol, Bishop Eldad and Gruffudd had travelled to Darioritum to attend the wedding, which delighted both Ceredig and Lavena.

The bishop even insisted on officiating at the wedding for his nephew, which delighted Lavena and Ophelia's mother. Lavena had also arranged a great banquet to celebrate the wedding, with great merriment all round, resulting in some sore heads the next morning.

Two days later, Ceredig made some time to meet with Eldol, Gruffudd, Madog and Arturius in the great hall. After some gentle ribbing of Ceredig about his wedding night, they settled down to discuss the latest developments in Britannia.

Ambrosius had already told Eldol about the battle against the Goths, the favourable peace terms offered by the King of the Wesi Goths and that Ceredig was now chieftain of Darioritum. Therefore, Ceredig brought Eldol and Gruffudd up to date on the Gewisse recruitment and search for larger transport ships.

Eldol then told Ceredig about the antics of Ambrosius after he returned from Armorica with the 200 men that followed him. Ambrosius won a number of small battles against the Saxons near Noviomagus, then Calleva. This had only emboldened Ambrosius more, so he recruited more men from the western province and pushed deeper into Saxon territory, towards Cantia.

Unfortunately, Hengest had heard of Ambrosius's return from Armorica, so was prepared for his approach towards Cantia. Hengest and Æsc were waiting for Ambrosius near Calleva, with almost double the number of men, and it was a rout. Ambrosius barely made it out alive, fleeing from the battle back to Dumnonia with just over a hundred men out of his original 1,000.

After taking some time to recover and recruit more men, Ambrosius and his band of warriors changed their tactics and were now undertaking another militia campaign, this time hitting and running Saxon and Angle border communities up and down the country.

Ceredig considered this news for a moment, then said, "It is going to take a tremendous army of Britons to defeat the Saxons. If I bring 1,000 Gewisse warriors to Britannia, will the other kingdoms be able to increase that number tenfold?"

"Yes, it is possible," Eldol replied. "However, they will need to commit to training enough warriors over a period of time, like the Gewisse, as well as gaining some real battle experience against the Saxons. Whilst we may suffer losses, the outcome will be an army of real warriors with the skills to take on the Saxons in a final battle."

"Perhaps we need to start thinking in terms of a long-term plan to defeat the Saxons. How long would training such a force take?" asked Ceredig.

"I have no idea," replied Eldol. "We first need a leader to bring all the kingdoms together under one vision."

"Ambrosius could be that man," said Ceredig. "He has the battle experience and will have learned a lot from his battles against the Saxons. He has the ear of King Erbin of Dumnonia and could bring the Durotriges with him. If you can bring the western kingdoms round to following him, that would be a significant force against the Saxons."

"That might work," said Eldol. "I will discuss this with King Erbin on my return to Britannia. We will keep you updated on any developments, either through Madog, or my next trip here."

With everyone in agreement, it was time for Ceredig to return to his new wife. Eldol, Eldad and Gruffudd would be leaving in the morning, returning to Glevum, with Eldol and Gruffudd refreshed and invigorated with a new plan towards ridding Britannia of the Saxons.

*

The next two years flew by, as Ceredig and Ophelia settled into their marriage. There was good news on the family front, when Ophelia announced that she was pregnant.

Ceredig felt helpless as the birth approached, so left her in the care of Lavena, and Ophelia's mother, who both went into full mothering mode and helped Lavena throughout her pregnancy.

Meanwhile, Ceredig spent most of his time travelling around Armorica, identifying potential recruits for his Gewisse warriors, especially from families with British heritage, and bringing them back to the estate, which was being expanded to cope with the planned increase in their numbers.

When winter came, trading missions across to Britannia became more hazardous, but Madog managed five trips to Dumnonia and Glevum. On his return from the last trip of the year, he brought news from Eldol.

Ambrosius had agreed to the proposals that Eldol brought back with him on his last visit to Armorica. Eldol had then convinced the people of Glevum to support Ambrosius as leader of the rebellion against the Saxons, and Dumnonia was already behind Ambrosius. The kingdoms of Guenta, Pagenses and Glywysing were easily persuaded to support the plan, but Eldol only had to offer the opportunity to avenge their rulers who had been killed by the Saxons.

Ambrosius was now the *de facto* High King of the Britons. His mission was to co-ordinate the revolution against the Saxons. He created several militia forces to pillage the kingdoms to the east under Saxon control, while he went north in an attempt to persuade the northern kingdoms to support a unified army of Britons against the Saxons and Angles.

*

In the second month of the new year, Ceredig and Ophelia welcomed the birth of a healthy son, after a short period of labour without any complications, thanks to the local birth mother who had been brought up from Darioritum nearer Ophelia's due date.

Ceredig was delighted to have a son and heir, who might succeed him as ruler one day, while Lavena was so happy that her grandson was healthy. She would never forget the challenges that Caradoc had to overcome.

Ceredig and Ophelia decided to call their new son Cunorix, meaning 'wolf king', in the hope that he would make a mighty leader one day.

A week later, when Ophelia had fully recovered her health, there was a great banquet, to which all the great and good people of Darioritum were invited. Eldol, Eldad and Gruffudd had also made the trip over the sea from Glevum, after hearing the news from Madog on his first trading mission after the birth.

At the start of the banquet, Bishop Eldad stood up and called for quiet. When there was silence in the hall, he welcomed everyone on behalf of his nephew, Ceredig, and Ophelia.

"We are all here to welcome their new son, Cunorix, into this world," he continued. "This celebration of new life gives us all great hope for the future, as well as continuity for our family, which has faced, and overcome, a number of great challenges over the years, including the brutal murder of Cunorix's grandfather, Elisedd, and is gradually rebuilding a life in Armorica.

"Now that Ceredig has a son and heir, I can see my nephew gaining a new drive to restore his family's fortunes, to ensure that his son, an Armorican by birth, has a legacy to build upon when his time comes to lead the Gewisse."

At that point, the Gewisse began slamming their goblets down on the table and cheering, which prompted baby Cunorix to start crying at the loud noise.

After Ophelia had calmed Cunorix down, Eldad continued, saying, "No one knows what the future will bring for Ceredig and Cunorix, but if I have learned anything about my nephew it is that he is intelligent, determined, fair-minded and respected, like his father. And I have no doubt that Ceredig will ensure that his son grows up with these same values. God willing, together they will change the history of Britannia. So, I ask you all to raise your goblets and hail Ceredig's son and heir."

Eldad held his goblet up high and called, "Cunorix!"

Everyone responded in unison, with a chorus of "Cunorix!"

At that point, Cunorix began to cry loudly and was not easily settled this time, so Ophelia took him out of the great hall, before returning to Ceredig's side having handed Cunorix to his nurse, who would take him to the villa and put him down to sleep.

With Cunorix asleep elsewhere, the banquet resumed its celebratory flavour, as Ceredig, Flavius and Eldol also gave speeches before, finally, Arturius stood up and spoke on behalf of the Gewisse.

He recalled the impact of a very young Ceredig on life at the fort of Portus Adurni all those years ago, how he had everyone wrapped around his little finger as he explored every single part of the fort. Like his father, Ceredig also loved to climb the steps up to the southern wall and look out over the estuary, listening to the sounds of the sea. Arturius said that, even then, he knew that this young man would be special, but never expected him to rise to become the great warrior he was, and he reassured everyone that the Gewisse would ensure Ceredig's son received the best training they could give him, so that he would make his father and grandfather proud when the time came.

Once Arturius finished speaking, the Gewisse showed their support by banging their goblets on the table.

Before returning to Britannia, Eldol and Gruffudd were able to catch up with Ceredig, Arturius and Madog to discuss recent news from Britannia, with a promise to keep in touch with regular trips each year.

*

Four years later, Eldol arrived in Darioritum during the autumn, having heard that Ceredig and Ophelia had been blessed with the birth of another strong and healthy son. Eldad was unable to attend as he was in Rome on pilgrimage.

Ceredig and Ophelia had named their second son Cunedda, after his grandfather's former commander of Portus Adurni, who had been killed by the Saxons alongside Ceredig's father over thirty years ago. For a lot of the older Gewisse, including Madog, it was an appropriate tribute to their former colleague.

After they had celebrated the birth, Ceredig, Arturius and Madog gave Eldol a tour of the new barracks and training area that had been built in preparation for the continued expansion of the Gewisse in Darioritum. While they were alone, Eldol took the opportunity to inform them of devastating news from Britannia.

The small militia raids by Ambrosius had been achieving great success, and the Saxons were unable to see any pattern in his attacks. In an effort to counter these attacks, the Saxons went on an offensive themselves in the early summer, before the harvest.

The first Saxon attack, three years previous, had coincided with a fresh influx of Saxons, led by a man called Ælle, who had landed near Andredescæster and defeated a force of Britons at Andredeslea.

Then, a few months ago, there had been another battle, near Portus Adurni, Ceredig's birthplace on the south coast of Britannia. It involved a force of Britons from Dumnonia, led by the king's elder son, Gereint, who had been given command of the Dumnonians by King Erbin to help him gain battle experience.

Gruffudd had led his force of Gewisse warriors from Glevum into this battle, alongside Gereint and the Dumnonians. They were attacked by Ælle and his South

Saxons, and it was a massacre, with very few survivors amongst the Britons.

Amongst the dead were Tudwal, King Erbin's younger son, but there was even worse news for Ceredig. Gruffudd and most of the Gewisse had also been killed in battle.

When Ceredig, Arturius and Madog heard the news from Eldol, they were stunned into silence. Although they were both used to seeing death in battle, the loss of Gruffudd, a man that Ceredig had known since birth, and so many of their Gewisse friends, hit them very hard.

Seeing how much this news had affected them, Eldol suggested they take time to reflect on this news and he would be ready to tell them the details later, once their minds were clearer.

Later that evening, in the great hall, whilst having an evening meal of cold meats, bread and cheese, accompanied by a goblet of light ale, Ceredig said they were ready to hear more about the massacre at Portus Adurni.

Eldol told them that the details were provided by one of the few Gewisse warriors to survive the battle, a scout whom Gruffudd had sent to a safe position so that he could observe and report back what happened, if no one else could.

King Erbin had brought his two eldest sons, Gereint and Tudwal, along with 300 Dumnonians to join the Gewisse, under Gruffudd, as they patrolled along the southern coastline. They had defeated the Saxons in a number of smaller battles, managing to push them back as far as Andredescæster, before this new influx of Saxons under Ælle retaliated and took the battle to the Britons.

King Erbin and Gruffudd had withdrawn their forces back as far as Portus Adurni. Although the fort buildings had been destroyed, they had camped inside the walls whilst they decided what action to take.

After discussing their situation, it was agreed that King Erbin would take a small protective guard back with him to Dumnonia, to secure reinforcements before returning to take the battle to Ælle and his Saxon force. King Erbin left Gereint in charge of the Dumnonian forces, while Tudwal also asked his father for permission to remain with his brother. The king agreed.

When scouts reported back that Ælle was leading a large force of Saxons towards Portus Adurni, Gruffudd had argued that they should remain within the fort, which they could defend until reinforcements arrived from Dumnonia. However, Gereint said it was better to face the Saxons in battle than cower behind the walls.

Since the Dumnonians were the larger force, and Gereint's commanders were making the necessary arrangements, Gruffudd felt obliged not to leave the Dumnonians to the mercy of the Saxons in battle, so he followed, in the hope that they would be able to retreat westwards if the battle became a lost cause.

They headed out of the fort, up the peninsula, and were still within sight of the fort when the Saxons came into view from the east, but it was too late to return to the safety of the fort. The Britons had no choice but to turn and fight the Saxons.

The battle that ensued was brutal, but the Britons fought well, including Gereint and Tudwal, so the losses were pretty even on both sides. Then disaster struck. Tudwal was isolated with two of his Dumnonian protectors, and the Saxons were quick to pounce, killing all three men in a flurry of axe attacks.

Gereint saw it all happen and was overcome with grief, leaving the Dumnonians in disarray. Gruffudd sensed that the battle was turning against them, so he ordered one of his scouts to leave the battle and find a safe place from which to watch, then report on events to Eldol in Glevum. He also told Gereint to go with the scout, so he could live to tell King Erbin the news about Tudwal's death. After they had reached safety, the scout and Gereint both watched as Gruffudd, the Gewisse and the rest of the Dumnonians fell under the overwhelming number of Saxons.

After making their escape, the scout and Gereint headed for Dumnonia, coming across King Erbin and his reinforcements on the way. The scout gave his version of events to the king, then took his leave and returned to Glevum. When he arrived back in Glevum, the scout informed Eldol that the king did not take the news of his son's death well and the colour visibly drained from his face.

Eldol heard later that King Erbin had suddenly dropped down dead, grabbing at his heart, just after returning to his palace. Eldol said he suspected that King Erbin must have been overwhelmed with guilt for leaving his youngest son to face the Saxons when he was clearly not ready.

When Eldol had finished, there was silence, as Ceredig and Arturius had nothing to say.

Eventually, Ceredig reached for his goblet, raised it up high and said, "To Gruffudd and our fallen Gewisse warriors. They were the best fighters and their deaths must be paid for in blood.

"To Gruffudd and the Gewisse!" he cried.

"Gruffudd and the Gewisse!" cried Eldol, Arturius and Madog.

*

Five years later, Madog returned from a trading mission with the Goths in Hispania with some important news that would change everything for Ceredig.

King Euric of the Goths had died in the last month of the old year. He had been in his sixties and had died peacefully in his sleep. Euric's son, Alaric, had succeeded him as the new King of the Vesi Goths.

For Ceredig, this brought mixed feelings. His fealty to King Euric was now ended, and he had never made the same oath to his son. However, this freedom would not come without a price if the new king decided he needed to assert his overlordship of Armorica.

Ceredig ordered his scouts to head to all the regions of Armorica to let the chieftains know of King Euric's death and alert them to the possibility that the new king, Alaric, may head north to Armorica at some point.

It was while these scouts were spreading the news that Ceredig received further news that encouraged him. In the four years since Clovis had become King of the Franks, he had expanded Francia's control over the kingdoms in Gaul, retaking a large region from the Goths.

It looked like King Alaric and the Goths had bigger fish to fry, so Armorica would be relatively safe for now, although it may be that they should be more concerned about King Clovis and the Franks in the longer term.

Although his oath of fealty was ended, nothing really changed for Ceredig. His priority was still about making sure that he had 1,000 Gewisse warriors in Armorica, ready to return to Britannia and take on the Saxons when the time was right.

That figure had originally included Gruffudd and the Gewisse warriors from Glevum, who would have joined up with Ceredig and his Gewisse when they reached Britannia. However, their massacre at the hands of the Saxons, near Portus Adurni, had left the Gewisse warriors in Armorica as the only survivors of the finest, fiercest and toughest warriors in Britannia. Therefore, Ceredig had increased the recruitment and training of as many new Gewisse warriors in Darioritum as he could find across Armorica.

Madog had been struggling to find five ships large enough to be capable of transporting 1,000 men and equipment across the sea to Britannia. However, he had found a ship builder who had been one of the last of his profession to build a large Roman-style merchant ship of the size they needed.

Deciding that he needed to give Ceredig some good news, Madog commissioned the ship builder to travel to Darioritum to design and build five new large cargo ships, which would take five to seven years to complete.

Although Ceredig was impatient to return to Britannia and face the Saxons, he understood the need for everything to be in place before the ships could set sail.

*

A year later, an extremely happy Eldol arrived in Darioritum. He was greeted by Ceredig, who took him up to the villa to see Lavena and Cunedda.

Later, Ceredig took Eldol down to watch Cunorix in training with Arturius. When Cunorix had turned ten years of age, Ceredig instructed Arturius to oversee his son's Gewisse training. Cunorix was excelling in his academic education with the monks from the monastery in Darioritum, so it was time for Cunorix to learn to become a Gewisse warrior. According to Arturius, Cunorix already showed tremendous promise as a swordsman.

Later that evening, Madog and Arturius joined Ceredig and Eldol at the family meal. After eating their meal together, Lavena and Ophelia retired to another room in the villa, leaving the men to discuss matters at hand.

"I can tell by that permanent smile on your face that there is some good news from home, uncle," said Ceredig. "What has happened?"

"Well, in short, I have avenged your father and brother's murders. Hengest is dead," said Eldol.

"What?" exclaimed Ceredig, almost spitting the ale he had just drank out of his mouth. "That is wonderful news. How did this all come about?" he asked.

"It started when the Saxons responded to the renewed hit-and-run tactics by Ambrosius's small militia forces," said Eldol, who then described the events that followed in detail.

Hengest commanded an army of 1,000 Saxons that had attacked and destroyed the old Roman citadel at Calleva. When Ambrosius's scouts reported back, the Britons gathered as many men as they could from the kingdoms around Glevum and the western provinces. Ambrosius also sent word to Dumnonia and, within days, they had marched to Searobyrg, to meet up with the Dumnonians. At that stage, there were 2,000 men under the command of Ambrosius ready to take the fight to the Saxons.

Hengest and his Saxons must have wanted a fight because, when they realised that the Britons had gathered at Searobyrg, instead of retreating back to the safety of their own lands, they came south towards the Britons.

When the Britons reached Maesbeli, the plains north of the temple of Cor Gawr, the Saxons were spotted to the east, having ravaged Leucomagus en route to facing the Britons.

The two sides came together in battle on the plains of Maesbeli, and it was typically brutal. However, the Britons had the overwhelming numbers this time, and, after a couple of hours, the Saxons started to fall in greater numbers and were close to defeat.

Hengest must have eventually realised that defeat was imminent because he turned and fled the field of battle with his fifty-strong personal guard. They all mounted their horses and rode away. Ambrosius and Eldol both spotted Hengest's escape, so they took over one hundred men with them and pursued him. Bishop Eldad, who had observed the battle from camp, had seen these events take place and followed the pursuit.

Hengest and his men headed north, so Eldol sent some scouts ahead to keep a close eye on them without being seen, just to make sure the Saxons were not drawing the Britons into a trap.

After ten days' pursuit, the Britons finally caught up with Hengest at Caer Conan, in the northern kingdom of Elmet. Hengest and his men decided it was time to face the Britons. In the battle that followed, Eldol eventually found himself facing Hengest, with most of the Saxon's personal guard dead.

At that point, Ceredig asked, "What about Ambrosius? Surely he would have wanted to fight Hengest?"

"Yes, of course," replied Eldol. "We had discussed such an eventuality on the journey to catch Hengest. However, I insisted that, because he was responsible for your father and brother's deaths, I had a greater right to face Hengest on our family's behalf. Eventually, he accepted my rightful claim."

Eldol explained that, having found himself face to face with the man who was directly responsible for Elisedd's murder, he reminded Hengest of that fact, and that he had been the Briton who killed his men and escaped that day at Vespasian's Camp. He then told Hengest that he would take great pleasure in avenging his brother's death.

Eldol saw Hengest smile, but was pretty sure it was nervousness he saw in his opponent's eyes. Hengest had decided that there was no point in delaying the fight, so he attacked Eldol, who managed to deflect his initial attack.

Hengest had his axe and shield, while Eldol had his sword and shield. Eldol explained that he knew the axe was heavier, so Hengest would tire before him, if he could withstand the Saxon's attacks until then. The problem was dealing with the extra force that came with the stronger axe.

They fought for what seemed like ages, before Eldol noticed the swings of Hengest's axe had lost a small amount of their strength, as well as accuracy. When Hengest next swung his axe, Eldol easily deflected it with his shield, but swung his sword upwards instead of down, which Hengest would not have anticipated.

Eldol's upward swing with his sword caught Hengest's arm. Whilst his leather padded jacket meant that the sword did not draw blood, Eldol had put sufficient strength in his sword swing to break Hengest's arm. As a result, Hengest dropped his axe, which fell to the ground. Hengest could no longer fight.

Hengest's men must have realised what had happened as they all stepped back from the fight. Their leader was down. The battle was over.

Eldol had defeated Hengest, ruler of the Cantia Saxons, the man who had murdered his brother, as well as all the other leaders of Britannia, that day at Vespasian's Camp with the treachery of the Saxons and their long knives.

However, having beaten Hengest, Eldol was left confused about what to do next. He turned to Ambrosius and asked what they should do with Hengest, expecting

Ambrosius to want Hengest as a high-value prisoner to get the Saxons to withdraw back into Cantia and remain there, or leave Britannia.

What he did not expect was his brother, Eldad, Bishop of Glevum, to interrupt him and tell Eldol to kill Hengest, for the murder of Elisedd and Caradoc, as well as his crimes against the Britons. Eldol had then looked towards Ambrosius, expecting him to disagree with the bishop.

However, Ambrosius agreed, saying that, with Hengest dead, the Saxons would have lost their most valuable leader, and, knowing that the Britons were powerful enough to defeat Hengest, should put any thoughts of immediate revenge out of their minds.

Sensing what was about to happen, Hengest dropped to his knees to take hold of his axe. Even though he had no way to lift it, he would die with his weapon in his hand.

Eldol said that he did not want to draw out the discussions any longer so, seeing that Hengest was kneeling down holding his axe, Eldol immediately swung his sword as hard as he could, removing Hengest's head from his body.

The Saxon warriors, who had been watching the discussions over Hengest's fate, screamed in rage as they saw Hengest's head fall to the ground, followed by his headless body. They suddenly attacked the Britons with as much force as they could, but were vastly outnumbered and were all killed straight away.

Eldol concluded his story, saying, "The last news we heard was that Hengest's son, Æsc, had succeeded his father as King of the Cantware, as they were now calling themselves. While they appear to be remaining within their own lands for now, I have no doubt that Æsc will want revenge of his own at some point."

When he had finished his story, Eldol turned to Ceredig, who appeared overwhelmed, staring into the distance as he was imagining the events as they had taken place. Eldol decided that his nephew needed time to digest everything he had just heard, so suggested to Ceredig that he would go and see Lavena, but they could talk more later.

Ceredig was experiencing a real mix of emotions, whilst also working through the ramifications of Hengest's death in his head, but told his uncle that he was fine and that he needed to bring Eldol up to date on the Gewisse's preparations for returning to Britannia, so he could let Ambrosius know on his return to Glevum.

Ceredig started by telling Eldol about the recruitment of young fighters around Armorica to become Gewisse warriors. He said that they were still on track to have 1,000 warriors if they continued to attract recruits at the rate they were going. The last group of new recruits had just joined up with the Gewisse training camp, and assuming that one tenth would fail to meet the required levels, there could be as many as 1,200 Gewisse warriors ready to travel within five years.

Arturius then confirmed that he had smiths and armourers manufacturing the weapons and protective clothing for such numbers. He then told them that he was confident they would have enough horses trained for every Gewisse, if he could get more land for stables and training space.

Ceredig was delighted with this news, as was Eldol, who said, "If we have over 1,000 fully trained Gewisse warriors in our numbers, I am sure Ambrosius will want to ensure he brings ten times that to fight alongside them."

Madog then confirmed that a suitable location had been found to build the five large merchant ships for their journey across the sea to Britannia. The shipbuilder and Madog had also found an experienced team of shipwrights from across Armorica who would help build the ships. Arrangements had been made for sufficient wood to be felled from the forests of Armorica. The shipbuilder estimated that it would take at least five years to build and test the five ships, if everything went to plan.

"Is there any chance that we may not have all five ships ready on time?" asked Ceredig.

"There is a possibility that at least one of the ships might fail the final tests, although we will have enough of our fleet of trading ships available to cover any shortfall," said Madog. "However, if we plan for a defining battle against the Saxons in seven years' time, I am sure we will have all five ships ready."

Eldol considered the information he had received, then said, "If I understand everything I have just heard, Ambrosius is going to have to plan on a final battle against the Saxons in five to seven years if he wants the Gewisse to fight with the Britons."

"Yes," said Ceredig. "That would be a reasonable timescale. If we push to bring it forward, we could have fewer numbers of ships to transport them over to Britannia. That would reduce our chance of a decisive victory over the Saxons and force them into a peace treaty on our terms, not theirs."

"I will relay all this to Ambrosius on my return," said Eldol. "We can start our preparations on the same timescale, although I suspect that he will continue the small militia raids."

"That will do no harm," said Ceredig. "It will keep the Saxons from thinking about our longer-term plans, and it will give our warriors plenty of fighting experience."

*

Shortly after Eldol had returned to Glevum with the seven-year plan for Ceredig and the Gewisse to return to Britannia for a great battle against the Saxons, a messenger arrived in Darioritum.

Eldol had sent the sad news that Bishop Eldad, Ceredig's uncle, had died whilst Eldol had been in Darioritum with Ceredig. The abbey in Glevum had given their bishop an excellent burial service, which they had to hold while Eldol was out of the country. Since Eldol was unable to attend the service, Ambrosius had attended on Eldol's behalf and given a great eulogy about the bishop.

At least my uncle lived long enough to see his brother Elisedd's death avenged by Eldol, thought Ceredig.

10

RETURN FROM EXILE

The *Anglo-Saxon Chronicle* records that, in AD 495, "came two leaders into Britannia, Cerdic and Cynric his son, with five ships, at a place that is called Cerdicesora".

The next seven years passed quickly for Ceredig and his family, but not without a great sadness for everyone at the estate.

Ceredig's mother, Lavena, had died peacefully in her sleep a few years previously. Lavena had been in her late sixties and her health had been slowly failing over the past five years, as she lost weight and all her energy. She became a shell of her previous self and complained of stomach pains that the local healers could not cure, so it was not unexpected when she passed away in her sleep one night.

Eldol returned to Darioritum to be at Ceredig's side as Lavena was buried in a barrow mound in the centre of the orchard. The Gewisse used some of the older apple trees to create a small wooden henge around the barrow as a monument to the wife of the Gewisse's former ruler and the mother of their current ruler.

A few days after Lavena's burial, Eldol sat down with Ceredig, Arturius and Madog to discuss the latest news from Britannia. Eldol informed them that Ælle, King of the South Saxons, had shown himself to be more brutal than the Saxons of Cantium. Ælle had attacked Andredescæster and massacred every single one of the Britons who were living there.

Man, woman or child, it made no difference to King Ælle. The bodies were then piled up in an area to the north-east of the town and burned to ashes. Ælle wanted Andredescæster as his Saxon stronghold and he did not want any survivors bearing a grudge against these Saxons.

Ceredig was livid. These were peaceful, hardworking people who had been under his father's protection, and the Saxons just killed them without a second thought. Ceredig hated these Saxons with such venom that he could not wait for the opportunity to destroy them in battle.

On a more positive note, Cunorix was now nineteen years of age and had excelled in his training under Arturius, who said Cunorix was even better than his father had been at that age, when he became ruler of the Gewisse.

Cunorix was now considered a fully-fledged Gewisse warrior, which delighted Ceredig, who immediately began to involve his son in the preparations for their return to Britannia.

Arturius had informed Ceredig that he had just under 1,000 Gewisse warriors ready to fight. He admitted to Ceredig that he had been stricter in his training as he preferred quality over quantity when facing the Saxons in battle. Those who had just failed to meet the levels required had been formed into a separate militia unit who would remain in Darioritum to defend the region for the new chieftain.

Arturius reassured Ceredig that they had sufficient horses, weapons and equipment ready to take with them. Meanwhile, Madog confirmed that the five ships were finally ready to sail, having been thoroughly tested over the past year.

Eldol returned to Glevum with the great news for Ambrosius and the other British leaders that they could now prepare to take on the Saxons in battle.

*

Later that month, Ceredig informed the local elders that he would be leaving Darioritum in the near future and was unlikely to return. He proposed Ophelia's brother, Flavius, whose father had been chieftain before Ceredig, to be his successor as chieftain. Since Ceredig's opinion carried a lot of weight, Flavius was accepted by the elders to become the next chieftain without any dissent.

Ophelia and Cunedda would remain in Darioritum, under the protection of Madog and the Gewisse militia unit, until it was safe to travel to be with Ceredig in Britannia.

Ceredig had already had a difficult conversation with Madog, who was approaching his seventieth year, telling him that he wanted Madog to oversee the journey to Britannia, but then return to Darioritum to continue the trading business, which would be his to run, along with the estate.

This was more out of Ceredig's concern that Madog would not have survived the first wave of any attack, but also out of a genuine desire for Madog to live out the rest of his life in peace. He had earned it!

Madog had initially pleaded with Ceredig to be given the opportunity to fight the Saxons, but could not disagree with his leader's assessment. If he was not permitted to take part in the battle, Madog would do his best to ensure they made it over to Britannia safely.

*

Over the following months, Eldol and Ambrosius made several journeys to Darioritum to discuss their plan of attack against the Saxons with Ceredig, Cunorix, Arturius and Madog.

Ambrosius was going to send all his militia units on raids against Saxon settlements to the west of Lundein to attract Saxon attention on this region. These raids would commence on the day after the next spring solstice and continue until they had attracted the attention of the Saxon leadership, which would be confirmed by an increase in larger Saxon patrols in that region.

At the appropriate time, the militia would make a final series of raids then slowly withdraw, making it easy to track them as they travelled to Durocornovium, which was now deserted. It should appear to the Saxons that this former Roman settlement was the base of operations for Ambrosius's militia units.

Meanwhile, Ambrosius and Eldol would lead their

forces to Corinium and wait while the forces from Dumnonia, led by King Gereint, would be camped at Aquaesulis.

Eldol's scouts would be watching to ensure the Saxons' scouts confirmed that the militia units were all congregated in Durocornovium. With over 500 Britons camped there, Ambrosius thought that this would be too much temptation for King Æsc of Cantia, and King Ælle of Suth Seaxna, to resist. The Saxons would surely send the majority of their forces to Durocornovium, with the aim of finally ending this tactic by the Britons once and for all.

As soon as the scouts reported back that the Saxons were on their way from Cantia and Andredeslea, Ambrosius and King Gereint would meet and combine their forces to the west of Durocornovium. When the Saxons approached Durocornovium, the militia units were to retreat west into the safety of the larger force of Britons.

The role of Ceredig's forces would be to reach the battle site at the last minute, creating a new threat to the Saxons, from the south. An added bonus would be that Ceredig's 1,000 Gewisse warriors would take care of any additional Saxon forces that had their own plans to arrive from the south.

One of Madog's ships had travelled over to Britannia several times in advance of the Gewisse, landing near Durnovaria. On board had been several Gewisse scout units who had been tasked with identifying the best landing spot along the coastline on the western side of the island of Vectis. Ceredig already knew that the Saxons had left the island in peace, so the islanders would not be an issue.

Ceredig wanted to avoid the coastline east of Vectis, especially Portus Adurni, as he was aware that the Saxons had taken control over this fort. If he could avoid conflict with this group, he would. His priority was getting inland to join the battle against the main Saxon forces. He would deal with the Saxons of Portus Adurni once the Britons had secured victory.

The scouts returned to report that there was a shingle beach shoreline on the mainland, below a set of high cliffs to the west of Vectis. A river had carved a gully between the cliffs that Ceredig and his men could use to get up to the higher ground. From there, they could follow an old trackway for nearly thirty miles that would take them to the hillfort at Searobyrg.

After Ceredig confirmed that this would be the perfect landing spot for his return to Britannia, the scouts returned to Britannia to inform Eldol and Ambrosius of this news. They would then head down to the place they were calling 'Ceredig's shore' and would remain there to protect the surrounding area until the expected day of arrival.

The plan was that, when the scouts spotted Ceredig's five Gewisse ships arriving in the bay, they would set three bonfires along the coastline to indicate it was safe to land, with the middle bonfire signalling the landing spot. No bonfires would signal danger, and the five ships would divert to the port near Durnovaria, although this would require Ceredig to increase the pace of the next step of their journey.

*

One morning, three days after the spring solstice, Ceredig and Arturius led over 1,000 Gewisse warriors out of the estate and down to the port at Darioritum, where Madog had berthed the five large merchant ships, each one bearing Ceredig's flag.

The sight of the flags brought a huge smile to Ceredig's face, just as it had done when he first arrived in Darioritum all those years ago. The Gewisse quickly boarded the ships, which had customised stables built into the cargo area to safely secure their horses.

Ophelia and her brother, Flavius, had joined a crowd of exiled Britons at the port to cheer Ceredig and the Gewisse off on their mission to take back control of Britannia from the Saxons. Ceredig had been a good and fair ruler of the kingdom, so they wanted to send him off as a celebration.

Madog had appointed his best commanders as masters of the other ships. When it was time to leave, he ordered one of his men to blow the ship's horn to signal their departure.

Each of the five large merchant ships was slowly pulled away from the port by three of Madog's trading ships. The smaller ships were being rowed by Madog's strongest rowers, until the large ships were able to hoist their sails to pick up the wind and head out into the gulf that protected the port from the ocean.

The fifteen smaller ships would accompany the five large ships across to Britannia to support the fleet. Madog had a suspicion that the smaller ships would come in useful when they reached their planned landing spot.

The journey over to Britannia took three days. Ceredig's ships hugged the coastline as they travelled north, around the Armorican peninsula, then north-east to the islands off the Gaul peninsula that lay to the south of their intended target.

When crossing the sea to Britannia at this time of year, the winds would take them naturally eastward as they travelled north, in a counterclockwise direction. The journey was smooth, which was easier on the horses and also minimised the number of men who suffered from seasickness.

Once they reached the shallow shelf of the Britannic coastline, Madog could see the high cliffs of the southern coast, and the island of Vectis on his right. He signalled for his ships to drop anchor and wait.

After waiting for an hour, they saw a fire beacon on the eastern edge of their intended landing spot by the high cliffs. Then another bonfire appeared on the western edge of the coastline. Finally, a third bonfire became visible a bit higher on the headland, identifying the best landing spot.

One of Madog's smaller ships beached itself on the shingle, and a small group of warriors made their way onto the shoreline, to meet up with the scouts and ensure that this was a genuine signal and there was no danger from waiting Saxon forces. It did not take long for a spear bearing Ceredig's banner to be waved, indicating that all was safe.

Madog gave the signal and the ships started to move closer to the shore. It had not long passed high tide, so he knew the larger ships would get close to the coastline before having to drop anchor again.

The shingle shore would make it easier to beach the large ships, but the smaller ships would also be helpful in keeping the beached large ships upright at low tide. The rest would remain afloat in case of an emergency, until the tide returned to allow the large ships to float again.

Once the large ships began to scrape on the shingle, Madog signalled for them to drop anchor and the smaller ships to come alongside, one each side of a large ship.

When the tide had gone out further, Ceredig's men started their preparations to disembark. The wooden ramps were lowered and half the warriors made their way onto the shore, forming up in a defensive formation, just in case a Saxon patrol arrived. The rest of the men then took the horses and equipment off the ships onto the shore.

When all the men, horses and equipment were safely on the shore, Ceredig turned to Madog and said, "Well, this is it, my friend. I do not know if we will meet again, but if it is my destiny to rule my father's lands again, I will send word. In the meantime, take good care of yourself, and my family."

They gave each other a hug, then Ceredig left for the shoreline.

Cunorix then hugged Madog, saying, "Thank you for everything you have done for me, Madog. I am only here because you have served my father and grandfather well, but I know that they considered you a great friend, as do I. I hope to see you again."

Cunorix then disembarked the ship and joined his father.

Lastly, Arturius said his farewell to Madog. "I have known you since I was a child, Madog, and want you to know that I considered you and Cunedda the fathers that I never had. More importantly, I wish you a long and happy life, my friend."

They gave each other a large hug, then Arturius left the ship to catch up with Ceredig and Cunorix.

While Ceredig, Cunorix and Arturius were saying their goodbyes to Madog, a single horse rider had suddenly appeared from along the coastline near the cliffs.

At first, he caused a stir amongst the Gewisse, until they noticed that he was holding a spear bearing the flag of Eldol so, once he had been confirmed, he was escorted into the camp.

As Ceredig joined his men, Eldol's messenger was led towards him. The messenger addressed Ceredig, saying, "Greetings, my lord, from your uncle, Lord Eldol. He charged me with finding you after you had arrived on shore, as there have been developments of which you need to be aware."

"What developments?" asked Ceredig.

The messenger continued, "Lord Ambrosius has amassed a total fighting force of over 12,000 men, and they are camped about twelve miles to the west of Durocornovium, hidden from view by woodland. The Saxons have been slow to react to the raids and have yet to pursue the raiders back to Durocornovium. Lord Eldol asks that you delay, or slow down, your advance north by at least two days. He suggests that you use the extra time available for whatever you think would be beneficial in our battle against the Saxons. He told me that you would know what he meant."

Ceredig considered the message, then said, "Thank you. You may return to Lord Eldol and tell him that I understand his message. I will see him on the battlefield. Get some food and refreshment before you leave."

As the messenger turned and left to find Ceredig's prefect, who was in charge of food supplies, Ceredig turned to Arturius and said, "Arturius, see to it that one of our scout units – fifty men should suffice – escorts this messenger north to the Britons, to ensure his safety. After that, they should swing round and check out our route up to Cunetio, from Vespasian's Camp, for any possible Saxon presence. You should also send another scout group of fifty men to head up to Searobyrg, to confirm that there are no Saxons operating in that area. If they come across any Saxons, I do not want even one Saxon to survive. Kill them all!"

Since they had time to waste until the battle, Ceredig ordered his men to head onto the higher ground and they would camp there overnight, before heading up to the old Roman legion road in the morning. Ceredig planned on making this a two-day trip, stopping overnight near the start of the old Roman legion road, then finishing the trip to Searobyrg on the following day.

*

Two days later, Ceredig's men arrived at Searobyrg. The scout group had arrived the day before and had confirmed that there were no Saxons in that area. The scouts had also organised a campsite for the men, just below the hillfort, near the road.

The local chieftain invited Ceredig and his commanders to be his guests of honour for their evening meal. During the meal, the chieftain and Ceredig discussed events that had taken place over the past few years and how the chieftain had managed to remain in control over Searobyrg, while Ceredig told the chieftain of his exploits in Armorica.

The next day, Ceredig and his men left Searobyrg and headed north towards Vespasian's Camp. The other scout patrols had returned from there and informed Ceredig that there were over one hundred Saxons camped inside the hillfort at Vespasian's Camp, 200 at the most.

It was a very short journey to Vespasian's Camp, so Ceredig split his men into four units. One group of 200 men, led by Arturius, travelled west around the south of Searobyrg hillfort and would eventually sweep round and come in on Vespasian's Camp from the west and north. Another force of 200 men, led by Cunorix, went south, then swept around to the east, so that they cut off the easterly escape route from Vespasian's Camp.

Ceredig and the remaining 400 men were last to leave their camp at Searobyrg, marching north up the short road to Vespasian's Camp, so that when they arrived at the hillfort, they would be seen by the Saxons watching from the palisade walls. Ceredig ordered that the men make camp on all four sides of the hillfort, within view, but out of reach of any spears or arrows.

The next morning, Ceredig walked up to the main entrance to the hillfort, on the south-east side, taking a protective guard with shields, just in case things got ugly.

He shouted to the guards on the gate, asking if there were any Britons inside.

"No," said one of the Saxons, "but you are welcome to come inside and check."

The other Saxons on the gate all laughed.

Ceredig also laughed, then said, "Thank you for the offer, but I will take your word for it."

He then turned and walked back to his men.

What the Saxons inside the hillfort did not know was that, in all four camps, during the night, Ceredig's men had gathered any branches, twigs and other flammable materials and wrapped them into bundles. When each man had a bundle prepared, they sneaked up to the hillfort and then placed their bundle at the foot of the wooden palisade that surrounded the hillfort.

While Ceredig was up at the fort, each camp set a bonfire going and created arrows that would carry a flame. When Ceredig returned, he gave a signal and the archers shot their flaming arrows at the bundles around the hillfort.

The Gewisse then watched and waited as the bundles caught light and the flames started to rise up the wooden palisade. The archers then fired more flaming arrows inside the hillfort, aiming at the buildings and the stable area, where dry grass would be stored for the horses. Within thirty minutes, all the buildings in the hillfort were ablaze.

Ceredig's men formed up, waiting for the moment that

the Saxons decided facing the Gewisse was the preferable option to being burned alive.

The men in Arturius's camp, on the westerly side of the hillfort, were also prepared for any Saxons to leave the fort using the gate on the other end of the old Roman road that cut through the hillfort.

Suddenly the gates flew open and the Saxons charged out of the hillfort towards both Ceredig and Arturius's men, with their axes and shields raised for attack.

Ceredig had given his men clear instructions earlier that no Saxon would be allowed to survive this day. For Ceredig, Arturius and the five older Gewisse warriors, who had been in Vespasian's Camp on that fateful day nearly forty years previous, this was vengeance for Elisedd, their father and ruler, Cunedda, their commander, and Ceredig's brother, Caradoc, who had been brutally slain by the Saxons in this fort.

In the end, it was a massacre!

The Gewisse moved all the dead Saxons' bodies back into the hillfort and piled them up, with more bundles of branches and straw then set alight.

Normally, Arturius would have pointed out the risk of leaving the hillfort alight to Ceredig, just in case the glow of the blazing hillfort in the dark skies brought a Saxon patrol to investigate it. However, he knew what his friend, kinsman and ruler needed, and was prepared to deal with the consequences.

Instead, Arturius had a large sentry group patrolling the area that night. Meanwhile, Ceredig slept really well, especially in the warmth of the smouldering hillfort.

*

The following day, Ceredig woke up to the news that the scout unit, which had travelled to Eldol's camp with his messenger, had returned during the night, and they had news.

Ceredig called a meeting of his commanders to hear the news first hand. The news from Eldol was that the Saxons had finally reacted to the raids by the militia units. The two rulers of the southeastern kingdoms, Æsc and Ælle, had gathered a force of over 10,000 Saxons at Calleva.

This was a larger force of Saxons than the Britons had expected. Ceredig felt that their intention was clear. The Saxons intended to destroy the raiders, then move towards Corinium, and then Glevum, to defeat the Britons, including Ambrosius and Eldol, once and for all. The Saxon forces were expected to leave Calleva at some point today and head to Durocornovium, arriving there tomorrow to take on Ambrosius's raiding forces.

Ceredig told his commanders that the Gewisse forces should travel up to Cunetio that day, but, instead of camping at the old Roman town, they would keep to the south of the town, using the forest there for cover. They would also have to keep their bonfires low that night, just in case there were other Saxon forces in the vicinity.

Arturius told the scout leader to give his scouts a well-earned break. The remaining three scout patrols would be sent ahead of the main forces, to secure their overnight campsite and form a perimeter of the surrounding area.

An hour later, the main Gewisse force left their campsite beside Vespasian's Camp to head north towards Cunetio. Their journey would take most of the day, and they wanted to be in position for tomorrow's battle.

*

The following morning, Britons and Saxons in various camps, east, west and south of Durocornovium, awoke with the expectation that the day would see the final major battle that would determine the future of the kingdoms of central and southern Britannia.

The day was bright and clear for a spring morning, and it would warm up later. However, for the men who were preparing themselves for battle, the temperature was still quite chilly.

Twelve miles to the west of Durocornovium, Ambrosius Aurelianus, Eldol and King Gereint led a force of 12,000 men as they marched towards the old hillfort at Badonbyrg, a few miles south of Durocornovium.

Ambrosius was now in his sixties, while Eldol, who had been his strongest commander and warrior during the British-Saxon wars, was in his early seventies. Their role in this battle was to command, not fight, which would have been foolish and short-lived.

They had 8,000 Britons on foot, who were well-trained and well-equipped warriors, most carrying long spears and oblong or round shields, with axes in their belts. These men wore basic armour, consisting of long leather padded overcoats, with gloves and helmets, for protection. Some had chain mail vests over their coats for added protection. Among this group of warriors were 250 men carrying bows, with arrows in the quivers on their backs and more tied bundles of ten hanging from the quiver.

It had been a long time since bows had been used in battle in Britannia, but both Ambrosius and Eldol felt it would be a useful tool against the Saxons, who had never been seen using this weapon since they arrived in Britannia.

The remaining 4,000 men were mounted warriors, each carrying a shorter spear and shield, with their sword sheathed. Most of these men wore similar armour to the foot soldiers, although the overcoats were shorter and they had extra protection on their legs. Most of their fathers or grandfathers had been amongst the nobles killed by the Saxons that treacherous day at Vespasian's Camp.

A mile away to the east, around 10,000 Saxons stood in front of the hillfort of Badonbyrg, having camped there overnight and decided to use the hillfort as a base if the battle lasted longer than a day. They were led by King Æsc of the Cantware and King Ælle of the South Saxons.

Two miles to the south, at the top of a ridge and hidden from view of the Saxons by the treeline, Ceredig, Cunorix and Arturius could see the two main forces move closer to each other, while the rest of the Gewisse warriors remained hidden in the valley behind the hill.

The Gewisse would not be fighting from the start. Instead, they would join in the third phase of battle that day, as part of a second front, hopefully when the Saxons were in disarray. For now, Ceredig and his men had to get into position, so they headed east along the small valleys between the rolling hills in the area.

Further north, Ambrosius called the Britons to stop and ordered them to form a shield wall when the Saxons were within the range of his archers. The Saxons also halted, expecting the Britons to launch an attack. Æsc and Ælle considered attacking, but were confused by the Britons' tactics, so held their men back until they could work out why the Britons had stopped and formed their shield wall. They did not have long to wait.

Suddenly, a wave of arrows, rising from behind the shield wall, created a dark band across the sky as they quickly flew over the short distance between the Britons and the Saxons.

The Saxons had little time to put up their shields before the arrows rained down on them. While some arrows hit shields, the majority of the arrows hit their targets, felling over 200 Saxons.

Cheers arose from the Britons, seeing a large number of their enemy fall under the blanket of arrows.

Warily, the Saxons stood up from behind their shields, unsure whether another wave of arrows would be heading their way, or if the Britons were about to attack. They were right to be concerned. Almost immediately, another wave of arrows was heading towards them from behind the Britons' shield wall.

The front group of Saxons put up their shields to protect themselves from this next attack. However, the archers had gone for distance this time and the arrows flew past the front wave of Saxons, hitting their comrades behind them, who had realised too late that more arrows were coming. Over 200 Saxons were felled by this attack.

While the Saxons were rising back to their feet, they suddenly realised that two groups of 500 mounted warriors, led by Gereint, King of Dumnonia, were galloping towards them at speed.

The horsemen kept a tight formation and hit them as a wave, and with such force, that the Saxon shield wall buckled, then the spears were stabbing downwards, ferociously piercing any unprotected areas of the Saxons' bodies. If a Briton lost his spear, he simply removed his sword and continued stabbing from his position of height.

Nearly 1,000 Saxons were killed in this one single attack, before the sound of a horn from the British side signalled the horsemen to turn their horses and return to join their own side. The horn had also been a signal to Ceredig and his men that the third wave would begin shortly.

As soon as the horsemen returned to the ranks, 4,000 Britons marched towards the Saxons, making as much noise as they could. This was an instruction from their commanders, to attract as much attention from the Saxons as they could.

On command, the Britons started running towards the Saxons. As the two sides met, the Saxons' shield wall buckled, but did not break and, eventually, the Saxons managed to compose themselves and push back, ensuring the Britons also suffered some losses, before a second wave of 4,000 Britons joined the fight.

Æsc and Ælle were concerned that the Saxons' losses were starting to mount up. However, before they could make any decision, they realised that there was another attack wave coming at them from behind the old hillfort. This time it was over 1,000 Britons on horseback, who carried a red banner with the gold rampant dragon, but it was not a flag that Æsc and Ælle could recall seeing before.

Ceredig and the Gewisse were tightly packed, co-ordinated and ruthless, using their horses to crush the Saxons, and their height to stab, slice and hit them from above. Ceredig and Arturius were thinking of Elisedd, Caradoc, Cunedda, Gruffudd and the other Gewisse whom the Saxons had brutally murdered at Vespasian's Camp, or killed in battle at Portus Adurni. As a result, this was the most vicious of all the attacks on the Saxons.

After two hours of intense fighting, another horn signalled for the Britons to withdraw back into their ranks. The mounted Gewisse, who had all raised their spears bearing Ceredig's flag, were cheered by the Britons as they joined their compatriots.

The Saxon forces had been decimated, with nearly half of their number lost in the first fight of the battle, while the Britons had lost only 600 of their ranks. The Britons now outnumbered the Saxons by more than two to one.

With the element of surprise lost, Ambrosius realised that the next phase would not be as effective, although their sheer numbers should prevail. His primary concern was whether the Saxons would retreat, sensing they were in a battle they could not win.

Ambrosius called for the Britons to bring their camp closer, so the sheer number of Britons would be a constant visible reminder to the Saxons of their opponents' strength.

Ceredig raised his concern that their closeness meant that they would have less time to react to an attack by the Saxons, especially as they had nothing left to lose. However, Ambrosius felt the Saxons would not be able to make a battle-winning move, so, in an effort to placate Ceredig, he set up a rotating perimeter to alert the Britons, just in case there was an attack.

For their part, the Saxons did not withdraw. Instead, they camped inside the hillfort overnight, for safety. They had suffered huge losses and needed time to regroup and plan their tactics for the next day. The hillfort would provide protection against a night attack by the Britons.

The Saxon leaders knew that the battle would be won or lost the following day. Given their losses, they would have to try something unexpected and, knowing the Britons would feel confident after their victories that day, they would be feeling more relaxed about claiming overall victory the next day. That might be a weakness that the Saxons could exploit.

Back in the Britons' camp, Ambrosius took the opportunity to discuss the next day's battle tactics with Eldol, King Gereint and Ceredig, as well as the other rulers who had brought men to the fight.

Ceredig and Eldol favoured an early attack just after first light, while the Saxons were still in the hillfort, with the aim to surround them and force a siege that they knew the Saxons would not have enough provisions to hold for long.

Ambrosius and Gereint felt that, after the early march that morning to reach the Saxons, he wanted his men to have a decent night's sleep and nourishment the next morning, in case the battle lasted well into the afternoon again. In the end, it was the support of the other commanders that determined they would go with Ambrosius's plan.

Ceredig then suggested sending a group of horsemen out to the west in the moonlight, to swing round the north overnight and come round behind the Saxons by mid-afternoon. He even said the Gewisse would be willing to take on this role.

It came as no surprise to Ceredig that this was also rejected by Ambrosius, who said that the horses would be needed for an attack the next day.

However, it was agreed that Ceredig should send his scout groups out, under the cover of darkness, to head south to Cunetio and then head east and north, behind the hillfort, up to Durocornovium, to make sure that there were no other Saxon forces preparing to reinforce Æsc and Ælle.

*

The following morning was bright but cold, a consequence of another spring night without clouds.

The Saxons woke early and prepared for battle whilst inside the hillfort. It was their plan to use the early morning to get back on the front foot against these Britons. When Æsc and Ælle saw that the Britons had not even taken up any position of battle, they decided on an early attack, so they sent their warriors to charge towards the Britons' camp.

As the Saxons charged, they could hear the Britons' sentries, suddenly shouting and calling out for everyone to prepare for battle. The Britons barely had time to take up their positions before the Saxons reached the Britons' camp. This early attack by the Saxons surprised the Britons and, initially, led to heavy losses for them. However, the Britons finally managed to get themselves organised and began to counter the Saxon attack, with the Saxons losing men quickly.

Realising that they could be trapped and massacred, the Saxons fought their way back from the dangerous position they were in and quickly retreated back over the open ground towards the safety of the hillfort of Badonbyrg. They did not expect the Britons to pursue them.

They were correct. Whilst the Britons initially started to follow the Saxons as they retreated, a horn sounded on the orders of Ambrosius, calling a halt to their advance.

Ceredig could not understand Ambrosius's reticence, and was extremely vocal in telling him that they had the advantage and needed to pursue the Saxons into the hillfort and kill them all.

Ambrosius might have been persuaded to agree with Ceredig, until a large number of rulers from the other kingdoms, mostly from the regions that had never been affected by the Saxons' expansion across Britannia, proposed permitting Æsc and Ælle to surrender and agree to a binding peace treaty.

King Gereint, who had never spoken up to that point, then said that such a move might be accepted by the Saxon rulers and finally bring an end to fifty years of war.

Ceredig could not believe what he heard. Had they never learned from past events? He could not contain his anger any longer. In a raised voice, he asked, "How can we trust the Saxons? They ignored the original treaty agreed between Hengest and King Wyrtgeorn, and then brutally killed nearly all our rulers almost forty years ago. They killed my father and brother, and my family's lands have been taken over by the Saxons. Am I going to get these lands restored to my family's control?"

Ceredig had a lot to get off his chest, so continued, saying, "There was also the battle at Portus Adurni, King Gereint, where they killed your brother, as well as Gruffudd and the Gewisse there. Gruffudd sacrificed himself and his men for you, my lord."

He also felt the need to remind these commanders of recent events, so added, "What about the attack on Andredescæster only a few years ago? They massacred every single man, woman and child who was living there. Who speaks for them?"

There was complete silence.

Finally, Ambrosius spoke, saying, "Lord Ceredig is right. None of us have suffered as much as his family and their people. I suspect that not many of you would disagree with him if you had also suffered similar losses."

A murmur of agreement circulated around the tent.

"However, I have to accept that there is no appetite for a massacre," continued Ambrosius. "Therefore, we first need the Saxons to surrender, then we can discuss terms. So, let us end this battle now. Lord Ceredig and King Gereint should lead our attack with their mounted warriors and head straight towards the Saxons, forcing them into the hillfort. The rest of our forces will follow and enter the hillfort to ensure their surrender."

Ambrosius then turned and addressed Ceredig directly, saying, "I know you would like to kill them all, Lord Ceredig. However, I need you to agree that the Saxon leaders, including Æsc and Ælle, will be allowed to live, so they can make the peace pact and ensure it is enforced. If they flee, make all effort to capture them.

"My lords," he continued, raising his sword. "To victory!"

The other rulers all responded, saying, "To victory!"

Shortly after giving their orders to the Gewisse and the Dumnonians, Ceredig, Gereint, Cunorix and Arturius led their mounted warriors off at a gallop towards the hillfort, as the rest of the Britons started marching in their wake.

Seeing the mounted attack, and with defeat inevitable, a small number of Saxons began to flee, heading eastward. When King Gereint saw this, he took his 200 mounted Dumnonians and pursued the fleeing Saxons, then killed them all.

Most of the remaining Saxons decided that attack was the best form of defence. However, Ceredig, Cunorix and Arturius led the Gewisse as they pounded through the Saxon warriors, slashing and hacking at any who stood in their way.

As they reached the hillfort, the mounted warriors carried out Ceredig's orders to form a guard at the entrance to the hillfort and stop any Saxon attempting to flee, killing them, only if necessary.

As the remaining force of Britons approached the hillfort, Ceredig ordered the Gewisse to create an opening for the Britons to march in and surround the group of Saxons waiting for them.

They included Æsc, Ælle and two other nobles. Ambrosius recognised them as rulers of other regions the Saxons had overwhelmed, like Ēastengla. They were protected by one hundred Saxon warriors.

Fifty Saxon warriors chose to attack. It was a foolish move and they were simply cut down by the Britons, leaving the Saxon rulers and the remaining fifty Saxon warriors.

Ambrosius addressed Æsc and Ælle, saying, "You are defeated, my lords, and you know it. Do you concede, or do you wish to see Valhalla this day?"

Both Æsc and Ælle looked around at the Britons, then at their own men, then turned back to see Ceredig, Cunorix and Gereint join Ambrosius and dismount from their horses.

"Yes, we concede," said Æsc, followed by Ælle and the other two Saxon leaders.

"Then you will all lay down your weapons, now," replied Ambrosius.

The Saxons hesitated, but then dropped their weapons on the ground, which were all gathered up by some of the Britons, while a group of other Britons were searching around the hillfort for any other weapons.

Ambrosius then told them that they would remain in the hillfort under guard, while the Britons considered the terms of their surrender. Ambrosius and the British leaders then turned and left, returning to their camp to discuss what terms they would require from the Saxons.

*

Back at their camp, Ambrosius ran through a basic set of terms of surrender that he wanted the Saxons to accept. He had listened to Ceredig's earlier comments about his family's sacrifices and wanted to go some way to giving them something they could accept.

When he was finished, most of the leaders were nodding in agreement before Ceredig spoke with restraint clear in his voice, saying, "What about the lands south of Calleva, down to Portus Adurni and the coastal region? Is King Ælle to be rewarded for his offences by keeping the lands he took with murder?"

"I am sorry, Lord Ceredig," said Ambrosius. "I doubt we would get King Ælle to simply get up and leave the whole region of Suthseaxna. These lands have Saxon chieftains and settlers, who have lived there for at least thirty years. That is why your route here was further west."

"These were my family's lands," said Ceredig. "I was born there. Portus Adurni was my home first. Do you deny me my homeland? Would you compensate me by handing over the land of your birth? I do not think so!"

"What about limiting the extent of King Ælle's lands as far west as Noviomagus?" said Ambrosius. "That leaves the lands between there and my kingdom as unclaimed or disputed. You would then be free to stake your claim as overlord with these chieftains once the Saxons agree to the terms and after a period of settlement."

Ceredig considered this for a few moments, then said, "For the sake of peace, I could live with that, but claim the right to take these lands earlier if King Ælle strays beyond his lands."

Ambrosius asked everyone else if they agreed with these terms and found there was general consent. He ordered his scribe to draft four copies for the Saxons and as many copies as required by the British leaders.

He was told they would be ready by morning.

*

The following morning, the four Saxon leaders were brought to Ambrosius's tent.

Ambrosius addressed them, saying, "Our terms are simple, but non-negotiable. You will accept them in whole, or you can return to the hillfort and face the might of Britannia's force in one very short battle that will end with your own deaths today."

"What are your terms?" said Ælle.

Ambrosius then explained the terms of their surrender.

He said, "First, Lord Ceredig, son of Elisedd, ruler of the Gewisse, will be granted lands between Lactodurum and Calleva, and five leagues either side of the old Roman road between these two settlements.

"Second, I, Ambrosius Aurelianus, son of Aurelius Ambrosius, will take over the region previously held by my father, in the lands of the Durotriges that stretch from

Searobyrg, in the east, to the mouth of the river Hafren, in the west.

"Third, you will be permitted to retain your current lands in Cantia, Est Seaxna and Est Engla, but must never leave these lands, or seek to expand them.

"Fourth, the western boundary of Suthseaxna will stop at Noviomagus, with lands to the west of this boundary treated as a neutral province for the next ten years, when Britons will make the final decision over its ultimate future.

"Fifth, there should be no further migration of Saxons into Britannia to form a new Saxon force, or seek an excuse to expand your current borders.

"Sixth, you will acknowledge the sovereignty of Britons over all the lands westwards, and north of your four Saxon kingdoms, up to and including the kingdom of Rheged.

"Seventh, each ruler of the Saxon kingdoms must hand over their eldest son, or daughter if they have no son, to act as a hostage for ten years. Alternatively, you can each pay 5,000 pounds in weight of gold and 5,000 pounds of silver instead.

"Finally, if any of these conditions are violated at any point over the next twenty years, the war that will follow will not end until every single Saxon has been killed. King Ælle brought this fate upon the people of Andredescæster, so that will be the consequence of any action that breaks the terms of your surrender."

The Saxon rulers considered this for a few seconds, then Æsc said, "Your terms sound reasonable, but may we discuss this in private before making our final decision?"

"Yes, by all means," replied Ambrosius. "You can return to the hillfort, but will remain under guard. When you have made your decision, let the guards at the gate know and you will be escorted down to my tent."

11 CEREDIG THE REGIONAL RULER

The *Anglo-Saxon Chronicle* records that "they (Cerdic and Cynric) fought with the Britons (at the battle of Badonbyrg)", and Ceredig becomes ruler of his own region in Britannia.

Ceredig wished he could have been a fly on the wall during the Saxons' discussions. He guessed it must have been heated, as it was not until the following morning before the four Saxon rulers were escorted into the tent by Arturius and a protective guard.

Sitting behind his table, Ambrosius greeted them.

"Have you considered the terms of surrender that I explained to you yesterday and are now willing to sign your agreement to them?" he asked.

"Yes," said the four Saxons.

"Excellent!" said Ambrosius, pointing to ten documents on the table. "In anticipation of your agreement, I have had ten copies of the treaty drafted. Once these documents have been signed by all rulers of regions here, both Britons and Saxons, a copy of each document will be retained by each regional ruler, so there will never be any doubt as to the terms that you have accepted."

The Saxon rulers stepped over to the table, each one reviewing a copy in front of them before nodding their acceptance.

The documents were then signed and sealed by Ambrosius, Ceredig and all the other rulers of Britannia. Then the four Saxon rulers signed the documents. Once they were finished, they stepped back.

Ambrosius reviewed the ten signed treaty documents before handing over a copy to each signatory and then handed the final copy to his scribe for safekeeping.

"Now," he said, "under the seventh condition of the terms of the agreement, who will act as your respective hostages?"

Æsc spoke first, pleading, "I have no children, my lord, so will pay 5,000 pound weight of gold and 5,000 pound weight of silver."

Ælle then said, "I have lost two sons in this battle, so my eldest, Cissa, is my only surviving son. I too will pay the required weight in gold and silver."

The other two rulers of Estseaxna and Est Engla also claimed to have no children, so offered gold and silver too.

Ambrosius then said, "Since you are all offering gold and silver instead of hostages, you will remain as our hostages until the 20,000 pounds of gold and 20,000 pounds of silver has been paid, to prevent any thoughts of deception. You can send a messenger back to your respective regions to bring back the amount of gold and silver to secure your release."

Arturius left the tent and returned with a Saxon

messenger for each ruler. Ambrosius, Ceredig and the other British rulers insisted the four Saxon rulers give their instructions in front of them, before the messengers left, mounted their horses and rode off towards their respective territories.

*

While they were all waiting for the Saxon messengers to return with their ransom, the Britons remained camped at Badonbyrg and used that time to gather their dead and bury them in a mass grave near the hillfort.

The Saxons, who were kept hostage in the hillfort, were allowed to gather and bury their dead, with their seax long knife in hand, to allow them the chance to enter Valhalla. This was all done under supervision by the Britons, to ensure the Saxons could not arm themselves. The Britons kept any remaining weapons and precious metals, such as gold or silver, from the dead.

Ambrosius arranged for the British rulers to share a main meal with the four Saxon rulers every day, in an effort to show them that it should be possible for Britons and Saxons to co-exist, if the Saxons would simply accept the borders of their kingdoms.

Whilst Ceredig attended these meals, he could not bring himself to engage with either Æsc or Ælle. Like Hengest and Horsa, he held them responsible for the brutal deaths of his father, brother, Cunedda and the people of Andredescæster. If it had not been for the explicit command by Ambrosius that they must survive, he would have cut them down without a second thought.

Instead, Ceredig talked to the other two Saxon rulers from Estseaxna and Est Engla, on the basis that they were Angles, not Saxons. He found them perfectly reasonable people, who were convinced to join in the battle after Æsc told them that their lands would come under threat if the Britons won. They just wanted to live in peace, if allowed. They also helped Ceredig understand the differences between Saxons, Angles and Jutes, who made up the 'Saxon' population in Britannia.

*

Two months later, Ceredig's scouts reported back that a train of 200 Saxons on horseback were within a day's ride from the Britons' camp. They were armed, but were bringing what looked like a large amount of gold and silver. Ceredig understood their need to be armed for their journey, to protect their precious cargo.

However, Ambrosius was not taking any chances, so he sent 1,000 men, armed for combat, to meet the Saxon group. Ceredig had dispatched his scouts in other directions to make sure there were no other forces of Saxons in the region. Meanwhile, the rest of the Britons prepared for battle, just in case the Saxons had plans to ambush the Britons.

The four Saxon leaders were also removed from the hillfort and taken under a large armed guard into Ambrosius's tent, so they were hidden from view.

Later that day, the Saxons carrying the gold and silver ransom drew closer to the camp. They were now being escorted by the force of 1,000 Britons, who were holding the Saxon weapons in the air to show the Saxons were unarmed.

They stopped within a hundred yards of the Britons' camp, and each ruler's group brought forward their gold and silver ransom, which was checked to make sure the correct weight of each precious metal had been given, all in front of Ambrosius, Ceredig, Gereint and the other rulers of the Britons. When this had been confirmed, Ambrosius called for Æsc, Ælle and the other two rulers to be brought forward.

Ambrosius addressed them, saying, "I hope this can be an end to future conflict between us, so that peace can once more return between the kingdoms of Britannia. If we ever need to fight again for the future of Britannia, be assured that we will bring the full force of our respective kingdoms against you and there will be no mercy shown to any Saxon we meet. However, I sincerely hope that it will never come to that. You and your men are free to return to your own lands, and I trust that you will remain there under the terms of the treaty that each of you has signed and sealed."

With his speech complete, Ambrosius stepped forward and gave each of the Saxon rulers a forearm handshake. The Saxon rulers left the tent and headed back to the hillfort, where their men were waiting under armed guard. After a short period, the Saxons left the area, heading eastward.

Ceredig had been watching these events unfold. As soon as the Saxons had left Badonbyrg, he turned to Arturius and told him to send the rest of his Gewisse scouts to meet up with the other scouts and track the Saxons all the way to Verulamium.

They were then to follow the Saxons as far as was safe into their territories to make sure there were no Saxon reinforcements ready to break the treaty as soon as their leaders were free.

When their task was complete, the scouts were to head for Durocastrum, the best-protected settlement in his new lands, as recommended by Arturius, who recalled an event during Ceredig's father's time, when the old Roman fort was able to provide sufficient protection for the locals after a Saxon attack. If Ceredig and the Gewisse were not there by then, the scouts were told to start scouting the area around Durocastrum for strengths and weaknesses.

Ambrosius had ordered the gold and silver ransom to be shared equally between the rulers of each kingdom that had joined the fight against the Saxons, including Ceredig who was now the ruler of a region, with lands on the boundary with the Saxons' kingdoms.

Ceredig wanted to start his rule by showing his people that he would be a fair and just ruler like his father, so he planned to use his share of the ransom to support the region he now controlled. However, he was also thinking about how he would reclaim the lands to the south that his father had once ruled.

*

Later that day, the Britons left the battlefield at Badonbyrg, with Ceredig and the Gewisse heading westwards into the lands that were now his to rule.

Ceredig planned to head to the former Roman fort at Durocastrum, after Arturius had advised him that it was a fortified settlement and would make a good base from which to operate.

On their journey to Durocastrum, they would visit as many settlements as they could, to make the local people aware that Ceredig was now their ruler after the battle at Badonbyrg.

Ceredig sent an advance party of three men ahead of his arrival to speak with the local chieftains to tell them of Ceredig's pedigree, as the son of Lord Elisedd, their regional ruler before the Saxons had expanded into their territory after the massacre of the Britons. They would also reassure the elders of each settlement that Lord Ceredig would be their protector, from his planned capital at Durocastrum.

Ceredig was received like a king at most of the settlements they reached, especially after he handed over some of the gold and silver to help each community, which delayed their progress as the elders insisted on sharing a meal with their new lord and protector.

At a small number of settlements, Ceredig and the Gewisse found a Saxon family in charge. Conscious of Ambrosius's ambition for peace to settle across Britannia, Ceredig reluctantly gave the Saxon families the opportunity to either accept him as their ruler and remain, or peacefully leave their lands behind and return to Cantia, or whichever Saxon kingdom they came from.

He reassured them that, if they stayed, they would have his protection as if they were Britons, but he would not accept them providing a safe haven for any other Saxons.

His conciliatory approach worked with these settlements, which meant that he was now a ruler of a region that included Saxons as well as Britons. This was something he had never imagined, and he wondered how his father and brother would feel about this.

On his arrival at Durocastrum, Ceredig was welcomed by the elders of the settlement, including an old man called Jemmett, who informed Lord Ceredig that he had known his father.

Jemmett recalled his ride to Portus Adurni with news of the Saxon attack on Durocastrum many years ago, before Ceredig was born, and the help provided by Lord Elisedd to rid them of the Saxon attackers. He had heard of Elisedd's demise, but was pleased to report that the Saxons had not chosen to destroy Durocastrum, although they had killed a number of Britons who managed estates in the area and installed new Saxon families in their stead.

Ceredig told Jemmett and the other elders that he had met some of them on their way to Durocastrum, but explained that Ambrosius, the High King of the Britons, had commanded that every effort be made to live in peace with the Saxons.

Ceredig said that these Saxons would be given a choice to remain and live in peace, under his protection, or return to their Saxon kingdoms. The elders accepted Ceredig's decision as a fair one.

That evening, a celebration banquet was held in Durocastrum's great hall to honour the new ruler and his Gewisse warriors.

*

Ceredig's first task after settling into life at Durocastrum was to decide where to settle the 1,000 Gewisse warriors who survived the battle at Badonbyrg, as well as ensuring there was sufficient protection across his lands.

He decided to split the Gewisse into three distinct units, with one at Durocastrum and the other two based at either end of the region they would need to protect.

Since Ceredig and his family would live at Durocastrum, Arturius would be the fort's commander, with 400 Gewisse warriors. The people of Durocastrum had established their own settlement outside the north gate of the old Roman fort, which was only used by the elders and as a sanctuary in the event of attack, so the fort would be large enough to house the Gewisse garrison.

The northern garrison would be based at Alaunacæster, which was a strategically important old Roman fort, close to the junction of the military road from Calleva to Lactodurum and the old Roman road which ran from Corinium to Verulamium.

The southern garrison would be at Calleva, which was equally strategic, at the other end of the Roman military road from Lactodurum, and at the junction with the old Roman road from Corinium to Lundein.

Ceredig realised why Ambrosius suggested he rule over this region. It formed a buffer between the Saxons in the east and the Britons in the west, which meant that, if the Saxons did decide to ignore the treaty of Badonbyrg, Ceredig and his men would be the first to know.

Ceredig did not ultimately trust the Saxons and anticipated that there would, at least, be some rogue groups who would ignore their rulers' commands to remain at peace with the Britons. Therefore, Ceredig and Arturius agreed that they would also need to organise regular patrols across Ceredig's lands.

Ceredig and Cunorix decided to accompany the northern group of warriors, with their new commander, north to Alaunacæster, calling in on any settlements on the way to make them aware that Ceredig was now their ruler, that they would be under his protection and that there would be a permanent force residing at the old Roman fort at Alaunacæster should they require help.

Just like their journey to Durocastrum, Ceredig and Cunorix found several settlements with Saxon chieftains, who received the same offer as their earlier compatriots. Either accept Ceredig as their overlord and protector, or leave the settlement and return to their original Saxon region.

The news of the Saxons' defeat at the battle of Badonbyrg was spreading around the country, so Ceredig found that these Saxons were more accepting of his overlordship, against returning to a Saxon kingdom where the shame of their defeat was causing a lot of tension, blame and recrimination.

A month after returning from this tour of his northern lands, Ceredig and Cunorix repeated the process with a journey to Calleva, and the settlements in between, with the southern forces and their new commander, who would be stationed at Calleva. It was the same story at settlements in the south too, with any Saxon chieftains accepting Ceredig's overlordship rather than returning to Cantia or Suthseaxna.

While Ceredig and Cunorix had been on these visits north and south of the region, Arturius had overseen the building of a new family villa on the foundations of the old praetorium in Durocastrum. Once the work was completed, word was sent to Madog in Darioritum, and a few months later, Ophelia, Cunedda and the other families of Gewisse warriors arrived in Glevum on one of the large merchant ships that Ceredig had used to bring his Gewisse to Britannia.

Ceredig and Cunorix travelled to Glevum, along with 200 warriors, spare horses and carts, to greet the women and children, and bring them back to Durocastrum.

The old Roman fort was not as big as the fort at Portus Adurni, so while the single men were housed in barracks within the fort, Ceredig decided that the men with families would be given property and land of their own to manage.

The elders informed Ceredig about two ruined Roman

villa estates six miles to the west of Durocastrum, and the surrounding lands there were quite fertile, so they were allocated to the family men of Durocastrum to develop into a small settlement.

Shortly after Ophelia and Cunedda had joined him at Durocastrum, Ceredig received some sad news when a messenger arrived from Glevum. Ceredig's uncle, Eldol, governor of Glevum, had died peacefully in his sleep. Eldol was an old man, in his early eighties when he died, so it was not entirely unexpected.

Eldol's status within Glevum merited a glorious funeral and burial in the abbey at Glevum, which was attended by Ambrosius and Gereint, as well as a number of other rulers who had fought with Eldol at Badonbyrg.

Ceredig spoke at the funeral about Eldol's life and the crucial role he had played in helping the Britons recover from the invasion of the Saxons over the past sixty years.

As his only living relative, Ceredig inherited his uncle's estate to the east of Glevum, as well as a property in the town near the west gate. He granted the latter to the church, but retained the villa estate that had been his home during the early years after leaving Portus Adurni.

The estate would be a useful retreat if he ever needed to escape from Durocastrum, as well as an inheritance for young Cunedda, if Cunorix fulfilled his destiny in succeeding Ceredig as ruler of the Gewisse.

*

The next twelve years passed quickly, as Ceredig, Ophelia, Cunorix and Cunedda settled into life at Durocastrum. The whole region was prospering under the new peace, people were happy again, and new settlements were growing.

Now well into his fifties, Ceredig was grateful that the Saxons had shown no signs of breaking the terms of the treaty of Badonbyrg. Whilst he did not trust the Saxon king, Æsc, given he was the son of Hengest, who had killed his father, Ceredig had found that the Saxon families living on his lands were pleasant people who offered no threat.

Cunorix was now taking a greater role in commanding the Gewisse forces, allowing Ceredig to spend more time with his family. With time on his hands, Ceredig began to think more about the lands south of Calleva that his father had once ruled. Ambrosius had given Ceredig tacit approval to pursue his claim to rule these lands after a ten-year period of neutrality, as part of the treaty at Badonbyrg.

Having consolidated his position as ruler of the lands he had been granted, Ceredig wondered whether it was time for him to make a trip to meet with Ambrosius in Aquaesulis. However, before he had any more time to consider his plans, there was sad news closer to home.

One morning, whilst overseeing training for the younger Gewisse warriors, Arturius suddenly collapsed to the ground holding his chest and was taken to his room.

By the time Ceredig arrived, his lifelong friend and

protector, Arturius, was dead. Although Arturius was elderly and had been showing signs of his age catching up on him, his sudden death came as a shock to Ceredig.

Ceredig knew that Arturius had made huge sacrifices in dedicating his life to ensure Ceredig's and his family's safety, foregoing the opportunity of marriage and children to continue his line.

Ceredig had relied heavily on Arturius throughout his life, as his protector, adviser, friend. Realising that Arturius would not be by his side anymore affected him more than he realised it ever would.

After he buried Arturius in the settlement's burial mounds, Ceredig spent the next week deep in thought as he walked the fort walls.

Ophelia had been trying to persuade Ceredig that they should take some time away from Durocastrum and visit the estate near Glevum for a change of scenery.

However, Ceredig quickly came out of his gloom when a messenger arrived from Aquaesulis to announce that Ambrosius, High King of the Britons, had died in his royal palace at Aquaesulis. Like Arturius, Ambrosius had been in his seventies, so his death, peacefully in his sleep, was no great surprise to Ceredig.

Ophelia had been concerned that this news would have compounded Ceredig's grief, especially losing another great ally. However, the more he heard, she could see his mind working overtime as he considered the ramifications.

The messenger reported that Ambrosius had already been buried in a simple ceremony in Aquaesulis, and his son had already been appointed his successor as King of the Durotriges.

Ceredig was both disappointed and concerned. A simple burial was not befitting a man of Ambrosius's status and achievements, so he decided to make the trip to Aquaesulis and pay his respects.

Ceredig could not remember ever meeting any sons of Ambrosius Aurelianus, or whether any of his sons had participated in any battles against the Saxons, especially the battle at Badonbyrg, so he was also keen to meet the new king of the region and find out more about him.

His primary concern was the potential of a power vacuum amongst the Britons that the Saxons might see as a weakness and an opportunity to set aside the Badonbyrg treaty.

This made Ceredig's journey vital, and urgent. He needed to know where he stood, given that his lands were on the front line against the Saxons.

12 CEREDIG REGAINS HIS HOMELAND

The *Anglo-Saxon Chronicle* records that, in AD 508,
"Cerdic and Cynric slew a British king, whose name
was Natanleoð, and five thousand men with him".

Ceredig was hugely frustrated when he returned from
Aquaesulis two months later and could not contain
himself when he told Ophelia, Cunorix and Cunedda all
about it when they greeted him back at Durocastrum.

"Ambrosius's son, Uthr, is a weakling," Ceredig told
them. "I cannot believe he has succeeded his father as
ruler of the Durotriges. No wonder we have never met
him before. He was as thin as a spear and was barely visible
under his father's thick cloak. To go from such a powerful
ruler to someone who would fall over in a strong wind is
incomprehensible."

Ceredig then told them that he advised King Uthr that
the Saxons, especially King Ælle of Suthseaxna, might see
King Ambrosius's death as a signal to set aside the treaty.
Ceredig informed the new king that he intended to show
strength against the Saxons by making his claim on the
southern lands that his father had once ruled, between
Calleva and Portus Adurni.

When the new king looked concerned, Ceredig was grateful that one of Ambrosius's commanders was present, who had been at the Badonbyrg treaty signing and was able to verify Ceredig's right, under the treaty, to reclaim his father's former lands between the kingdom of the Durotriges and King Ælle's lands of Suthseaxna.

King Uthr had asked whether Ceredig had the forces to defend his existing lands if the Saxons chose to attack, as well as the men required to enforce his claim over the southern region.

When Ceredig confirmed that he had sufficient Gewisse forces, unless all four Saxon kingdoms combined into a large force, as they did at Badonbyrg, the new king said nothing.

Ceredig then suggested organising a conference of the rulers of Britannia to discuss a co-ordinated response, in case the Saxons did rise up against the Britons. The new king seemed to mull it over, but would not give any commitment to this, suggesting they wait and see what the Saxons did first.

Ceredig said that he did not want to say something he might regret, so made his excuses and left, then immediately headed for Dumnonia to see King Gereint.

Gereint told Ceredig that he had a similar experience during his visit to Aquaesulis and shared Ceredig's feelings about King Uthr. Gereint promised he would send a force of men to support Ceredig if the Saxons began incursions into his lands.

"I did not even have to ask King Gereint for support," said Ceredig. "That shows the stark difference in attitude between these two kings. I am now firm in my mind that we need to start taking control over the southern kingdom. We will start next year with the lands between Calleva and Ventacæster."

After listening to his father's story, Cunorix said, "I would like to lead the Gewisse on this venture if you will let me, Father. It is time for me to take command of my own Gewisse forces."

"Of course, son," said Ceredig. "I was going to suggest that anyway. You can take 300 men from here, and you can draw another 200 men from the camp at Calleva."

Ceredig sat back in his chair in the great hall and relaxed, with satisfaction that the campaign for regaining control over his father's lands had begun.

*

The following year, Cunorix led 500 Gewisse warriors out of the fort at Calleva, heading south and visiting all the settlements on their way to Ventacæster, claiming them on behalf of Ceredig, ruler of the Gewisse.

Cunorix found that there was overall acceptance of Ceredig, son of Elisedd, as their ruler at each settlement they reached, until they arrived at Ventacæster. The Saxon chieftain there must have heard the Gewisse were coming and retreated into the hillfort, to the east of the old Roman civitas, which was now deserted.

Cunorix set up camp in the old Roman civitas of Ventacæster and then approached the hillfort. When the chieftain arrived at the hillfort gate, Cunorix explained about the treaty of Badonbyrg that the Saxon kings had accepted, which meant giving up any claim to these lands.

Then Cunorix offered the inhabitants the same terms that his father had made when he had claimed lordship over the settlements in his new lands many years ago. As a Saxon, the chieftain could either accept Ceredig as his overlord, or he could take his Saxons and leave the hillfort and these lands, to return to the Saxon lands of Suthseaxna to the east.

The Saxon chieftain asked Cunorix for time to consider the offer, so Cunorix agreed and withdrew back to his camp. In the end, the chieftain took seven days, before finally accepting the offer and wishing Cunorix good fortune elsewhere in the region. This response left Cunorix surprised and doubting that the acceptance was genuine, but wanted to give the chieftain a chance to prove it. Therefore, Cunorix commanded his forces to withdraw and head south.

When they were far enough away from the hillfort, Cunorix ordered his men to make camp, then sent three scout units to take up positions around ten miles to the east of the hillfort along various routes to Suthseaxna. If the chieftain sent any messengers for reinforcements from King Ælle and the South Saxons, the Gewisse were to kill them and bring the bodies to Cunorix's camp.

Cunorix was not surprised when the scouts returned, a few days later, with the bodies of three armed messengers, whom they had caught on the road heading south towards Portus Adurni. When another group of scouts arrived in camp with the bodies of three more messengers, caught heading cross-country towards Andredescæster, Cunorix decided to return to Ventacæster to remove the chieftain.

When they arrived back at the hillfort, Cunorix was not surprised to see that the Saxon chieftain had remained inside the hillfort and appeared set for a siege. However, Cunorix was in no mood to wait.

Having seen the impact of fire on a wooden palisaded hillfort in action at Vespasian's Camp, shortly after arriving in Britannia, Cunorix ordered bundles of wood and branches to be gathered and placed on a cart they had liberated from a nearby farm estate. That night, in the darkness, a group of Gewisse quietly made their way up to the gate and positioned the cart against the gate.

The next morning, as daylight broke, the Saxons were greeted with the sight of six heads of the messengers fixed atop spears outside the hillfort gate.

When the Saxon chieftain arrived at the palisade wall, he also saw Cunorix standing beside a large bonfire about a hundred feet away. The chieftain then noticed a length of rope leading from the Britons up to the gate, while Cunorix stood watching.

Cunorix then stepped forward, withdrew a branch from the bonfire and used it to set the rope alight. The rope had been purchased from a settlement further south and had been steeped in animal fats to make it burn faster. The Gewisse watched as the flame trail began its journey towards the hillfort.

On the wall of the hillfort, the chieftain and his men's attention was drawn to the line of fire edging closer to the gate. Meanwhile, on the other side of the hillfort, a small group of thirty Gewisse warriors were using the distraction to climb over the palisade wall. They had made their way around the hillfort under the cover of darkness and waited for the Saxon sentries' attention to be drawn to events at the hillfort gate.

Back at the entrance, the chieftain realised there was a cart full of bracken and branches up against the wooden gate, so he ordered his men to form up at the entrance. He had decided to open the gate and push the cart out of the way before the gate could catch fire.

Suddenly, there was a commotion on the other side of the hillfort, as a group of fifty Gewisse warriors had breached the rear wall and were attacking the Saxons. The chieftain and his men were temporarily distracted while he ordered some of his men to head over and deal with the rear attack.

That was the signal for one of Cunorix's men, who was holding onto a piece of camouflaged rope that had been attached to a log holding the cart in place. He pulled on the rope, which released the cart to roll down the ramp into the hillfort's defensive ditch. Cunorix's men were already charging the gate, which had been partially opened, making it easier for his men to enter the hillfort, ready for battle.

The diversion worked perfectly, and Cunorix easily gained control over the hillfort, with only a few superficial injuries to his men. The Saxon warriors had all been killed and the chieftain was taken captive.

Cunorix and his Gewisse commanders walked up the steps to the entrance of the great hall, with the Saxon chieftain as their prisoner. Cunorix ordered the Gewisse to ensure all the people living within the hillfort were present at the gathering place in front of the great hall.

When everyone was present, Cunorix called out in a loud voice, saying, "People of Ventacæster, this man has brought death to your settlement," pointing to the Saxon chieftain.

"Under the Badonbyrg treaty, signed by your Saxon leaders, these lands now fall under control of Lord Ceredig, son of Elisedd, former ruler of these lands," he continued. "I offered your chieftain the same peace terms that everyone, Briton or Saxon, living in this region has accepted. We are happy to allow you to remain and live in peace here, but you must accept Lord Ceredig as your ruler and protector. If that is unacceptable, we will allow you to leave peacefully, to return to your Saxon lands to the east of Noviomagus and never return."

He looked around the crowd, looking for acknowledgement before he continued, "Whilst initially accepting our offer to allow you to remain, your chieftain then sent two groups of messengers to King Ælle in Suthseaxna, requesting reinforcements to defend him against the Gewisse warriors of Lord Ceredig, which would have broken the terms of the treaty. For that crime, your chieftain must be punished."

Cunorix turned to one of his commanders, called Coel, who was holding the bound chieftain in front of him, and nodded. On the signal from Cunorix, Coel stepped back and thrust his sword upwards into the chieftain's back so forcefully that the sword appeared through the front of his chest. Coel withdrew the sword and the chieftain's body collapsed to the ground.

Cunorix then spoke again, saying, "Now, I offer the same terms to you, but with a difference. If you choose to remain, you will accept my appointment of a new chieftain. In addition, a cohort of my Gewisse warriors will remain here to maintain peace and order in this region."

He continued, "If you cannot accept my terms, you have one day to make your decision. We will remain here tonight and, in the morning, those who wish to leave will be escorted as far as Noviomagus. In the meantime, I want your elders to join me in the great hall now."

Cunorix then turned and walked into the great hall, followed by the commanders of his Gewisse warriors. The elders followed them into the hall shortly afterwards.

Cunorix sat in the chieftain's chair, while the elders stood before him, surrounded by the Gewisse commanders. He asked the elders to tell him about the people living within the hillfort, to gauge how many were likely to leave and whether there was likely to be any further trouble after he had appointed one of his men as chieftain.

The elders told Cunorix that they were simple Jutish farmers, who had relocated from Cantia many years ago, long before King Ælle came to Britannia. They had found the hillfort deserted, so they settled there and had been happy with their life there. Then, about twenty years ago, King Ælle came to Ventacæster and imposed the Saxon chieftain on them.

The chieftain had brought a number of Saxon warriors with him to enforce Saxon control over the area, but he had not been a good or fair ruler, so would not be missed by the Jutes. The elders were also pleased to report that neither the chieftain nor his men had any family living within the settlement either. They then reassured Cunorix that no one in the hillfort would bear any resentment towards him or Lord Ceredig. In fact, they imagined that everyone would accept the terms presented by Cunorix, to remain in Ventacæster under their protection.

Satisfied with the responses from the elders, Cunorix informed them that he was appointing Coel as chieftain of Ventacæster and commander of the forces, who would remain there to protect the region. It was accepted without objection.

The elders then insisted that Cunorix and his commanders accept their hospitality and were to be entertained in the great hall by the elders, who introduced Cunorix to their families, who served the meal to their new protectors.

During the meal, Cunorix found himself attracted to one of the servers, called Hildis, who was the daughter of one of the elders. Cunorix could not take his eyes off her. Hildis seemed to reciprocate and remained close to Cunorix, serving his food and refilling his goblet with mead whenever he came close to emptying it.

One of the elders must have noticed this and asked Cunorix if he had a wife yet. When Cunorix said he did not, the elder suggested that perhaps it was time to consider his future happiness, then suggested that Hildis would make a fine wife. When Cunorix and Hildis both appeared suitably embarrassed, the elder called for a toast to Cunorix finding a wife.

Towards the end of the meal, an elder took the opportunity to have a quiet word with Cunorix. The elder explained that he was Hildis's father and said that, if it was Cunorix's wish to take Hildis as his wife, he would have his blessing.

Cunorix was not used to such direct offers of a wife, so said he was not prepared to marry someone he did not know.

The elder then suggested that Cunorix delay his departure for a few days to get to know Hildis before making his decision. The elder said he was confident that once Cunorix got to know Hildis, he would want her for his wife.

Cunorix replied saying he would consider the elder's proposition and let him know in the morning. That night, Cunorix thought about the elder's proposal. He liked Hildis, so it would not do any harm to see if there was more than just an attraction there. Therefore, he decided to remain in Ventacæster for a few more days and would spend that time getting to know Hildis.

The next morning, the elders reported to Cunorix that, as predicted, all the residents of Ventacæster had chosen to stay and accept Lord Ceredig's protection.

Cunorix informed his commanders that they would remain in Ventacæster for three more days. In the meantime, the new chieftain, Coel, and his men should get to know the hillfort and its defences, identify any weaknesses, especially the way that Cunorix's men had found their way into the hillfort, and spend some time in the area around the fort.

The remaining Gewisse were to venture further afield, to see if there were any other settlements they had missed and assess any threats from Saxon warriors in the area, as well as arranging supplies for the return journey.

The elders had told Cunorix that several winter floods had made the lower half of the old Roman citadel uninhabitable for half the year, which is why they relocated to the hillfort, so he asked some of his men to assess the citadel's river defences and see what it would take to prevent further floods.

Cunorix planned to ask his father if he could be granted these lands in the south to rule in Ceredig's name. If the Ventacæster citadel was made inhabitable again, it would make a suitable base from which to rule.

Cunorix then asked one of the servants in the great hall to be shown to the home of the chief elder. When he knocked on the door, the elder invited him in. Cunorix came straight to the point. He asked the elder if he stood by his offer the previous night.

The elder said yes, so Cunorix told Hildis he felt an attraction between them and asked if she would like to spend some time getting to know each other. When she agreed, Cunorix asked her to show him around the area.

For the next three days, Cunorix and Hildis became virtually inseparable. She told him about her family's arrival in Britannia nearly forty years before, their life in Cantia, then Ventacæster, and her wishes for a more peaceful life between the Britons and the Saxons.

Cunorix told Hildis about his grandfather's rule over the region until he had been killed by Hengest's Saxons, his father's life in exile in Armorica, their return to Britannia, defeating the Saxons at Badonbyrg and his father being granted lands further to the north, with the treaty's agreement that control over the region came under the Britons a few years back. He also told her of his father's wish to fulfil Lord Elisedd's wish for his family to rule the region down to the coastline and his ambition to succeed his father.

Time seemed to fly and, before Cunorix realised it, the three days had passed and it was time to return home. He told Hildis he wanted her to return with him to Durocastrum and become his wife.

When she agreed, Cunorix said he would speak with her father and they would have a celebratory meal that evening in the great hall, before departing the next day. Naturally, Hildis's family were delighted and gave their blessing.

Cunorix wondered how his father would feel when his son brought home a Jutish woman as his wife!

The next morning, Cunorix and Hildis, together with 400 Gewisse warriors, left the hillfort, heading for Calleva via the old Roman settlement at Vindomis, but they did not anticipate any problems along that route.

A few days later, nine months after leaving, Cunorix, with Hildis by his side, led 200 Gewisse warriors into Durocastrum.

Ceredig was happy to see them return and eager to hear from Cunorix about their reception by the people of the southern region. However, the news that Cunorix had found himself a wife was more exciting, especially for Cunorix's mother, Ophelia.

Leaving Cunorix to tell his father all about the events during his expedition down south, Ophelia took Hildis under her wing and started organising a banquet that evening to celebrate their union.

The news about Ventacæster was mildly concerning for Ceredig as it looked like King Ælle had been imposing his own Saxon chieftains on the main hillforts in the region along the southern coastline. That would have implications when he tried to retake the more southerly fortified settlements, like Portus Adurni, Clausentum and Onna, as well as Leucomagus, given its strategic importance on the old Roman road to Corinium.

However, now that he knew the Saxons' tactics in that region, it would be easier to anticipate their reception on their next venture further south towards the coast.

*

Six months later, Ceredig decided that it was time to complete his southern expansion, to finally reclaim the lands that his father had once ruled. He decided that he would lead this expedition, but was happy for Cunorix to accompany him.

Ceredig also suggested that Hildis come too, so she could catch up with her family, especially as he planned to use the citadel of Ventacæster as their base. He had recently received news from Ventacæster that the community had relocated back into the citadel, after building up defences to stop the local river flooding again. It would be large enough to accommodate a large Gewisse force as well.

And so, after making all the necessary preparations, Ceredig, Cunorix and Hildis headed out of the fort at Durocastrum with 200 Gewisse warriors, bound for Calleva, where they would spend the night before heading south to Ventacæster.

During the evening meal, the group discussed the events in and around Calleva since they had last been there. The commander had reported only minor skirmishes with youthful Saxons who had ventured into the area. They did not live to report what they had found in terms of defensive forces.

The next day, Ceredig, Cunorix and Hildis, with a now larger force of 400 Gewisse warriors, left Calleva for the next part of their journey, arriving two days later at Ventacæster. A group of scouts had been sent ahead to inform Coel, the citadel commander, of Ceredig and Cunorix's imminent arrival.

*

When the group arrived at Ventacæster, there was a guard of honour waiting for them at the east gate as they crossed the bridge, through the gate and marched into the citadel, up to the old Roman forum.

After Coel and the elders welcomed Lord Ceredig and Cunorix to Ventacæster and they all exchanged the traditional greeting of a forearm handshake, Hildis ran to her father and threw her arms around him.

Meanwhile, Coel guided Ceredig and Cunorix into the great hall that had been built on the foundations of the old Roman Basilica. They exchanged news from their respective regions over a goblet of wine, while Ceredig explained the purpose of their visit.

Coel said that his scouts had been checking out the other settlements in the region as part of his remit from Cunorix when he had been appointed as chieftain. He revealed to Ceredig and Cunorix that, in the thirty years since King Ælle had taken control over the southern kingdoms, Saxon chieftains and their men had been installed at all the major settlements in the area.

The only exception was Leucomagus, a settlement to the north which was still populated by Britons, with a Briton as chieftain. That was some good news, so Ceredig decided that they would visit Leucomagus first, since it should be relatively easy to declare overlordship amongst his own kind.

Ceredig decided that they would choose whether to visit Onna or Clausentum after they had returned from Leucomagus. He had decided before leaving Durocastrum that they would tackle Portus Adurni last, as the final stage of reclaiming his father's lands, as he thought it might be the most difficult fort to breach.

Ceredig chose not to delay, so he left Ventacæster the following morning with his Gewisse warriors and headed north-west towards Leucomagus, leaving Cunorix to spend time with Hildis and her family.

While his father was away, Cunorix held a meeting with Coel to discuss protecting the region as it expanded and how to build their forces to replace the older warriors who would soon be more of a liability in battle.

He was pleased to learn that Coel had already considered this and his men had been training some of the younger Jutes to fight, just in case they were needed to defend the citadel. Amongst their number were two young men, called Wihtgar and Stuffa, whom Coel praised for their attitude and natural ability. They were the sons of one of the other elders, who was Hildis's uncle, making Wihtgar and Stuffa her cousins.

Cunorix raised his concern about the possibility that they might one day need to fight against Saxons, traditional allies of the Jutes, but Coel informed him that this would not be a problem. The Jutes had reassured Coel that they had seen enough brutality from King Ælle and his Saxons to know that Lord Ceredig and Cunorix were the better allies. After all, since Cunorix's wedding to Hildis, they now considered themselves as kinsmen with the Britons, which was a stronger bond in their eyes.

Later that day, Cunorix spent time watching Coel and his best warriors put the young Jutes through their paces in a training session. Cunorix was impressed by the strength and aptitude of the Jutes. It reminded Cunorix that the Gewisse had their own origins in merging the talents of warriors from many kingdoms from the Roman Empire.

*

The following day, as Ceredig and his Gewisse warriors were nearing the settlement at Leucomagus, Ceredig's advance scouts approached them from the settlement and stopped as they reached their ruler. They told Ceredig that the Leucomagus chieftain and elders were very wary of such a large group of warriors arriving from the south, having suffered from numerous attacks by the Saxons.

The chieftain wanted Ceredig's group to remain outside the settlement while he sent a team to listen to Ceredig's terms. Whilst Ceredig was a little impatient, he took the opinion of his scouts that this was simply a very cautious chieftain, who had done well to protect his people from the Saxons.

Ceredig accepted this, so ordered his men to set up camp and organise regular sentry patrols, and sent his scouts out to check the surrounding area, just in case there were any Saxon groups in the region.

An hour later, ten men rode out from Leucomagus. The group consisted of four elders and six armed warriors, an indication to Ceredig that the elders were used to negotiating with the Saxons.

Ceredig called for nine of his best men to accompany him out to meet the group. He carried a spear bearing his family's banner, the gold rampant dragon on a red background.

When the two groups met, Ceredig introduced himself directing his words to the elders, saying, "I am Lord Ceredig, son of Elisedd, once ruler of this region, before the Saxon treachery. After the Saxons lost the battle of Badonbyrg over ten years ago, I was granted overlordship of lands to the north, but with the right to reclaim my father's lands when I deemed it appropriate. Someone from your settlement may have even been present at the battle."

At that point, one of the elders said, "How does this affect us, my lord?"

"I am not here to attack or take control of your settlement," continued Ceredig. "All I ask is that you recognise me as your overlord and protector, as my father once was. I can see that you have created your own force of warriors to protect your settlement, which is impressive. If you accept me as ruler, we can provide training and weapons, and support from Ventacæster, as well as the opportunity for any of your men who have the right qualities to join my Gewisse warriors."

At the point that Ceredig mentioned the word 'Gewisse', one of the elders held up his hand.

"You are Gewisse?" he asked.

"Yes," replied Ceredig.

"Are you the miracle boy?" asked the elder, whom Ceredig surmised was the chieftain, as it was doubtful anyone but the chieftain would know about Caradoc's miracle healing.

"No," said Ceredig. "That was my older brother, Caradoc. He was also killed along with my father by the Saxons at Vespasian's Camp."

"I am sorry for your loss, my lord," said the chieftain.

He turned to the other two elders and they held a quick discussion, then the chieftain turned back to Ceredig and said, "My lord. We are satisfied that you are who you say you are and accept you as our overlord. Please join us in the settlement and honour us with your presence at a banquet to celebrate your family's return."

"Thank you," said Ceredig. "I would be honoured. I would like to hear your thoughts on how we can help you and whether there are any issues with the chieftains to the west now that Lord Ambrosius is dead."

With the business of negotiations complete, they all headed towards the gate to the settlement and the prospect of a banquet to recognise Lord Ceredig's overlordship over Leucomagus.

*

The next day, Ceredig left Leucomagus, having completed the first part of his mission. That was the easy part done, but he knew the next one would be much more difficult.

When Ceredig and his Gewisse warriors returned to Ventacæster, Cunorix informed his father about the work undertaken by the citadel commander in establishing a defensive force of Jutes, who now considered themselves part of Lord Ceredig's 'kingdom'.

At Cunorix's mention of the word 'kingdom', Ceredig said, "I do not think I am in a position to declare myself the ruler of a kingdom, son. We need to establish the borders of our planned kingdom first, which can only be achieved when the southern coast is under our control once more. Then we need loyal chieftains from the major settlements to become representatives of their region on a council of advisers, with their own force of warriors, willing to come to the defence of their neighbouring regions in my name."

"That might prove more challenging than we first thought, Father," said Cunorix. "However, the opportunity to test your authority might come sooner than anticipated."

"What has happened?" asked Ceredig, recognising concern in Cunorix's voice.

"Whilst you were at Leucomagus, a scout patrol had returned from their mission to explore the Saxon settlement at Onna, half a day's ride to the south-west," said Cunorix. "The scouts reported that the Saxon chieftain of Onna, who called himself Nætanleoð, must have heard about your intention to claim lordship over the region. He has gathered a Saxon force of nearly 5,000 men, presumably from other Saxon settlements in the region, like Clausentum, Portus Adurni and possibly from Suthseaxna. The only good news is that only one fifth of the Saxon force gathering at Onna are seasoned warriors."

As soon as he heard this, Ceredig halted the discussion and told his son that they would discuss this in the morning, with Coel and the scout commander who had accompanied Ceredig to Leucomagus. He wanted a good night's sleep before he tackled his next challenge.

*

The next morning, Ceredig, Cunorix, Coel and the scout commander gathered in the great hall. Ceredig asked Cunorix to update them on the news from Onna.

Once they were up to speed, Ceredig told the scout

commander to take his patrol group on an urgent mission back to Leucomagus to explain the situation and ask the chieftain if they would volunteer as many battle-ready men as they could spare. Ceredig said he should emphasise the risk of the Saxons attacking Leucomagus next, if needed.

Ceredig then asked Coel how many Gewisse warriors he could spare from Ventacæster. Coel said that there were 150 men, including a number of local Jutes who were ready for battle, although they were not experienced.

That gave Ceredig a total of 550 men, plus however many came from Leucomagus. This was clearly not enough. They would be vastly outnumbered.

During the night Ceredig had come up with an idea to increase their number and a strategy to defeat the Saxons.

"Coel, send your fastest rider up to Calleva," he said. "Tell them that we need as many warriors as they can spare, ready for battle against Saxons. They should travel here as fast as their horses can carry them."

He turned to Cunorix, saying, "Cunorix, my son, you shall wait here for the reinforcements from Leucomagus and Calleva."

"What will you do, Father?" asked Cunorix.

Ceredig said, "I am going to take 400 of our most experienced fighters with me to Searobyrg. The chieftain there knows me and I am confident I can persuade him to give me men to fight the Saxons at Onna, given it is only one day's ride away. Five hundred of his men should suffice. It will bring my numbers up to around 900, roughly the same number of experienced warriors as they will have."

He checked to see if Cunorix and Coel were following his train of thought, then said, "We will head south to the end of the old Roman army road, then turn east, making camp around five miles to the west of the fortified settlement at Onna. It is a flat area of land across the marshland from Onna, so it will make an ideal location for battle. We will make the camp look big enough that the Saxons are obliged to send their forces out to take us on in battle."

"That would work, but you would be hugely outnumbered," said Coel.

"Yes," said Ceredig. "Timing will be crucial. It will take us two days to reach our planned camp from Searobyrg, so when we leave the hillfort, I will send a mounted messenger back here. Use that as your signal to time your departure from Ventacæster and ride your men south, past Onna, to come in behind the Saxons. That second front should confuse them enough to give us an advantage."

*

Four days later, Ceredig, along with his 400 warriors and 500 men from Searobyrg, were camped exactly where he had planned. They had built a very large camp, with more fires than normal, suggesting a much bigger force than they actually had, so they would be seen from Onna.

Ceredig's scouts were set up around the Saxon settlement, ready to signal when the Saxon forces were leaving to face Ceredig and the 900 Britons.

At some time around noon, smoke could be seen from one of the scout patrols, followed quickly by another column of smoke from a second patrol. When there was a fourth smoke signal, Ceredig knew that the Saxons were sending all their warriors. He also knew that Cunorix and his reinforcements, coming down from Ventacæster, would also see the signals and know that Ceredig's plan was working.

As the Saxons crossed the marsh and set themselves up to face the Britons, Ceredig had his men form up in three rows, with his archers at the back. They would have a use in this battle, but not immediately.

The Saxons appeared to be assessing the size of the force facing them. Eventually, a large force of nearly 2,000 men marched out to face the Britons. They must have thought they could simply overwhelm the Britons in front of them.

Ceredig sent 700 warriors out to face them. The Britons were outnumbered, but the big difference was that they were experienced warriors. Ceredig knew that the first wave of Saxons would be the least experienced, used by their leadership to assess the skill of their opponents.

It was a massacre for all the wrong reasons. The Saxons did not expect to have any problems killing these Britons, given the overwhelming Saxon force. However, the Gewisse warriors led the Britons in a V-shaped formation, driving through the Saxon shield wall, leaving the Britons from Searobyrg to clean up the disorientated Saxons. The Gewisse then quickly turned and came in behind the Saxons, killing every single Saxon warrior.

The Britons cheered then returned to their positions, and Ceredig waited for the Saxons' next move, which he anticipated would be a full-on attack by the remaining 3,000 more experienced Saxons.

When it came, Ceredig watched them build up to a full-speed attack. When they were closing in on the Britons' front line, he ordered his warriors to kneel. This gave the archers behind them an unobstructed view to fire three sets of arrows in quick succession, taking out at least 500 Saxons. The archers dropped their bows, picked up their swords and shields, then joined the rest of the Britons as Ceredig ordered them to attack.

As the two forces met on the battlefield, a loud noise of screaming and metal clashing could be heard from behind the Saxons. Ceredig's pincer movement plan had worked perfectly.

Behind the attacking Saxons, Cunorix and 400 mounted warriors were using their natural height and weight advantage to barge, slice and stab at the Saxons who had turned to face his attack. Cunorix took great pleasure in killing any Saxon that came close to him.

While the front group of Saxons continued to run towards Ceredig's men, the others had turned round in an attempt to face the Britons on horseback, led by Cunorix. Ceredig's men easily defeated the first group of Saxons, then worked their way through the Saxon forces and came face to face with Cunorix and his mounted warriors.

There were only a few Saxons left fighting and protecting the man who was clearly their leader, Nætanleoð, who was, unusually for a Saxon, wielding a sword. The Britons had them surrounded, so there was no escape, and, one by one, they were killed, until only the Saxon chieftain was left.

Ceredig ordered a halt to fighting and stepped into the clearing along with Cunorix, and they both faced the chieftain.

"I am Ceredig, son of Elisedd, the ruler of these lands before Saxons murdered him whilst he was unarmed. Who are you?" asked Ceredig.

"I am Nætanleoð, chieftain of Onna," was the reply.

"Well, Nætanleoð, you are no longer chieftain of Onna," said Ceredig. "I am going to give you the chance to die in battle, but I do not care whether you die whilst wielding your weapon or not."

"Cunorix, he is all yours," said Ceredig, turning and joining his men.

Cunorix stepped forward, sword and shield in hand. He faced the Saxon chieftain and asked, "Ready to die, Saxon?"

Nætanleoð did not answer. His response was to swing his own sword at Cunorix, who simply deflected it with his shield. The Saxon chieftain continued to attack with his sword, but Cunorix's shield was an effective tool in deflecting any attacks. In reality, he was simply playing with the Saxon, who was older than him by at least a generation.

The onlooking Britons started chanting for Cunorix, with phrases like "Kill him" and "Cunorix".

Eventually, Ceredig began to get bored himself and said, "Enough, Cunorix. End this."

Cunorix was not going to disobey his father. He waited for the next attack by Nætanleoð, deflected it with his shield, turning the chieftain to his right, then brought his own sword underneath his shield arm to stab the sword into an unpadded part of Nætanleoð's body, just under his right shoulder. The sword went through the chieftain's jacket into his ribs, causing him to drop his sword and shield, and fall to his knees.

Nætanleoð looked down at his sword on the ground with a look of panic on his face. He was unarmed and about to die. However, he would not have long to think about that.

Cunorix dropped his shield, grabbed his sword in both hands, then pivoted round swinging his sword round with as much force as he could, slicing the chieftain's head clean off his body.

The chieftain's head fell to the ground and rolled down a small slope before stopping, face upwards. The Britons all started chanting Cunorix's name and then Ceredig's name.

Ceredig had won a great victory over the Saxons, against what most people would have considered insurmountable odds. However, Ceredig knew their work was not done. He raised his arm to call for quiet.

"Well done, men," he said. "We have won a great battle. Now, we need to take the settlement of Onna, which could contain more Saxons. We will head there now and, if anyone raises a weapon towards you, kill them. There could also be women and children inside. They must not be killed, or harmed in any way, unless they attack you. Does everyone understand?"

When it was clear what needed to be done, Ceredig, Cunorix and the Britons marched on the Saxon settlement at Onna. Inside the fortified settlement, they only found around fifty Saxon women and their children gathered in the great hall. They did not put up any fight when Ceredig's men entered.

The scout patrols arrived back in the settlement and reported to Ceredig in the great hall that there were no other Saxon warriors in the area, so the women and children were all that remained of the settlement's community.

Ceredig addressed the women and children, telling them none of the Saxons who left to fight would be returning. He told them that the settlement and these lands would fall under his control, and he would be sending a group of Britons to establish a new community there, with a new chieftain.

He added that they were welcome to remain in Onna, if they accepted his overlordship, but he understood if they would wish to return to their own people to the east. If they chose to return to Suthseaxna, Ceredig said his men would escort them, under his protection, to the border with Suthseaxna at Noviomagus.

One of the women spoke up, saying that, since their men were all dead, they really had no choice but to return to Suthseaxna.

Ceredig told the Saxon women and children to collect their belongings, then return to the great hall and spend the night there, which would be guarded by his Gewisse warriors to ensure their protection.

After sending them off with a select group of his men, Ceredig called for the scout patrols to head to Clausentum and Portus Adurni, to check whether there were any other Saxons still there. Given the number of Saxons they had defeated in battle, he was convinced they must have faced most of the warriors from these other two Saxon settlements, so did not expect to find many Saxons there.

Ceredig then sent a couple of his men out of the settlement on another mission for him.

*

By noon the next day, the first scout patrol returned from Clausentum, reporting to Ceredig and Cunorix that it was empty, with no other Saxons waiting to ambush the Britons arriving there. Ceredig suggested they head to Clausentum and camp there overnight.

Before leaving, he called for the commander of the forces from Searobyrg. Ceredig thanked the commander and his men, saying that he did not think they would be needed for the next stage of Ceredig's journey. He told them they were free to return to Searobyrg with thanks to their chieftain for his support.

However, before they left, as a reward for their support in battle, they were free to take whatever plunder they could find from the bodies of the dead Saxons on the battlefield, on the condition that they disposed of the dead bodies. The commander thanked Ceredig and wished him good fortune against the Saxons, then left to tell his men the good news.

Ceredig also released the warriors from Leucomagus so they could return to their settlement, with his thanks to the chieftain there.

As these warriors headed north, Ceredig and his Gewisse warriors, along with the Saxon women and children, left the hillfort heading east towards Clausentum.

Their short journey to the empty Roman fort only took a few hours and, when they arrived, they were greeted by the scout patrol that had returned from the area around Portus Adurni.

The scouts reported to Ceredig and Cunorix that there was a small contingent of Saxons based at Portus Adurni. The scout leader added that there was a Saxon ship berthed at the pier behind the fort.

Ceredig knew it would be difficult to breach the fort walls, or gates if they were closed. However, he had brought some battle plunder of his own from Onna that he hoped would help avoid any bloodshed, but wanted his Gewisse warriors behind him, just in case the Saxons did not surrender.

*

The next afternoon, Ceredig, Cunorix and a group of 500 Gewisse warriors arrived outside the fort at Portus Adurni and spread out across the peninsula. This was primarily a show of force for any Saxons inside the fort, but also served to cover any possible escape route by land.

When he was sure they had been seen, Ceredig took eight warriors and moved closer to the fort, then stopped. As Ceredig waited, he took in the view of his birthplace. It looked completely different compared to the last time he was there, over fifty years ago, so he closed his eyes and remembered the good days as he played with his friends and Arturius.

After a while, Ceredig was disturbed from his memories when the gates of the fort opened and a small group of Saxons rode out towards them. When they were close to Ceredig's group, they stopped.

One of the Saxons called out, "Who are you, and why do you threaten this fort?"

Ceredig said, "I am Ceredig, ruler of the Gewisse. These are no longer your lands, they once belonged to my father, Elisedd, and they now belong to me. You can remain here and die, or you will leave and return to your own people in the east. The choice is yours."

The Saxons remained silent, so Ceredig continued, "I would prefer you to live, because I want you to deliver a message to King Ælle in Andredescæster. Tell him that Ceredig of the Gewisse is now ruler of these lands, under the terms of the treaty of Badonbyrg. If there are any further Saxon incursions beyond Noviomagus, I will find these invaders and they will not live to see the next day."

Ceredig sat back and watched as the Saxons quietly discussed his words. The discussion became heated, until finally, the man who was clearly their commander held up his hand to silence them.

He turned to Ceredig and said, "You should be aware that over 1,000 Saxons will be returning to this fort very soon."

Ceredig replied, "If you mean the forces at Onna, all I can say is that dead men do not walk. We have come from Onna."

The Saxon was surprised by Ceredig's response, then asked, "How do we know that all the Saxons at Onna are dead?"

Ceredig turned to one of his warriors who was directly behind him and nodded. The warrior handed Ceredig a bloodied cloth bag, containing the item that his ruler had asked him to recover after the battle against the Saxons at Onna.

Ceredig then turned back to face the Saxons, reached into the bag and pulled out the head of Nætanleoð, Onna's Saxon chieftain, by his hair. Ceredig turned the head to make sure the Saxons could recognise Nætanleoð's face.

Ceredig said nothing, letting his actions speak volumes.

The Saxons tried to remain stony-faced, but Ceredig could clearly see them considering the ramifications and straining to show no emotion as they looked at each other. Nætanleoð was known to them.

The Saxon commander then spoke, saying, "We accept your terms and will leave the fort. There is a ship in port on the other side of the fort. If you will allow it, can we make preparations and we will all leave by ship on the next tide?"

"That is acceptable," said Ceredig. "You can start your preparations to leave. Meanwhile, we will remain camped here. You will keep the main gate open from now, so we can see through to the port gate."

"We accept that," said the Saxon commander, who turned round and led his men back to the fort, leaving the main gate open as instructed.

Ceredig ordered his men to make camp and arrange a sentry group to defend any attack from the fort, or the shallow waters around the peninsula.

Ceredig wanted to ensure that the Saxons left for their own lands as they had promised, so, while the Saxons were making their preparations to leave, he sent scout patrols around the eastern side of the estuary to ensure that when the ship left, it headed out of the estuary towards Andrédescæster.

With nothing left to do but wait, Ceredig went over and sat on a fallen tree trunk, facing the open main gate of the fort, watching the place where he was born, remembering how it looked then and recalling the happy memories of his early years living there.

It felt like everything had finally come round full circle. He had grown up and succeeded his father as ruler of the Gewisse, his uncle had killed the man who had killed his father and brother, and he had now reclaimed the lands his father had ruled when he was born. Ceredig felt very emotional, thinking of all those who had not been able to see this moment. He had fulfilled his destiny.

Ceredig sat there for what seemed like hours and was so lost in thought, that it took Cunorix calling his father's name to bring him back to the present.

"Father," said Cunorix, "the Saxon ship is leaving. I am taking fifty men into the fort to make sure that no Saxon remains to attack us. Do you want to join us?"

Ceredig said, "Yes, I will join you. Just give me a few minutes to get my old legs moving again."

Once he had stood up, Ceredig walked his horse into the empty fort of Portus Adurni. Gone were the older Roman buildings, including the villa that had been his home. In their place were some wooden-built Saxon houses, and a great hall for the chieftain.

Ceredig spent the rest of the day wandering around the fort, walking around the sections of the walls that remained passable and then walking around the outside of the fort, reminiscing about his early years at Portus Adurni, as well as that fateful day when he and Arturius had left the fort and headed into exile, with Arturius promising to make him a great warrior who would rid these lands of the Saxons. How Ceredig wished that Arturius had lived to be with him today.

By mid-afternoon, the remaining one hundred Gewisse warriors, who had been escorting the women and children from Onna, arrived at Portus Adurni. Ceredig had decided to remain in Portus Adurni for another night, before heading eastward to Noviomagus to return the Saxon women and children to their own lands.

That evening, whilst Ceredig, Cunorix, his commanders, and the women and children from Onna, were enjoying a meal in the great hall, the Saxon woman who had spoken for them previously approached Ceredig.

She told him that the women had been watching Ceredig and his men, since their 'capture' at Onna, and the kind treatment of the Saxon women and children by the Gewisse since then. They had been talking and decided that it made no difference to them where they lived. Therefore, if Ceredig agreed, they would like to remain in the nearest occupied settlement, and would serve the chieftain if he were agreeable and promised to ensure the safe upbringing of their children.

Ceredig was delighted with their request. He told the woman that he had planned to establish Portus Adurni as a permanent garrison for a group of Gewisse warriors to protect the southern coastline. It would make life easier for the men who were assigned to the fort if the women remained to help. When the woman agreed to this offer, Ceredig said that he hoped they would be happy with their new life.

*

The following morning, Ceredig appointed one of his commanders, Trystan, to be chieftain of Portus Adurni and assigned him command of an initial force of one hundred Gewisse warriors who would be stationed there. Ceredig also told Trystan of the Saxon women's agreement to remain as servants there, and wished him and his men good fortune in their new role defending the southern coastline from any Saxon attacks from the east, or by ship.

Content that he was leaving his birthplace in safe hands, Ceredig ordered the rest of the Gewisse to head back north to Ventacæster. Everyone was in good spirits after their victory, so the journey passed quickly and they were crossing the bridge into the citadel late in the afternoon.

Cunorix was delighted to see Hildis, so Ceredig told him to go and spend time with her. Meanwhile, Ceredig would hold a council meeting with Coel and the elders, to inform them of the events that took place, the clearance of the Saxon settlements at Onna and Clausentum, and the establishment of a Gewisse settlement at Portus Adurni.

Ceredig told them he was concerned that the fortified settlement at Onna was lying empty, and suggested that some of the younger Jutes might want to relocate to Onna and establish a community there. It would help if some of the Jutes who had trained as Gewisse joined them too. The elders said they would discuss this within their families and let Lord Ceredig know if there were any volunteers.

Coel then gave Ceredig an update on the ongoing improvements to the derelict buildings within the citadel, some of which needed demolition, whilst others could be repaired.

Satisfied that everything was in hand, Ceredig retired to his room. He realised that his age was catching up on him, as the last week had taken a lot out of him.

Two days later, Hildis's father came to speak with Ceredig. He informed him that a group of one hundred Jutes were interested in relocating to Onna.

Ceredig asked whether there was anyone in that group who would make an appropriate chieftain. The elder suggested one man from the group, a kinsman of Hildis, called Wihtgar. Ceredig remembered this Wihtgar distinguishing himself in the recent battle victory against the Saxons at Onna.

Ceredig thought he sounded perfect, but asked the elder to bring Wihtgar to him, so he could give Wihtgar's appointment as chieftain his approval.

Ceredig had an enjoyable discussion with Wihtgar and thought he would make a great chieftain for the new settlement at Onna.

*

A week later, Wihtgar led one hundred Jutes, mostly young families, as they left Ventacæster, bound for Onna. Before they left, Ceredig told Wihtgar that he should not consider himself in isolation, as he would have the full support of the Gewisse at Ventacæster or Portus Adurni to call upon if he ever needed help.

That evening, Ceredig hosted an evening meal with Cunorix, Hildis, her father and Coel and told them about his future plans. Ceredig told them that the past few months had made it clear to him that he was too old to be able to move swiftly around the whole of his territory as needed. Therefore, he asked Cunorix if he would be happy to remain in Ventacæster as regional chieftain.

Cunorix would have overall control over the southern region of his father's lands, from Calleva down to the coast, and would be tasked with increasing the size of the Gewisse force of warriors there. He would also be free to develop Ventacæster as his regional capital and establish a local council of chieftains to ensure security for the peoples of the southern region.

Naturally, Cunorix jumped at the chance to be his own ruler, especially of the lands where his father and wife were born. He did not mention that this was something that had been on his mind too.

Coel, the citadel commander, was also delighted to have Cunorix living in Ventacæster as his chieftain, especially as he had been reassured that his role in running the administration of the citadel would be unaffected.

And so, a few days later, Ceredig led 300 Gewisse warriors out of the east gate of Ventacæster, bound for Calleva, then home to Durocastrum.

Ceredig gave Cunorix and Hildis a hug before leaving, and wished them both peace, prosperity and happiness in their new life at Ventacæster, but reassured them that he and Ophelia would be regular visitors.

13

CEREDIG, KING OF THE GEWISSE

The *Anglo-Saxon Chronicle* records that, in AD 519, "Cerdic and Cynric undertook the government of the West Saxons" and Cerdic was crowned king at Ventacæster.

After Ceredig's victory against the South Saxons, King Ælle appeared to have received the message that the Gewisse controlled lands to the west of Noviomagus. As a result, there were no attempts by the Saxons to reclaim Portus Adurni, Clausentum or Onna over the next ten years.

Ceredig's younger son, Cunedda, was now into his twenties and was taking an increasingly more active role in ruling the northern region from Durocastrum on his father's behalf. As a result, Ceredig and Ophelia had more time to visit Ventacæster, especially when they received happy news from Cunorix and Hildis about the birth of his first son, called Ceawlin, followed two years later by a second son, called Cuthwulf.

Ceredig and Ophelia made the trip down to Ventacæster to see Cunorix, Hildis and their grandsons after each birth, with regular trips over the following years.

Sadly, after Ceredig and Ophelia returned from one trip to see Cunorix, Hildis and their grandchildren, Ophelia became gravely ill. Despite all the efforts of the local healers, they could not identify the cause and she died shortly afterwards.

Ophelia's death hit Ceredig very hard. She had been his friend in Darioritum before becoming his wife, so his bond with her was greater than love alone.

Ceredig mourned her loss heavily. After her burial, he retired to his room, rarely leaving it, and he ate very little of the food that had been brought to him.

Cunedda was concerned, so he sent word of his father's self-imposed seclusion to Cunorix, who came to Durocastrum and insisted that his father accompany him back to Ventacæster for a while, where he could spend time with his grandchildren. Eventually, Ceredig agreed to travel to Ventacæster with Cunorix and the fifty Gewisse warriors his son had brought for protection.

In the end, it proved to be the right decision, because it was the time that Ceredig spent with Ceawlin and Cuthwulf that slowly brought him out of his depression, so he was ready when the next challenge to his authority came from the south.

*

One afternoon, while Ceredig was walking around the walls of the citadel, he heard a commotion from the southern gate. When he reached the gate, he saw a messenger had arrived, and he looked terrified.

Ceredig hurried to the great hall, where he expected the messenger would be taken. As he arrived, Cunorix, Coel and the elders were also there, having heard the news of the messenger's arrival.

Hildis's father knew the messenger and asked him by name what was his news.

"We… we… we were attacked," he said, spluttering the words out.

"What happened?" asked Cunorix.

"I had been returning to the settlement when I saw it all happen," replied the messenger. "They killed over thirty of our people while they were out in the fields tending to the crops. Our people were unarmed and these Saxons murdered them in cold blood. Why would they do that?"

"Are there any survivors?" asked Hildis's father.

"Yes," was the response. "The rest of our people managed to reach the safety of Onna's palisade walls, but they are trapped inside under siege. I came straight here because I do not know how long they will last inside the wooden walls of the settlement."

"How on earth did Saxons get to Onna without being noticed by the patrols out of Portus Adurni?" asked Coel.

"Were they on horseback?" Ceredig asked the messenger.

"No, my lord," was the messenger's reply.

"How many attackers were there?" asked Ceredig.

"Probably no more than 500 men, my lord," said the messenger.

"I doubt it was Saxons," said Ceredig.

"What makes you think that, Father?" asked Cunorix.

"The Saxons have never made any attack in the past ten years," replied Ceredig. "Even after King Ælle died, his son, Cissa, has shown no sign of seeking to expand his kingdom in this direction. If he did, he would have tried to take Portus Adurni first, and 500 Saxons would have been seen travelling over land or sea if they had come either from Suthseaxna, or from Gaul. This is something different."

Ceredig was aware that King Uthr of the Durotriges, the weak son of Ambrosius, had died, or been killed, a few years ago. Uthr did not have any children or surviving brothers, so he left his kingdom without a natural successor. As a result, the regional chieftains were showing their own ambitions for independent rule and were seeking to establish, perhaps even expand, their own region. On that basis, Ceredig had a good idea where to look first.

He said, "We need to head down to Onna immediately to relieve those trapped there, but I want a scout patrol to head to Searobyrg to see what is happening there. There is a new chieftain of Searobyrg and, whilst the previous chieftain was a good ruler, I suspect the new one is more aggressive and ambitious. The scout patrols will be able to find out what type of chieftain we are facing, but I am confident that he is responsible for the attack at Onna, even if he is not leading it."

Turning to Coel, Ceredig said, "Prepare as many men as we can spare for battle. Cunorix and I will deal with these Britons. And send out the scout patrols immediately. We need to know what is going on at Searobyrg and Onna."

Cunorix was delighted to see passion from his father again. The great ruler of the Gewisse was back!

By early evening, Ceredig, Cunorix and 400 Gewisse warriors came upon the settlement at Onna, but found the people in the process of repairing damage to the settlement and burying the dead.

Wihtgar, the chieftain, informed Ceredig that the attackers had withdrawn as soon as they had seen the advance Gewisse scout patrol group appear on the hill that overlooked the settlement.

The scout patrol leader reported that he had sent some men to follow the direction that the attackers took, through the forest, possibly towards the old Roman army road that led to Searobyrg.

Ceredig told Cunorix and his commanders that they needed to pursue the attackers and catch them before they reached safety at Searobyrg. Since the attackers were on foot, they would not be travelling at any speed and would need to camp for the night, somewhere on the escarpment, before dropping down into the valley to join the old Roman army road to Searobyrg.

There were very few clouds in the sky, so Ceredig knew it would be a clear, albeit cold, night, with the moon providing light for their journey. They would use the forest to protect their approach, where possible, and rest for a few hours before attacking the Britons in the early hours of the following morning.

Ceredig's plan worked perfectly. One of the scouts who had pursued the attackers was returning to Onna and came across Ceredig and his men. He reported that it was

Britons from Searobyrg who had attacked Onna, and they had camped on the escarpment, roughly five miles north of their current position. He also confirmed to Ceredig that the Britons were not on horseback, so would not escape Ceredig's mounted Gewisse warriors in the event of an attack.

When they reached within two miles of the encamped Britons, Ceredig ordered a 'silent camp', which meant that there should be no fires or significant noise that would carry in the silence of the night.

As the morning birdsong started and first glimpse of light could be seen through the trees, Ceredig ordered his men to quietly mount their horses and ride towards the Britons' encampment.

The Britons from Searobyrg, who had camped overnight on the escarpment, were starting to wake and became aware of a rising noise coming from the forest behind them. Realising what the sound was, they immediately began to arm themselves, turning to look at their commander for orders.

They did not consider scattering into the forest, where being on foot might have given them a slightly better chance against men on horseback. Instead, their commander ordered them to run down the trail leading to the old Roman bridge across the river, which would act as a bottleneck for the advancing horsemen.

Sadly, his delay in making a decision came too late, as Ceredig and his warriors suddenly appeared out of the forest, riding at full gallop towards them, swords out ready to attack.

The Britons had nothing to offer against such a force of strength and speed from seasoned warriors like the Gewisse. As a result, Ceredig and his men carved through them with such ease that even they could scarcely believe it. It was a massacre!

After killing every single Briton, Ceredig's men searched for their chieftain, believing that he would have been the leader of these attackers. However, his body could not be found. *That probably explains why these Britons made such poor decisions*, thought Ceredig.

They found the five best-dressed warriors amongst the dead, identifiable by the higher-quality battledress and swords they carried, and put their bodies on a sled that they hastily made out of some trees that had been felled.

Having achieved their objective, Ceredig and his men took some time to rest and eat a morning meal, some of which was from the provisions they found in the Britons' camp. When they were ready, the Gewisse crossed over the old Roman bridge and headed north, up the old Roman army trackway to Searobyrg.

*

By early afternoon, Ceredig and the Gewisse had arrived at the flat plain to the south of the hillfort at Searobyrg and made camp.

Searobyrg hillfort had been built atop a large mound that overlooked the area. It was not the highest point, but the steep slopes of the mound were practically impossible to climb, making it easily defendable. There was also a large man-made ditch around the foot of the mound that made an ideal killing ground in the event of an attack.

Ceredig knew that his forces had no chance of overwhelming the hillfort at either of the entrance gates, so they remained and waited until they were spotted by sentries from the wooden palisade walls around the hillfort.

After an hour, a group of fifty men rode out of the hillfort and came towards Ceredig's group. In the middle of the group was the new chieftain, whom Ceredig recognised from the Britons of Searobyrg who had helped the Gewisse defeat the Saxons at Onna eleven years ago.

Ceredig took fifty of his men forward to meet them.

"What brings such a large group of Gewisse warriors to my lands, Lord Ceredig?" said the chieftain.

"We are just returning some of your lost property," was Ceredig's reply. "We found it to the south of here and thought we should return it to its rightful home."

"Well, what is it?" responded the chieftain.

Ceredig called to Cunorix within the main group of Gewisse warriors. Within seconds, one of Ceredig's men rode out from the group, pulling the sled. The rider swung round in front of Ceredig, releasing the rope that held the sled as he passed in front of his leader. The sled dropped to the ground, while the rider continued round the other side of Ceredig's group and returned to join up with Cunorix and the rest of the Gewisse.

The chieftain looked down at the five bodies of his dead commanders lying on the sled.

"I believe these are yours," said Ceredig, looking the chieftain directly in the eyes for any clue to whether any of the men were related, perhaps a son. There was only disappointment from the chieftain.

"I cannot believe that you did not know what your own men were doing when they attacked my settlement at Onna," continued Ceredig. "Eleven years ago, you and your men helped me defeat the Saxons who had taken over the settlement on lands that were mine, but that did not give you the right to plunder it whenever you wanted. If it ever happens again, the same thing will happen, only I will come for you too, and your hillfort will not protect you."

Again, Ceredig watched the chieftain take in the threat that he had promised in response to further incursions.

He then continued, "Whilst you are free to use the old Roman army trackway to reach your lands to the south, the lands on the escarpment and forest to the east of it are my lands and you will not venture there ever again. And while we are discussing our borders, Leucomagus is also within my borders and is protected, so I never want to hear that you have paid this settlement a visit either.

"Do we understand each other?" he added.

The chieftain looked up at Ceredig and said, "You are an old man, Lord Ceredig, so I will accept your terms for now. However, you will not be a ruler forever and, when you die, we will revisit the border lines between our kingdoms."

The chieftain signalled to one of his men, who rode forward, dismounted and picked up the end of the sled, attaching it to his horse's saddle, then mounted up and rode the sled back to the hillfort.

"You are not a king," said Ceredig. "However, if you ever rise to become king, you should know that my son, Cunorix, is a great warrior and will defend our lands with equal resolve. If you wish to dispute the borders after my death, do not underestimate Cunorix and the Gewisse."

The chieftain turned and led his men back to the hillfort.

Satisfied that his western land border had been clearly defined with his neighbouring ruler, Ceredig led his men away to the east, taking the old Roman road that led up and over the escarpment to Ventacæster. After they were out of sight of the hillfort, Ceredig stopped his forces.

He told one of his commanders to take one hundred men and head south to Onna. They were to remain there for the next month, just in case the chieftain from Searobyrg decided to make another attack there. It was just a precaution, and Ceredig did not expect any further attacks, but he was also going to arrange regular patrols to Onna.

*

Six months later, Ceredig was returning from a visit to see his youngest son, Cunedda, in Durocastrum. Cunedda had decided to accompany his father to Ventacæster after Cunorix had sent them a message to say he had called a council meeting of all the chieftains and fort commanders from the region, including those from Leucomagus, Onna, Portus Adurni and Vindomis, as well as commanders from Calleva, Durocastrum, Alaunacæster and Lactodurum.

Ceredig was confused by Cunorix's lack of information for the need to hold a meeting, so he went to look for Cunorix when he arrived in Ventacæster. Cunorix could not be found, but Ceredig found Coel and asked him what was going on. Coel feigned ignorance, but suggested they might find the answer in the great hall.

As Ceredig and Coel approached the entrance to the great hall, he could see large banners, bearing his family symbol of the gold rampant dragon on the red background, hanging all over the place. *Very extravagant for a council meeting*, thought Ceredig.

When Coel led Ceredig into the great hall, a huge roar arose from a huge crowd of people in the hall. At the end of the aisle, leading up to the dais where the top table would normally be located, stood a large ornate wooden chair that looked more like a throne. Ceredig could not remember ever seeing that chair as Coel led him up the aisle.

As he approached the dais, Cunorix and Cunedda stepped into view and stood either side of the ornate chair.

"Cunorix, what is going on?" asked Ceredig.

"Patience, Father," replied Cunorix. "Everything will become clear soon."

As Coel escorted him onto the dais towards the large ornate chair, Ceredig spotted the various chieftains and commanders sitting in chairs on both sides of the dais from the ornate chair, with an empty chair on either side for his sons.

Cunorix encouraged his father to sit in the ornate chair, then raised his hand to calm everyone down and bring silence to the room. When there was a hush around the room, he spoke.

"Thank you all for coming here today," he said. "It pleases me no end to see my father confused for once, given he has shown so much wisdom and foresight in ruling these lands over the past twenty-four years.

"For those who have known Lord Ceredig since he became ruler of the Gewisse in Darioritum fifty years ago, his leadership has been impressive. However, today's event has taken over sixty years to come to fruition, ever since, as a young boy, he was forced to leave these lands after my grandfather's murder on the order of the Saxon king Hengest.

"Six months ago, after defeating a challenge to his rule over these lands by the chieftain of Searobyrg, Lord Ceredig finally consolidated his control over the region that his father had once ruled. At that point, I was reminded of a comment made by one of the elders of this citadel many years ago.

"This elder described being part of Lord Ceredig's 'kingdom'. At the time, my father did not think it was the right time to proclaim himself king. Today is the right time. However, knowing my father, he would not consider himself a king unless it was by consent of the people he ruled.

"When I approached the chieftains and commanders of all the major settlements under my father's rule, there was immediate consensus with my plan. And that is what brings us here today.

"In this great hall are representatives of these settlements across my father's lands, from Lactodurum in the north, to Portus Adurni in the south. We have Britons, Armoricans, Jutes and Saxons who have all willingly accepted his rule. They are Gewisse warriors, farmers, craftsmen, servants, elders and chieftains. The one crucial thing is that they are all considered equal under my father's rule.

"The lands under Lord Ceredig's rule have no name to proclaim as a kingdom, but, knowing my father, he would not want to be known as king of a region. He would want to be known as a king of his people. This kingdom has emerged from a combination of people from different origins across Britannia, integrating to create something stronger than their individual communities. They share this identity and strength with the militia unit of elite warriors called the Gewisse, from which Lord Ceredig was descended. So, I think it only appropriate to call on everyone here to proclaim my father, as..."

Then unsheathing his sword and raising it up high, Cunorix shouted, "Ceredig, King of the Gewisse!"

Everyone in the hall shouted, in response, "Ceredig, King of the Gewisse!"

Then, everyone knelt down and bowed their heads. Cunorix turned to his father, then knelt and bowed his head towards him.

Ceredig stood from his chair and placed his hand on his son's shoulder to signal him to stand. He turned to everyone in the hall and commanded, "Arise, everyone!"

When everyone was standing, Ceredig continued, "I thank you for granting me this honour. However, I would not be here without the support of my eldest son,

Cunorix, who has been a great commander of the Gewisse in my name when needed, and taken steps to ensure the safety and protection of everyone who lives on our lands. Therefore, if you proclaim me as king, you also proclaim Cunorix as my rightful heir. So, if anyone would challenge his right as my successor, let them speak now."

There was silence within the hall.

Cunorix stepped forward, told his father to sit down, then turned to the audience and said, "We have a king, and he has a throne. But a king needs a golden crown."

He signalled to the side of the dais, where a goldsmith was waiting. The smith carried a golden band forward and handed it to Cunorix, then withdrew to the side of the dais. Cunorix held the crown aloft and, placing it on his father's head, he said, "This crown bears the image of a rampant dragon carved on the front to symbolise the origins of the family of King Ceredig."

Cunorix then produced a gold ring, which had a gold dragon carved in a roundel, with red glass insets. He pushed the ring onto his father's right middle finger.

Cunorix then knelt in front of the newly crowned king, held the ringed hand and kissed the ring, saying, "My king, I swear allegiance to you for as long as you reign."

He stepped back, then Cunedda, the chieftains and commanders all stepped forward one by one, knelt in front of Ceredig and swore their oath of fealty to King Ceredig.

The chieftains and commanders then raised their swords into the air and shouted, "All hail Ceredig, King of the Gewisse!"

The rest of the people in the great hall cheered the proclamation in response, then, over the next three hours, everyone who had been in the great hall stepped forward to kneel, kiss the royal gold ring and swear their own allegiance to the king.

That evening, there was a huge banquet in the great hall, with celebrations going on around the citadel. It had been a long day, but Ceredig went to sleep that night at peace with himself for the first time in many years.

The peace he had forged would reverberate across his new kingdom for the next nine years, bringing great prosperity to everyone.

14

A DYNASTY BEGINS

The *Anglo-Saxon Chronicle* records that Cerdic
reigned for fifteen years, until AD 534, when "this year
died Cerdic, the first king of the West-Saxons" and was
succeeded by his son.

Eight years after he was crowned king, and now in his
late seventies, Ceredig was spending most of his time
at Ventacæster with his grandchildren, while Cunorix and
Cunedda were ruling the kingdom in his name.

Cunorix was spending most of his time touring the
kingdom, making regular visits to all the major settlements,
hearing from the local chieftains about their communities,
resolving local disputes and identifying activities that
needed additional help. In every visit, he found a prosperous
community, with a growing populace and more young men
volunteering to become a Gewisse warrior.

The Gewisse were training these potential warriors in
Alaunacæster, Calleva, Ventacæster and Portus Adurni,
and the standard requirement to become one of the
Gewisse was becoming higher. Any men who were not
selected to become a Gewisse warrior became part of the
defensive militia within their own communities.

When Cunorix informed his father that he was making a trip up north to visit Durocastrum, Ceredig said he wanted to accompany his son. It had been many years since he had last visited the original capital of his lands, and he wanted to see how much it had changed. He also wanted to see his youngest son, Cunedda, who had been ruling the northern region in his father's name.

So, the following week, Ceredig, Cunorix and 500 Gewisse warriors travelled north to Calleva for an overnight stop, before heading to Durocastrum the following day.

When they arrived, King Ceredig was welcomed into Durocastrum by his son, the elders and the people of the settlement, who lined the streets to welcome their king.

Ceredig was amazed to see so many people living there and asked Cunedda for a tour of the whole settlement whenever possible. His youngest son told him he would need to do it on horseback as the settlement had spread north and west, beyond the walls of the old Roman fort, and there were a number of smaller settlements further away from the town that had been established to provide homes for the expanding population.

That evening, there was a banquet in the great hall to celebrate the visit of the king. During the meal, Ceredig heard that Jemmett, the town elder whom he had met when he first arrived in Durocastrum after taking control of these lands, had died a few years back. It was another reminder of the passing years and the mortality of man that was also Ceredig's ultimate destiny.

The next morning, Cunedda and his father rode out of Durocastrum for a tour of the settlement, heading out of the north gate, along with a protective guard of twenty Gewisse warriors. After visiting the houses north of the fort, they then followed a new road track to the west of the fort, finding a large settlement further out, where the married Gewisse warriors had originally established a small hamlet after Ceredig's arrival in Durocastrum. Ceredig was delighted to see such prosperity there and enjoyed talking to the people they came across on their tour.

Whilst Ceredig was getting to know Durocastrum again, Cunorix had left with 400 Gewisse warriors, heading for Alaunacæster, then Lactodurum at the northern border of their kingdom.

*

When Cunorix and his men arrived in Alaunacæster, they found the fort was abuzz, with the Gewisse warriors based there preparing to depart.

The commander was delighted to see Cunorix and especially the 400 men he had brought with him. He told Cunorix that a Gewisse scout patrol from Alaunacæster had spotted a large group of 500 Saxons, who had made an incursion into the Gewisse's lands, travelling up the old Roman road of Wætling Street from Verulamium, pillaging smaller settlements as they were heading north-west towards Alaunacæster. The scouts reported that they had stopped about a day's march from Alaunacæster, presumably to camp overnight.

The Alaunacæster commander knew that area, and

the location of the Saxons' camp also gave them the option to change direction the next day, to head west towards Durocastrum instead. Although he felt that they were more likely to target the more remote settlement at Alaunacæster first, to take out the Gewisse warriors based there, before heading south to attack Durocastrum, the commander felt it was important that they defeat the Saxons as soon as possible.

The commander informed Cunorix that the scout patrol had also sent a messenger to Durocastrum to warn them, just in case the Saxons decided to take the southwestern road to Durocastrum the next day.

Cunorix realised that the messenger would have reached Durocastrum by now and, as soon as his father heard the news, he would be preparing to lead a force of Gewisse warriors to face the Saxons.

"We need to draw the Saxons towards us," Cunorix said. "Since you are already prepared, send 200 men down the old Roman road immediately. These men should stop when they see the Saxon campfires, which I am sure the Saxons will be using, as they have no reason to hide their presence. The Saxons will have their own scouts watching for any potential attacks, and they will report an estimate of numbers far less than the Saxons."

"What if they decide to attack, my lord?" asked the fort commander.

"That is my hope," said Cunorix. "If so, it will be at first light. Your men should have scouts ready to warn them if the Saxons prepare to attack, so they can retreat, drawing the Saxons north. In the meantime, we will have rested and will follow in the early hours of the morning, arriving just in time to reinforce your men as the Saxons are heading north towards them."

Meanwhile, back in Durocastrum, the Alaunacæster messenger had arrived and reported the news about the Saxons being camped overnight about a day's march from Durocastrum, from where they could head in their direction in the morning.

As predicted by Cunorix, Ceredig and Cunedda immediately started organising as many Gewisse warriors as they could. In the end, they gathered 400 men, including Ceredig's own protective unit of one hundred men. Ceredig planned to lead the force from Durocastrum out at first light, so they were halfway towards the Saxons before they headed on the road towards Durocastrum. Either way, Ceredig and his Gewisse warriors would be ready for them.

*

The Saxon leader was awoken by a scout in the early hours and told that a force of Britons from Alaunacæster had been spotted about five miles away from their position and appeared to be waiting for something.

The Saxon leader thought the Britons must have come from Alaunacæster and stopped as soon as they had seen the fires from the large camp ahead of them, and had most likely sent for reinforcements, having realised they were near a large Saxon camp.

Since they had lost the element of surprise, the Saxon

leader felt that heading for Durocastrum would be the better way to go. It was unlikely to have more than 300 men and may not have been warned of the Saxons' presence in the area yet.

The Saxon leader ordered his men to quietly prepare to leave, and they headed west towards Durocastrum. They would leave the campfires lit, to make it look like they were still asleep and prevent an attack before they were well away.

He had decided that they should take a route less travelled to Durocastrum that would keep them off the main road, hoping they might avoid any possible reinforcements heading from Durocastrum in the unlikely event that they had been pre-warned.

When Cunorix and the Gewisse warriors reached the advance group from Alaunacæster, just after first light, they discovered that the Saxons had not taken the bait. A scout patrol had just arrived back in the camp to say that the Saxons had left their camp during the night, presumably heading west towards Durocastrum.

Cunorix sighed. He knew it was highly likely that his father and his Gewisse forces would be on their way from Durocastrum, but he did not know how many men would be with him.

"We need to head across country to cut the Saxons off," he said. "We may have time to catch them. We may even meet at the same time as the force coming from Durocastrum and would have superior numbers that will overwhelm the Saxons. Tell the men to head south, down that trackway, and send the scouts ahead to find the Saxons, and the king. Make sure the king knows we are on the way."

The Gewisse scouts headed off immediately, with Cunorix and the rest of the Gewisse, now numbering 800 men, following behind.

*

The Saxons were just over seven miles west of their overnight camp, when their scouts reported a very large number of Britons on horseback were heading towards them from the north.

The Saxon leader decided that they must be the reinforcements from Alaunacæster that he had suspected would be coming. He had no choice now, so he ordered his men to stop and prepare for battle.

When he saw the river nearby, the Saxon leader ordered his men to cross over it. Since the Britons were on horseback, the river would force them to halt any downhill charge to cross the river, as they would not know how deep it was. This would give the Saxons a slight advantage, so they picked the best position that they could, set up their shield wall and prepared for the onslaught they were about to face.

When the Britons appeared at the top of the hill, the Saxon leader realised that they were greatly outnumbered. He was confused. Where did the Britons from Alaunacæster get such numbers? It was too late to retreat, and there was nowhere to go, even if they wanted to run. All the Saxons could do was face up to the Britons and hope for a miracle.

The Saxon leader watched as the Britons came charging towards the Saxon shield wall with their spears at the ready, but smiled as they had to slow down as soon as they saw the river.

Unfortunately, the Saxon leader then noticed another group of Britons on horseback, coming at them from behind. It must be the force from Durocastrum. Outnumbered and outflanked, he realised that they did not stand a chance. With resignation, he ordered his men to set up shield walls on both flanks. He knew they were facing defeat and, most likely, death.

In the end, it was an easy victory for Ceredig, whose men picked off the Saxons before they could organise their shield wall against the new front, with Cunorix's forces crossing the river to pick off any retreating Saxons.

Father and son met each other on the battlefield when every Saxon warrior was killed. After removing any valuables, the Gewisse took the dead Saxon bodies up to the top of the nearest hill, piled them up high and set them on fire.

After they had discussed what had happened, Ceredig and his men left, returning to Durocastrum. Cunorix and the men from Alaunacæster returned there, and Cunorix continued with the final stage of his tour up to Lactodurum, the most northerly settlement in the kingdom.

Cunorix returned to Durocastrum a few weeks later to collect his father, and then they headed back to Ventacæster.

*

Over the next seven years, there were no further incursions by Saxons or Britons into Ceredig's kingdom. This peace allowed his people to prosper and expand their settlements.

Ceredig was now in his eighties, and his age was definitely catching up with him. He began to rely more heavily on Cunorix, who was now the effective ruler of the Gewisse, and had learned to delegate a lot of the work to his chieftains and commanders in each of the major settlements up and down the kingdom.

Ceredig rarely left Ventacæster, preferring to spend most of his time telling his grandsons, Ceawlin and Cuthwulf, about their family's history and the origins of the Gewisse. They learned about their great-grandfather, Elisedd, who ruled the Gewisse from Portus Adurni before his murder by the first Saxons to come to Britannia, as well as Ceredig's own life growing up in Armorica, then as Gewisse ruler and chieftain of Darioritum, before returning to Britannia to help Britons defeat the Saxons at the battle of Badonbyrg, and the expansion of the lands under his rule before he became King of the Gewisse.

Ceawlin and Cuthwulf loved hearing their grandfather's stories as they were growing up, but were now in their late teens and had become Gewisse warriors. This meant that they had less time to spend with Ceredig.

*

One morning, the sentries around the walls of the citadel were surprised that Ceredig had not made a tour of the walls like he did every other morning. When Coel, the citadel commander, appeared on the wall, they asked him if there was any reason why the king had not made an appearance that morning.

Meanwhile, the servants had become concerned that Ceredig had not called for food, so one of them informed Hildis just in case she had an explanation. She had no idea, so made her way to the king's room.

She met Coel in the corridor as they were both heading to see why Ceredig had not risen that morning. They both entered the king's room and found Ceredig motionless in his bed. He appeared to have died peacefully in his sleep during the night.

Hildis and Coel immediately found Cunorix and explained what had happened. After confirming with his own eyes, Cunorix informed Ceawlin and Cuthwulf, and sent a messenger to Cunedda at Durocastrum with a sealed letter to let him know of his father's death.

The elders were called to the royal villa and informed of the news. Then, the household staff were told what had happened, and word quickly spread around the citadel that the king was dead.

The scout patrol commander was tasked with sending messengers to every settlement of Ceredig's kingdom to let his people know of the king's death. They were informed that a royal burial would take place in a week's time.

The elders, chieftains and fort commanders were also advised that a council meeting would be held the day after the king's burial, to discuss the kingdom's succession and confirm Cunorix as the next King of the Gewisse, in line with Ceredig's wishes when he was crowned king.

*

A week later, all the chieftains, commanders and elders and their families and representatives from settlements across the kingdom, were gathered in the great hall of Ventacæster, where Ceredig's body had lain since his death, allowing the people of his kingdom to come and honour their king if that was their wish.

It was a fine, sunny day, and the streets of the citadel, from the great hall up to the western gate and beyond, were lined by the public, waiting to see the procession as the king was taken to be buried.

Cunorix was grateful that his father had shown the foresight to consider his death at some point in the future and already chosen the location for his burial place.

Five miles to the west of Ventacæster, there was a long ridge that was visible from the old Roman road to Searobyrg. Ceredig had found the highest point in the area around Ventacæster, with wonderful views over the region, and decided that it was the perfect location for the burial mound of a king.

As soon as Ceredig died, Cunorix ordered the land around the planned burial barrow to be cleared, including the felling of any trees that would hinder the view of the burial barrow. Within the week, a large round burial barrow had been partially built, around a wood-walled box-like space, ready to receive the king's body and his traditional burial goods.

Although the burial space was only an eight-foot by eight-foot square, the overall burial barrow would be over a hundred feet wide and twenty feet high once finished, with a ditch around the outside.

When as many people as possible were crowded in the hall, Cunorix stepped up onto the dais, beside the body of his father, and raised his hand for silence. When the great hall was quiet, Cunorix spoke.

"Thank you, everyone, for coming here today to celebrate the life of my father, Ceredig, first King of the Gewisse, who has ruled these lands for over twenty-five years, although only fifteen years as king.

"King Ceredig lived for a magnificent eighty-four years, which has been filled with great and happy occasions, although he also faced some significant challenges. Yet, it took all of these events to create the man who has single-mindedly devoted his life to restoring his father's lands and creating the kingdom of the Gewisse.

"He was the youngest-born son of Elisedd, ruler of the Gewisse, and the chieftain who ruled these lands over eighty years ago, and protected his people from the Saxons, who first came to Britannia to help defend us from invaders and then began to oppress us.

"The king was only a young boy when his father and brother were brutally murdered by Hengest and the Saxons at Vespasian's Camp, forcing Ceredig to flee Portus Adurni, his place of birth, with his mother, Lavena, great friend and protector, Arturius, and the Gewisse warriors, when the Saxons threatened their very lives.

"After spending a few years at Glevum, the king and his

mother were forced to flee again, this time for new lives in Armorica, where Ceredig grew up to become leader of the Gewisse, succeeding his father, then becoming chieftain of Darioritum. Whilst living there, Ceredig met and married my mother, Ophelia, who sadly died seventeen years ago.

"Ceredig returned to Britannia and led the Gewisse, fighting with the Britons, under King Ambrosius Aurelianus, against the Saxons at the battle of Badonbyrg. My father's reward for his role in their victory, was to be granted lands to the north, around Durocastrum, and the promise he could, one day, reclaim the rest of his family's former lands.

"In the following thirty-nine years, Ceredig consolidated his control over the lands that his father had once ruled and was appointed our king, by proclamation, fifteen years ago.

"During these years, King Ceredig has been a strong, fair and wise ruler, protecting the people of this kingdom from anyone who threatened our peace. As a result, we are a prosperous kingdom, with a growing population and a powerful army of Gewisse warriors to defend our people from any threats to our peace.

"The king is survived by his two sons, myself and Cunedda, as well as two grandsons, Ceawlin and Cuthwulf, who are all dedicated to continuing his legacy. So, for the last time, I ask you all to proclaim him…"

Cunorix then removed his sword, raised it upwards and shouted, "Hail, Ceredig, King of the Gewisse!"

The whole crowd in the great hall responded, shouting, "Hail, Ceredig, King of the Gewisse!"

Cunorix turned towards his father's body and bowed to it, then knelt down, still holding his sword in his hands, and bowed his head. The crowd also knelt down and bowed their heads.

After a moment of contemplation, Cunorix stood up and the crowd also stood.

Cunorix, Cunedda, Ceawlin and Cuthwulf, along with Coel, the citadel commander, and Trystan, the chieftain of Portus Adurni, gathered round Ceredig's body, lifted it up and carried it through the crowd, out of the great hall and outside into the streets, where they laid it on a decorated long cart.

In front of the funeral cart, one hundred Gewisse warriors prepared to lead the royal procession to the burial site. Cunorix and his family, Cunedda and all the chieftains, commanders and elders mounted their horses and took their place behind the cart, followed by another one hundred Gewisse warriors.

When everything was in position, Cunorix raised a pole bearing Ceredig's banner as a signal, and the procession started moving slowly up the main street of the citadel as thousands of people joined in, following the procession as it headed out of the citadel's west gate, onto the old Roman road to Searobyrg.

Just over an hour and a half later, the procession reached the burial site. Ceredig's body was removed from the cart and carefully placed on a bed-like structure in the burial room. His sword was in its scabbard, and his brooch was fastened to the cloak that he always wore. His shield was placed on top of his body, then one of his large banners, bearing the gold rampant dragon on a red background, was placed over the body and shield.

Hildis placed some flowers over the banner, and then they all withdrew from the burial mound.

Fifty Gewisse warriors moved in and closed off King Ceredig's burial chamber, then started covering it in the earth that had been brought to the site for the burial mound.

After two hours, the chamber was covered and the burial mound was complete, so the men withdrew to their position with the other Gewisse. Then, four bonfires around the mound were set on fire, and fifty Gewisse warriors took up their position to guard the burial site.

The public crowd, chieftains, commanders and elders then returned to Ventacæster, escorted by one hundred of the Gewisse warriors, leaving the king's family to spend private time at the burial site, before they returned to the citadel with the other fifty Gewisse warriors.

*

The following day, Cunorix, Cunedda, Ceawlin and Cuthwulf, as well as all the kingdom's chieftains, commanders and elders, attended a council meeting in the great hall at Ventacæster.

Cunorix opened the meeting by thanking them all for coming to Ventacæster for King Ceredig's funeral. He then reminded them that it would not serve the kingdom well to delay appointing a successor to Ceredig as King of the Gewisse.

Cunedda then spoke, saying that the king had always intended that his elder son, Cunorix, should succeed him and he saw no reason to change that. Cunedda reminded them that Cunorix had been the kingdom's effective ruler these past few years as the king's health was failing, and had shown his leadership capabilities in dealing with the Saxons in battle. He concluded by saying he supported Cunorix's right to succeed his father as King of the Gewisse.

When no one spoke up to challenge Cunedda's words, he asked the attendees to say "Aye" if they agreed to Cunorix becoming King of the Gewisse.

Every single man there shouted, "Aye!"

And so, a week later, a large crowd assembled in Ventacæster's great hall to witness the ceremony to crown Cunorix as second King of the Gewisse. His reign would last for twenty-six years, before his eldest son Ceawlin succeeded him.

Ceredig's legacy was so great that all subsequent rulers of the kingdom that became known as 'Wessex', from Ceawlin through to King Ælfred at the end of the ninth century, would claim their ancestry from Ceredig, or 'Cerdic' as the *Anglo-Saxon Chronicle* called him.

Ceredig, the first Wessex king!

KEY REFERENCES

This is a selection of the historical and academic publications that I have used in my research for this novel:

Burne A.H. (1945). 'The Battle of Badon: A Military Commentary' in *History*, Volume 30, No. 112, pp. 133–144.

Constantius of Lyon (c. AD 480). *Vita Germani* (*Life of Germanus*).

Giles, J.A. [*Translated by*] (1848). 'Geoffrey of Monmouth's British History', in *Six Old English Chronicles*.

Giles, J.A. [*Translated by*] (1848). *History of the Britons* (*Historia Brittonum*) by Nennius.

Howorth, Henry H. (1898). 'The Beginnings of Wessex', in *The English Historical Review*, Volume 13, Issue 52, pp. 667–671.

Hughes, John (1819). *Horæ Britannicæ*, or *Studies in Ancient British History*.

Ingram, Rev. James [*Translated by*] (1823). *The Saxon Chronicle*: with an English translation, and notes, critical and explanatory.

Marren, Peter (2006). *Battles of the Dark Ages: British Battlefields AD 410 to 1065*.

Martin, C.T. (1891). 'Hengest (d 488)', in *Oxford Dictionary of National Biography*.

Mierow, Charles C. [*Translated by*] (1908). *The Origin and Deeds of the Goths by Jordanes, c. 551 AD.*

Myres, J.N.L. (1986). 'The English Settlements', in *The Oxford History of England*, Volume 1B.

Thornton, David E. (2004). 'Vortigern [Gwrtheyrn] (fl. 5th cent.)', in *Oxford Dictionary of National Biography*.

Yorke, Barbara (1992). *Kings and Kingdoms of Early Anglo-Saxon England.*

Yorke, Barbara (2004). 'Cerdic (fl. 6th cent.)', in *Oxford Dictionary of National Biography*.